T0129227

No Place for Fear

OTHER BOOKS BY AL LACY

Angel of Mercy series:
  A Promise for Breanna (Book One)
  Faithful Heart (Book Two)
  Captive Set Free (Book Three)
  A Dream Fulfilled (Book Four)
  Suffer the Little Children (Book Five)
  Whither Thou Goest (Book Six)
  Final Justice (Book Seven, March 1998)

Journeys of the Stranger series:
  Legacy (Book One)
  Silent Abduction (Book Two)
  Blizzard (Book Three)
  Tears of the Sun (Book Four)
  Circle of Fire (Book Five)
  Quiet Thunder (Book Six)
  Snow Ghost (Book Seven)

Battles of Destiny (Civil War series):
  Beloved Enemy (Battle of First Bull Run)
  A Heart Divided (Battle of Mobile Bay)
  A Promise Unbroken (Battle of Rich Mountain)
  Shadowed Memories (Battle of Shiloh)
  Joy From Ashes (Battle of Fredericksburg)
  Season of Valor (Battle of Gettysburg)
  Wings of the Wind (Battle of Antietam)
  Turn of Glory (Battle of Chancellorsville)

Fort Bridger Series (with JoAnna Lacy):
  Under the Distant Sky (Book One)
  Consider the Lilies (Book Two)
  No Place for Fear (Book Three)
  Pillow of Stone (Book Four, April 1998)

NO PLACE FOR FEAR

B O O K   T H R E E

AL AND JOANNA LACY

Multnomah® Publishers *Sisters, Oregon*

NO PLACE FOR FEAR
© 1998 by Lew A. and JoAnna Lacy
published by Multnomah Fiction
a division of Multnomah Publishers, Inc.

Cover design by Left Coast Design
Cover illustration by Frank Ordaz

International Standard Book Number: 9781590528372

For information:
Multnomah Publishers, Inc., Post Office Box 1720, Sisters, Oregon 97759

LIBRARY OF CONGRESS CATALOGING-IN -PUBLICATION DATA

Lacy, Al.
No place for fear/Al and JoAnna Lacy
p.cm.—(Hannah of Fort Bridger)
ISBN 9781590528372
I. Lacy, JoAnna. II. Title. III. Series; Lacy, Al. Hannah of Fort Bridger.
PS3562.A256N6 1998
813'54—dc21   97-32512
                                               CIP

146651086

To my beloved Patty O'Brien Lacy,
who in reality is the mother of the special man I'm married to, but in
my heart of hearts is my mother-inspiration, teacher, and friend.
I am deeply grateful to you, Patty, for "training up a child in the way
he should go." And I am grateful to my husband for listening and
learning at his mother' knee.
In this series, our Patty Ruth Cooper bears a strong resemblance in
her personality and her precocious ways to this one-of-a-kind, very
precious lady.
I love you.
Josie
Proverbs 31:28

God is love;

and he that dwelleth in love dwelleth in God,

and God in him.

There is no fear in love;

but perfect love casteth out fear:

because fear hath torment.

He that feareth is not made perfect in love.

1 JOHN 4:16, 18

PROLOGUE

No western Indian was more hostile toward the white man, who invaded their land, than the Blackfoot tribe. They were called Blackfoot because they wore black-dyed moccasins. This large tribe inhabited a massive territory in the early nineteenth century around the upper Missouri and North Saskatchewan Rivers, along with their friends, the small Gros Ventres (Big Bellies) tribe.

Both tribes migrated in the middle of the century to what is today southern Saskatchewan, Canada, and Montana and Wyoming.

Early American trappers knew the Blackfoot and Gros Ventres Indians as desperate and implacable enemies, with the Blackfoot being the fiercest fighters.

John Colter, one of the earliest mountain men, was the first American trapper to face the furious Blackfoot warriors when he helped a large band of Crow repulse a Blackfoot attack in 1808.

Repeated Blackfoot and Gros Ventres attacks prevented white men from gaining a foothold in or near their country for the next thirty years. However, the whites eventually came in greater numbers, with more powerful weapons, driving both tribes farther westward.

When the two tribes settled in Montana and Wyoming territories, the white hunters came there, killing the buffalo by the thousands for their hides. This greedy slaughter infuriated the Blackfoot people and spawned a deep hatred toward the white man.

In the 1860s and 1870s, as whites began to settle in large numbers in Montana and Wyoming, they met with fierce opposition from both tribes, especially the Blackfoot. By this time, there were also Cheyenne, Arapaho, Snake, and Shoshone tribes to reckon with. Thus came the U.S. Army, building forts and attempting to push the Indians onto reservations. This only served to further infuriate the red men. History records the bloodshed that resulted until the late 1800s, when finally the white men so grossly outnumbered the Indians that they were defeated and placed on reservations where their descendants still live today.

We read much in history of the fighting men of the U.S. Army, and the men who trapped, hunted, and settled in the Wild West. But little is said about the gallant women who did their own kind of fighting and settling. The wives of the soldiers would stand at fort gates and watch their uniformed husbands ride out to battle the fierce tribes, knowing that this might be the last time they saw their husbands alive. Many times their fears were well founded.

The wives of the settlers often were killed by attacking hostiles, as were their children and husbands. If the families were not massacred, they survived only to see their homes burned to the ground.

Fear of the hostiles was a part of everyday life, and most vulnerable were the naturally tenderhearted wives and mothers. Some of them learned that in only *one* place could their fears be relieved—the perfect love of God. As the beloved apostle John wrote long ago, under the inspiration of the Holy Spirit, "Perfect love casteth out fear."

CHAPTER ONE

High atop Luther Pass, in the rugged Sierra Nevada Mountains of California, the first pearly ghost of day lightened the eastern sky. Birds twittered in the branches of the towering pines, welcoming the dawn.

On a lofty promontory, a great bald eagle lifted his majestic head and spread his powerful wings, then plunged downward into the deep shadows before swooping upward in graceful flight and winging his way eastward.

There was a stirring inside the main building of Wesson's General Store and stagelines office, as well as the cabins that flanked it. The eastbound stagecoach was scheduled to pull out at 8:00 A.M., and the agents, stage crew, and passengers had plenty to do before then.

Judy Charley Wesson rolled out of bed, looked down at the lump under the covers next to her, and smiled as she said, "You awake, sweet stuff?"

The lump moved slightly, then the covers came off a head that was bald as an egg. Sleepy blue eyes squinted in the direction of her voice. "What say, honey pot?"

"I said, are you awake?" Judy chuckled as she padded to the bedroom window and raised the shade. Dawn's light flooded the room.

"Wal, I wasn't awake before, but I shore am now!" Curly Wesson said.

Judy peered out the window. "Oh, c'mere an' look at this sunrise!"

While Curly was throwing back the covers and padding over to the east window, Judy hurried around the bedroom, raising the other shades, then went to stand by her husband.

"Look at that!" she exclaimed. "What a pitcher! My heavenly Father painted that pitcher!"

"Ya know what?" said Curly. "*My* heavenly Father painted that sunrise too!"

Judy chuckled. "I guess that not only means we are husbin' and wife, but we're also brother an' sister in Jesus, 'cause we both been borned-agin an' have the same heavenly Father!"

"That's right!" Curly said, nodding his head.

"Well, sweet stuff, do ya want a wifely kiss or a sisterly kiss this mornin'?"

Curly grinned. "I'll take one o' them *wifely* kind!"

Afterwards, the two of them held on to each other and gazed at the changes in the sky beyond the window. A bank of long-fingered, fleecy clouds in the east turned a beautiful shade of rose. To the south and west, the dark sky began to brighten.

Later, when Curly and Judy entered their kitchen, Judy went to the big calendar that hung on the side of the cupboard and noticed that she'd forgotten to put an X through the previous day. She picked up the pencil off the cupboard and made the X, saying, "My, how time flies. Here it is the seventeenth of September 1870. I reckon you know what tomorra is?"

"Shore do. Tomorra is Sunday, an' we'll be havin' church services as usual fer any an' all o' them folks down there in that there wagon train who wants to come."

Curly, who stood about five feet, five inches in height and weighed barely 110 pounds, went to the stove and began building a fire. The room had turned as silent as a sealed tomb. He looked back at his wife and said, "You're shore awful quiet. Somethin' wrong?"

Judy laid the pencil down and stared at him in mock contempt. Her eyes tended to look in opposite directions, and Curly couldn't tell which one was focused on him.

"So that's what tomorra is, eh?" she said, wagging her head. "Sunday?"

"Yep. Is it somethin' else?"

"Yes, it is!"

Curly scratched his hairless head. "Well, let's see...it ain't Groundhog Day, an' it ain't our weddin' annivers'ry. It ain't July fourth, an' it ain't George Washin'ton's birthd— Oh, I know what it is! It's my *sweet thing's* twenny-ninth birthday!"

Judy laughed, and they met in the middle of the room for a tight hug. Curly was careful to place his feet so she wouldn't step on them with her high-topped, lace-up work shoes. The ankle-length dress she wore looked as if it were hanging on a scarecrow, she was so thin.

"What'd ya git me?" she asked.

"Oh, no ya don't!" Curly said. "Ya ain't findin' out till tomorra!"

The sun had barely lifted above the mountain peaks when Mitch Glover and Jim Dutton, who were hiding in a dense stand of trees, gazed at the buildings across the road. A large sign on a post read:

WESSON'S GENERAL STORE
and
CALIFORNIA STAGELINES
Curly and Judy Charley Wesson
Proprietors and Stagelines Agents

A California Stagelines coach was parked in front of the

small building marked "Stage Office," which stood adjacent to the general store. Passengers were beginning to board.

Just down the road, toward the east side of the pass, a wagon train was parked in a circle beneath the tall pines. This would be the last wagon train until spring. Even early October could bring heavy snows to the high country.

"The stage'll be gone in a few minutes," said Dutton, "but it's gonna take the folks in the wagon train awhile to turn their wheels."

"They're bustlin' about, though," said Glover, who was the taller of the two. "Probably be gone in an hour or so."

Dutton nodded. "We hit it good, ol' pal. With that wagon train havin' stopped here, the store will have lots of money from sales."

Glover, who was as dirty and unkempt as his partner, grinned, showing a mouthful of crooked buckteeth stained with tobacco. "And we'll take it all," he said. "I told you all that's here to run the place is an ugly old woman and that scrawny old man. They'll be pushovers. We'll make a haul here and have enough money to do us all winter."

Curly Wesson followed the stage driver and shotgunner out of the small station building. As they climbed up to the box, he said, "You boys be careful. We'll see ya next week."

Curly couldn't see the passengers inside the stagecoach, but he heard a female voice say, "Isn't that Curly just darling? I love his winsome smile."

Another woman's voice replied, "Yes, he's as cute as a bug's ear. Too bad he's married!"

Curly blushed, and the shotgunner atop the stage laughed.

The driver turned to his partner and said, "Now, Harley,

you're just jealous. When did a lady ever say that about you?"

The shotgunner shrugged and picked up his double-barreled shotgun.

The driver grinned down at Curly and said, "Good-bye, cutie!"

Wesson made a fist in mock anger and shouted, "Get outta here!"

The stage was still in sight when a second stage came over the crest of the pass from the east. The two crews shouted at each other and waved, and the westbound stage rumbled to a stop at the station. Curly was there with his winsome smile to welcome them.

Across the road, in the shadows, Jim Dutton swore. "Now, we've got another bunch of people to worry about!"

"They won't stay long," Glover said in a calm voice. "Stage pullin' in this early sure ain't staying for the night."

Dutton wiped a hand across his mouth. "Tell you what. Since there's quite a few wagon train folks in there, and now there'll be them stagecoach passengers, let's you and me go in and just buy some little thing or two. You know, sorta let the old man and the old lady see our faces. We'll tell 'em we're campin' close by for a few days and will be back to buy some more stuff. That way, when we come back later, we'll have 'em off guard. We'll just tell 'em we thought of somethin' else we wanted to get…then put our guns on 'em and tell 'em what we want is all the money."

"Good thinkin'," Glover said with a grin. "Let's just do it right now."

The two men wheeled about and went deeper into the woods to get their horses.

Inside the general store, Judy was cracking jokes with customers from the wagon train when six stagecoach passengers came through the door, followed by the driver and shotgunner. Curly walked in behind them, carrying a small canvas bag.

Judy looked up and showed the passengers her snaggletooth smile. "Howdy, folks! Welcome to the Wesson Gen'ral Store! Jist feel free to browse around."

The passengers were a bit taken aback at the sight of the old woman. Her scarecrow form was rare enough, but during business hours she also wore an old Stetson that looked ancient enough to have belonged to her grandfather. Her coarse gray hair stuck out from under the hat in strands of varying lengths. And on her narrow hips hung a Colt .45 in a leather gunbelt.

Judy looked more closely at the driver and shotgunner. "Well, dog my tootsies, if it ain't old Bart Fletcher and his little boy, Freddie! You guys doin' okay?"

"Fine, Judy," Bart said. "And Curly tells me you're doing all right."

"Couldn' be no better if'n I was twins!" she said with a laugh. "And how's your wife, Freddie?"

"She's doing quite well, ma'am," said the younger Fletcher. "Baby's supposed to arrive in about six weeks."

"Wunnerful! You wantin' a boy or a girl?"

"Doesn't matter, ma'am. Just so the baby's healthy."

Judy clicked her tongue. "That's the ticket, Freddie!"

Curly joined his wife behind the counter and placed the small canvas bag on a shelf underneath. "Mail fer us offa the stage," he said.

Judy nodded, and Curly turned toward a customer who had just come to the counter.

Dutton and Glover rode up outside and dismounted at

the hitch rail. The men entered the store and moved around slowly, finally picking up one item each before getting in line at the counter. When Curly told the wagon master he was looking forward to having all the folks from the wagon train in the Sunday services in the morning, the outlaws exchanged wooden glances.

Curly finished taking care of the wagon master and said to Judy, "Well, flower pot, it's time to send the stage off. See ya later."

"You do that, snookums."

Curly glanced at Dutton and Glover, gave them a friendly smile as he rounded the end of the counter, and said, "My missus will take care of you two fellers in a jiffy."

Both men nodded, forcing smiles, and seconds later the customers in front of them moved away.

Judy grinned at them and said, "Howdy, gentlemen. Find what ya needed?"

Mitch Glover nodded. "Yes'm. We'll probably be back in before we break camp in a day or two."

"Oh, so you're campin' close by, eh?"

"Yes'm."

"Doin' some huntin'?"

"That we are," Jim Dutton said. "Huntin' bears."

Judy nodded. "Oh, I see. Black b'ars or brown b'ars?"

"Either kind, ma'am," said Dutton. "You ever eat bear meat?"

"Oh, shore. I'm kindly like you…don't matter to me what color the hide is. Meat tastes the same."

When the transaction was finished, Judy said, "You gentlemen come on back now, y'hear?"

"We'll do that, ma'am," said Glover. "You can bank on it."

When they were outside and mounted on their horses, Dutton said, "Did you see that cash drawer when she opened it?"

"We're gonna make us a real haul tomorrow."

That evening, after supper, Curly and Judy sat down at the kitchen table to go through the mail. Curly tipped the bag and dumped the envelopes onto the table. They each grabbed a pile to work on. As Curly began sifting through his pile, he picked up an envelope and waved it. "Lookee here, dumplin'. We got a letter from that there Wells Fargo vice president in Cheyenne City, Mr. Winn Haltom."

"Well, open it up and see what he says."

Curly ripped the envelope open, unfolded the letter, and began to read silently. He looked at her with twinkling eyes. "Looks like we might just have ourselves a deal."

"Okay," she said, wringing her hands. "I'm all ears."

"Well, Mr. Haltom is offerin' us a better salary than we're gittin' from Californy Stagelines, and a far better percentage of the profit. I'd say, offhand, it'd make up fer what we're makin' on the store. An' he says they're buildin' a stage office with an apartment upstairs fer the agents to live in."

"Sounds good to me," said Judy. "With what we make offa sellin' the store, we could build us a house right there in Fort Bridger if'n we had a mind to."

"No reason we couldn't, honey," Curly said with a nod. "Since both those businessmen from Placerville have made us offers, we could have 'em make offers one more time. See which one comes up with the best offer, and sell it to 'im."

Judy rubbed her pointed chin thoughtfully. "Well, you know we both have talked about how bad last winter was, and that we ought to get to where the winters don't get us snowed in like here. I know Wyomin' gets lots of snow an' cold, but it wouldn't be like bein' on Luther Pass on top o' the high Sierras."

"Let's pray about this offer, an' see if the Lord gives us

peace in our hearts 'bout writin' Mr. Haltom and tellin' him we'll take the job in Fort Bridger."

"Let's jist pray right now," said Judy, reaching across the table to take Curly's hand.

The next morning, Judy woke to find a box lying on a straight-backed wooden chair that Curly had moved close to her side of the bed. The box had a red ribbon wrapped around it with a bow on top.

"What's this?" she said, raising up on one elbow.

"Yore birthday present, honey bunch! Happy birthday!"

Judy rolled over, wrapped her arms around Curly's neck, and kissed his cheek. "Well, bless your bones! You couldn't even wait till I was up an' dressed."

"Nope. I want you to open it now!"

Judy sat up on the side of the bed, and Curly joined her, watching as she ripped the ribbon loose and opened the box. She gasped when she saw what was inside.

"Oh, Curly!" she said excitedly. "A new skillet! Just what I been needin'! Thank ya, darlin'!"

Across the road from the general store and stage station, Jim Dutton and Mitch Glover watched the occupants of the wagon train move toward their wagons after the singing and preaching service, which was held inside the store. Curly had led the song service and done the preaching, too.

Finally the wagon train disappeared over the crest of the pass, heading toward Placerville.

"Okay, Jim," said Mitch. "Let's go fatten our pockets before somebody else shows up."

The words were hardly out of his mouth when a wagon came up the trail from the east side of the pass, driven by a lone man.

"Probably just a quick customer," said Dutton. "We'll move in as soon as he's gone."

Curly looked out one of the front windows when he heard the rattle of a wagon. Judy was on her knees behind the counter. "Who's that?" she asked.

"Zach Palmer."

"Tell ya what. I'll go to the kitchen and fix us some lunch. You take care of Zach."

As she rose to her feet, the door came open and Zach Palmer, who owned a small ranch a couple of miles east of the pass, came in. Judy was halfway to the rear door when she looked over her shoulder and said, "Howdy, Zach."

"Howdy, Judy. I was going to see if I could borrow your husband for a while." Palmer moved toward the counter where Curly stood, and said, "I'm putting a new gate on my corral, but it's just plainly a two-man job. Could you come and help me?"

"Why, shore," said Curly. "How long you think it'll take?"

"Probably about an hour. Hour and a half at the most."

"I can wait that long to fix lunch," said Judy. "Or if you'd like, I could whip up somethin' real quick and feed you an' Zach both right soon."

Curly looked at his friend. "You name it, Zach."

Palmer chuckled. "Judy, you know I can't pass up your cooking. Martha isn't planning to start a meal till after I get the gate on. So if you want to fix us a little something, I'd just love it."

"Well," she said with a grin, "I can whup up some pea soup and a san'wich o' some kind right fast. Sound all right?"

"Sounds great!"

Glover and Dutton peered through the trees, waiting for the man in the wagon to come out of the store and give them free access to rob the old couple.

When a half hour had passed, Glover said, "I'm tired of waitin', Mitch. Let's just go do it."

"Patience, ol' pal. The fewer people inside that store when we rob it, the less chance of trouble. We can wait a little longer."

Finally, the door of the store opened, and the outlaws recognized Curly Wesson with the man who owned the wagon. Both men climbed into the wagon, and with a snap of the reins, they headed off.

"Looks like this'll be easier'n we thought," Dutton said.

Judy was on the back side of the counter, taking items from a box and placing them on the shelves behind her, when she heard the little bell above the door give off its familiar tinkle. She recognized the two men from yesterday and smiled. "Oh. There's them there b'ar hunters. You boys find ya a b'ar yet?"

Judy felt a crawling uneasieness when neither man smiled. Suddenly Dutton's gun was out, cocked, and aimed at her midsection.

"What's this?" Judy said.

"We're takin' all your money, that's what," said Dutton. "First thing, I want you to take that .45 out of your holster real slow-like and hand it to my partner."

Judy kept her eyes trained on the robbers and pinched the butt of the revolver between her thumb and forefingers, slipping it free of the holster.

Mitch Glover closed his hand around the gun and then tucked it under his belt, saying, "That's a good old lady. Now, if you'll just keep cooperatin', we won't shoot you."

Glover reached behind his back for the canvas moneybag tucked under his belt and swung it in front of Judy's face. "Here, grandma. Fill it up. Cash drawer first. Wherever else you keep the rest of it, we want that too. If you don't do as we say, September 18, 1870, will be carved on your gravestone as your last day on earth." Glover shook the bag in front of her eyes and snapped, "Take it, grandma!"

Judy made her hand tremble as she pulled the cash drawer open, then took the bag from the robber's fingers. "Whoops!" she said, as the bag slipped through her fingers. She pretended to be afraid as she stuttered, "S-sorry, mister," and bent down as if to pick up the bag. Instead, she thrust both hands under the counter.

From where Dutton and Glover stood, they could see only the crook of her arms at the elbows.

Judy set her jaw, got a steely look in her eyes, and said, "I've got you both covered with revolvers, you dirty skunks! Now, I want ya to put your guns on the counter. An' I want my Colt .45 back. Put all three of 'em on the counter. *Right now!*"

Dutton looked at Glover. "She's bluffin'. And even if she's got revolvers trained on us, the hammers ain't cocked. We'd have heard 'em if she cocked 'em. I can shoot her down before she can cock the hammers and fire."

A slow grin curved Glover's mouth and he turned to Judy. "Pick that bag up, old woman, and empty the cash drawer into it like I told you."

Judy's jaw jutted stubbornly. "You and your pal are gonna have September 18, 1870, carved on *your* grave markers, mister, 'less ya put them guns on the counter like I tol' ya!"

Jim Dutton laughed. "Yeah, grandma, and I say you're bluffin'. Now let's have that bag filled up. *Right now!* I mean it!"

"So ya think I'm bluffin', do ya?"

Dutton's laugh died out. "Yeah."

She shifted her gaze to Glover. "You think so, too, right?"

"Yeah."

Judy fixed them each with a piercing eye. "You dudes willin' to gamble on it? I mean, if I'm tellin' ya the truth, ya honyocks are 'bout to get gut shot."

Glover nervously licked his lips. His gun was still in its holster. If the crusty old woman was telling the truth, she had him cold.

Judy's face turned a darker red as she gusted, "Well, what is it? Do you birds feel like gamblin', or are ya gonna do as I tell ya? Ya better make your move quick, 'cause I'm about to start shootin'!"

Sweat on Dutton's brow ran down his forehead. "We're gonna feel like fools if she ain't got those guns under there," he said.

Glover licked his lips again. His voice croaked a bit when he said, "Yeah, but I'd rather be a live fool than a dead doubter."

Without another word, both men laid their guns on the counter. Glover removed Judy's gun from under his belt and placed it beside them.

Judy's gaze remained on the two men as she said, "All right. Now I want you two to lay facedown on the floor. Put your heads and palms flat on the floor. We're gonna wait till my husbin' gets back, an' we'll decide what to do with ya."

When the outlaws lay facedown, hands pressed flat on the floor, the old woman walked around the end of the counter and stood over them. Cold chills raised goose bumps on their skin when they saw two cocked Colt .45 pistols in her hands.

An hour later, Judy and Curly stood on the front porch of the general store, watching Zach Palmer and two neighboring ranchers drive away with the outlaws bound in the back of Palmer's wagon.

"Well, honey lamb," said Curly, "I'm shore the marshal down in Placerville will know what to do with them skunks."

Judy chuckled. "I'm sure o' that. An' ya know what?"

"What?"

"I'm a thinkin' that this here episode was allowed by the Lord to tell us we need to move to where there's more people. Fort Bridger's got the army post an' all them citizens."

"Nex' stage headin' east, I'll send Mr. Haltom a letter acceptin' the job."

CHAPTER TWO

O n a cool Wednesday night in Fort Bridger, Wyoming, young Hannah Cooper and her four children were walking home from the midweek church service with Gary and Glenda Williams. An October harvest moon hung in the sky, and above it was an infinitude of winking stars.

The town's street lamps cast circles of yellow, and dim lights shone in the windows of houses and the second-story apartments of the commercial buildings.

Hannah's three oldest children—Christopher, fourteen; Mary Beth, twelve; and Brett Jonathan, eight (better known as B. J.)—were discussing the special speaker who would address the students at school the next day. Civil War veteran Major Clint Barker, the fort's newest officer, was going to tell them about the Battle of Gettysburg.

Major Barker had fought as a lieutenant under the now famous Colonel Joshua L. Chamberlain, commander of the Twentieth Maine Regiment. It was this regiment that had courageously withstood the repeated efforts of the Confederate forces to capture the strategic rocky and wooded hill known as Little Round Top and ultimately turned the Gettysburg battle to victory for the Union army.

Little five-year-old Patty Ruth walked beside her mother, holding Tony, her stuffed bear, in her arms.

Hannah listened to her children talking and then glanced at her oldest son before saying, "I'm sure all of you will enjoy Major Barker's talk about his army experiences. I met the entire Barker family when they came into the store this morning. They're Christians and will be attending our church starting this Sunday."

"I heard they have two kids, Mama," said Mary Beth. "Is that right?"

"Yes. A thirteen-year-old girl named Dorine, and an eleven-year-old boy named Donnie. Nice-looking children, and very polite. Mrs. Barker, whose name is Alice, told me that tomorrow will be the first day of school for her children. They could've started today, but they asked if they could start the same day their father spoke to the students."

Glenda Williams, who was Hannah's best friend, said, "I have to hand it to Miss Lindgren. She must have met the major at the gate when they arrived, to line him up so quickly to speak at the school."

Hannah laughed. "Well, almost. It just so happened that Colonel Bateman and Sundi—Miss Lindgren—got to talking a few days ago in the store. Colonel Bateman mentioned that Major Barker had been assigned to the fort and that he had fought in the battle of Gettysburg. That's all it took for our illustrious schoolmarm to turn on her sweet charm and talk the commandant into letting her speak with Major Barker as soon as he arrived."

Gary Williams laughed. "That little gal could charm an Indian out of his tomahawk!"

When they reached the corner where the Uintah Hotel stood, and next to it the café called Glenda's Place, Gary squeezed Glenda's hand and said, "Honey, I've got to work on the books in the hotel office for a while. I'll be home in a couple of hours." He bid the Coopers good night and entered the hotel.

Hannah turned to Glenda. "I need to talk to you for a little while. Could I come down to the house after I get the children in bed?"

"Sure," Glenda said. The light from a street lamp danced in her big blue eyes. "I'll put some spicy tea on. How soon will you be down?"

"Oh…let's say half an hour or so."

"It's a date," said Glenda. She patted Hannah's shoulder then turned toward home. The Williamses' house was on the next street, directly behind their hotel.

The Coopers entered the hotel, spoke to the night clerk, and climbed the stairs. As they approached the doors to their rooms, Hannah said, "Children, I'd like you to come into my room for a few minutes before you get ready for bed. There's something I want to tell you."

"Is this the same thing you're gonna talk to Miss Glenda about, Mama?" asked Chris.

"Well…yes, it is. I just want to tell you about it first."

Mary Beth smiled to herself. Her mother had shared the secret with her almost three weeks ago.

Hannah motioned for the children to sit on her bed, then pulled up a straight-backed chair. "Chris, B. J., Patty Ruth…what I'm about to tell you I already shared with Mary Beth a few weeks ago. I did that because she was having such a difficult time missing Papa, and after praying earnestly about it, I felt I should tell her."

"Mama," said Chris, "you don't have to explain all that. We always trust you to do the right thing. What is it you want to tell us?"

Hannah smiled, then bit her lip as tears misted her eyes. "Well…you see…there's going to be a new addition to our family."

Patty Ruth looked puzzled. B. J. frowned. Mary Beth smiled.

Chris's eyes widened. "Mama, are you telling us you're going to have a *baby?*"

Hannah pressed her fingers to her lips and nodded. Tears began to flow down her cheeks.

Patty Ruth blinked and said, "Mama, is there a baby in your tummy?"

"Yes, honey." Hannah cupped the child's chin in her hand. "Jesus is going to give you a new little brother or sister."

"Do we get to choose which we want?" Patty Ruth asked.

"Well, no, honey. The Lord has already made the baby whichever it is."

"Oh. Well, I was gonna ask for another sister."

"And if we could put in an order," said B. J., "I'd order another brother."

"But you *will* love it, whichever it is, won't you?"

Both B. J. and Patty Ruth assured their mother they would.

"Mama…" said Mary Beth. "Tell them about Papa."

Hannah brushed tears from her cheeks. "Yes, I must do that. You see, children, when we were coming here in the wagon train, I began to have signs that maybe I was expecting another baby. I knew for sure just about the time the wagon train stopped near Devil's Gate. That night, before—before Papa was bitten by the snake, I told him about the new baby. He was so happy he almost shouted."

Chris smiled in spite of the pain he felt, and said, "He was the best papa in all the world, Mama. Just like you are the best mama."

There were tears in Mary Beth's eyes as she wrapped her arms around her mother's neck and kissed her cheek, telling her she loved her. The other three took their turns to do the same.

Glenda Williams opened the front door before Hannah knocked.

As Hannah entered the house, she said, "You must have been standing there with your hand on the doorknob."

Glenda chuckled. "Not quite. I was just closing the closet door in the foyer when I heard your footsteps on the porch. Here, let's go into the parlor."

The aroma of hot, spicy tea filled the room. Glenda had three lamps aglow, and a bright fire burned in the fireplace. In front of the loveseat that faced the fireplace was a coffee table on which sat a tray with a steaming teapot and two dainty cups and saucers to match.

"Sit down, Hannah," said Glenda as she started to pour the tea.

Hannah accepted the cup of tea and inhaled the aroma. "Mmm. This will hit the spot."

Glenda smiled, then turned to study her friend's face. "You look awfully tired, Hannah. I've noticed the pinched look around your mouth the last few days, and even a slight slump to your shoulders. You need to get some help in the store. It's just too much for you."

Hannah smiled. "It wouldn't really be too much under normal circumstances, but things aren't exactly normal right now."

Glenda's brow knitted. "I don't understand."

Hannah smiled again. "This is exactly what I wanted to talk to you about." She took a sip of tea, then set the cup and saucer down. "It's really quite simple, Glenda. I'm expecting my fifth child."

Glenda's mouth dropped open. "Hannah...you *are?*"

Hannah nodded and told Glenda about her suspicions that she might be with child as they traveled the Oregon Trail.

When she finished her story by saying that she'd given Solomon the news on the last night of his life, and how excited he had been, tears were on her cheeks, and Glenda reached out to pull her close.

Hannah took in a couple of deep breaths and said in a trembling voice, "Oh, Glenda, I'm so happy about this baby. Of course I have the other four, but the way the Lord brought this about, so that I would have just a little bit more of Solomon, is such a blessing."

"I'm so glad, honey," said Glenda, patting her back.

"Glenda, I…"

"What is it?" Glenda pulled her head back to look into Hannah's dark brown eyes.

"I have to be strong and positive in front of my children, but…"

"Yes?"

"You're my very best friend, and…well, I can tell you what's heavy on my heart." Hannah moved back so she could look into her friend's eyes. "I mean it when I say I'm happy about this baby, but the baby…the baby is going to bring on more responsibility. And I already have enough to stagger any woman."

Glenda squeezed Hannah's hand and nodded. "You're going to have to have some help. Especially when the birth draws nearer and *after* the baby's born. You know I'll help you in every way I can. I'll certainly work the counter at the store for you as much as possible."

"But that throws too much of a load on you," Hannah said. "You've got the café to look after, and Gary often needs you at the hotel. I just can't ask you to—"

"You haven't asked me. I'm volunteering. And when I'm tied up at the café or the hotel, I'm sure the other women who fill in on Saturdays can jump in there and take my place. That baby is going to demand your attention, as you well know, and you're not going to be able to handle the store and the baby at the same time. At least not for a couple or three months after the baby comes."

"I know. But it bothers me to have to ask for help."

"You won't need to. I'll be a committee of one to line up help among the women who already know how to run the store."

"I appreciate it, Glenda. And you know I'll pay every one of them who will let me."

"Of course. Now, don't you fret. Your best friend here will go to work on it right away. You'll have help starting tomorrow. I may be an hour or so late for work in the morning, boss lady, because I'll be recruiting, but you just rest your sweet self about it. You're going to be taken care of. And just so there are no arguments between us, missy, you are not paying me a dime."

"But—"

"But nothing."

"But Glenda, you and Gary are already letting us stay in our hotel rooms without charge. I can't let you work in the store and not pay you!"

"No arguments, Hannah Marie Cooper," Glenda said in mock anger, "and I mean it! End of discussion."

Hannah wept again, and threw her arms around her friend. "Oh, Glenda, I'm so glad the Lord brought you into my life!"

Hannah walked down the long hall in the hotel. When she came to the boys' room, she inserted the skeleton key in the lock and quietly slipped inside. Light from the street lamps illuminated the room enough for her to see the boys in their beds, fast asleep.

She moved like a shadow and bent over to kiss Chris's

temple, whispering softly, "I love my big boy."

Then she glided to B. J.'s bed, with her skirts rustling like a breeze through the branches of a tree, and kissed his forehead. "I love my little boy, too."

Moments later, she slipped into the girls' room. Patty Ruth's bed was closest to the door. Hannah smiled as she looked down at the sleeping little redhead. Tony the Bear was tucked close by her side. Hannah brushed a stray lock of hair from Patty Ruth's brow and pulled the quilt up close under her chin, then kissed her chubby, freckled cheek. "I love my little girl," she said.

Then she rounded the foot of the bed and moved up beside Mary Beth, who lay on her side, facing the wall and window. She kissed her temple and whispered, "I love my big girl, too."

When she turned to tiptoe away, a sweet whisper came from Mary Beth. "And I love my precious mama, too."

Hannah turned, bent down, and said, "You're supposed to be asleep, young lady."

"I had to wait till I got my good night kiss, Mama. Was Miss Glenda glad about the baby?"

"Very. Now you get to sleep."

"You did say it's all right for me to tell Miss Lindgren on Friday?"

"Yes."

"Okay. Good night, Mama. I love you."

"And I love you so very, very much."

Hannah slipped into bed in her own room and sighed, knowing it would be some time before sleep claimed her, even though she was bone tired. Her nightly custom for the past several weeks had been to talk to Solomon as if he were there and could hear her.

"Sol, darling, I miss you terribly. The Lord has been so good to give me Glenda and our many other good friends. The children are adjusting to your absence—a little more each day. We'll always miss you, but the Lord is proving that His grace is sufficient.

"Sales are getting better all the time, even though we're still in the sutler's. The new store is coming along real good. Should be in it soon. I love you, my darling."

She then prayed and thanked the Lord for the strength He had given her that day, and for His bountiful blessings. Soon Hannah grew drowsy, and refreshing sleep claimed her.

She dreamed of Sol. To be close to him even in a dream would give her courage to go on another day.

Saturday morning in Fort Bridger was a glorious fall day. Sundi Lindgren, the town's only schoolteacher, left her sister's dress shop and started down Main Street toward the fort, letting her gaze take in the beauty of God's handiwork.

The tall cottonwoods and weeping willows were dressed in their finest array of gold, russet, red, and yellow leaves, which stood out in breathtaking contrast to the towering green pines.

Sundi herself, though unaware of it, was a vision of God's handiwork. The sun's rays turned her blonde hair to burnished gold, and the new dress her sister had just finished making for her perfectly complemented her coloring. The dress of green and black watch plaid, exquisitely trimmed with black collar and cuffs, was a perfect fit. The morning sun had warmed the air enough that she wore only a light shawl to protect her from some unexpected breeze blowing in from the surrounding prairie.

Sundi greeted the people she met on the boardwalk. Though she and her sister had been in Fort Bridger only a few months, they felt at home and had been warmly welcomed into the community.

As Sundi drew near the Fort Bridger bank, Alice Barker emerged and stepped onto the boardwalk, closing the door behind her. Alice saw Sundi immediately and smiled. "Good morning, Miss Lindgren. Beautiful day, isn't it?"

"That it is. And how are you, Mrs. Barker?"

"Fine, thanks to Calvary," said Alice, her face shining.

Sundi nodded. "Amen to that."

Alice gestured toward the bank. "Nice to be able to do my banking on a Saturday."

"Mm-hmm. Mr. Dawson is very much community-minded. He knows the people at the fort sometimes need a few hours on Saturday to do their banking, as well as to shop in the stores. And for that matter, it helps the ranchers and farmers too. I understand he's been keeping the bank open on Saturday mornings ever since he opened it." Sundi paused. "You heading back to the fort?"

"Yes, I am."

"Well, let's walk together. I'm going to see Mrs. Cooper at the general store. Have you met her yet?"

"Yes...very sweet lady. And a fine Christian, too. I could tell that right off. And bless her heart, a widow with four children to raise all by herself."

"Hannah's had some real bumps, Mrs. Barker, but she's shown the rest of us in this town the kind of strength the Lord can give us when we let Him."

They met up with a rancher and his wife on the boardwalk. Sundi introduced the new major's wife to them before the two women continued on toward the fort.

"Mrs. Barker, I want to tell you what a joy your husband was to my students and me," said Sundi. "We really enjoyed his visit."

"Not as much as he enjoyed being there," Alice said. "And let me tell you, Donnie and Dorine just love you. They say they've never had a teacher who cares so much about teaching her students."

Sundi smiled. "That's good to hear. All the children took to Donnie and Dorine quickly. I must commend you; they are so polite and mannerly."

"Maybe it's the military aspect. Clint keeps a pretty tight rein on them."

The new general store building came into view. Two men were applying paint to the outside, and the sound of pounding hammers came from inside. As they approached, a tall, slender man with sunken cheeks, deep-set eyes, and a bony, hawklike nose emerged from the building, carrying a bucketful of wood shavings and sawdust. He paused when he saw the two women and smiled, saying, "Good morning, Miss Sundi."

"Good morning, yourself, Alex. I want you to meet Alice Barker. Her husband is Major Clint Barker—the newest officer to the fort. Mrs. Barker, this is Alex Patterson."

"I'm happy to meet you, sir," said the major's wife.

"The pleasure is mine, ma'am," said Alex, touching his hat brim. "My children are singing your husband's praises. They said he really held their attention when he told them about the Gettysburg battle the other day."

Alice smiled in acknowledgment.

"The Barkers are Christians, Alex," said Sundi. "They'll be coming to church on Sunday."

"We'll sure look forward to seeing you in the services, ma'am," Alex said.

As they moved on down the street, Alice said, "That's a very nice man."

"Thanks to the Lord," said Sundi. "As of a few weeks ago, he was anything but a nice man."

"Oh, really?"

"You know Mrs. Cooper's store was burned down, didn't you?"

"Yes."

"Alex is the one who set the fire."

"Oh, my!"

"Everyone in the town and fort knows Alex was a hard and bitter man."

"So tell me how he got saved."

"Well, Hannah—bless her heart—had witnessed to Nellie, Alex's wife, on several occasions, and finally led her to Jesus. Then Pastor Andrew Kelly led their three children to Jesus. This set Alex off. He was like a madman. On a Sunday night, during church services, he set Hannah's barn on fire to pay her back for 'making' his family become Christians. But a stiff wind came up and carried the flames to the store building, too, which also housed their home—an upstairs apartment. They lost it all."

"Oh, how terrible!"

Sundi's face broke into a wide smile. "Well, that isn't the end of the story. The Lord is so good! I won't go into it now, but out of the blue Hannah was given enough money to rebuild the store, restock it, refurnish the apartment, and buy new clothes for the entire family."

"Amazing! He's a great and mighty God, isn't He?"

"Amen to that. Now most people—even Christians— would've hated Alex for what he did. But not Hannah. Alex's conscience finally ate him alive, and he went to her and confessed that he was the arsonist. He asked her to forgive him and told her he wanted to be saved. Hannah readily forgave him, and because she had explained the gospel to him many times before, she was able to lead him to the Lord right then and there."

"Wonderful!"

"So…when Alex got saved, he was ready to confess his crime to Marshal Mangum and take whatever punishment he had coming. Hannah pled leniency on Alex's behalf. And Judge Carter sentenced Alex to six months in the town jail but made allowance for him to be out ten hours a day to help rebuild the store. And he can go to church twice on Sunday and on Wednesday nights."

"That's quite a story."

"Yes, it is. And Marshal Mangum even lets him out in the evenings to eat supper with his family. And what a change in that family! The Lord did a mighty work there!"

"All I can say, other than 'Praise the Lord,' is, God give us more Christians like Hannah Cooper!"

CHAPTER THREE

Inside the old sutler's building, Hannah Cooper and Sylvia Bateman stood behind the counter waiting on customers. Sylvia was the wife of Colonel Ross Bateman, the fort's commandant.

News of Hannah's forthcoming baby had spread through town and fort, and while customers paid for their goods at the counter, conversation centered on Hannah's pregnancy. She was looking a bit tired and peaked from the lingering effects of morning sickness. Nevertheless, she was cheerful and her usual warm self as she talked with her customers and answered questions concerning the baby's due date, whether she wanted a boy or a girl, and how her children had taken the news.

Hannah was just beginning to show a slight thickness at her waistline, but as always, she was neat and tidy. She wore a pretty gingham-checked dress of green and white, covered with a crisp white apron. Her long, dark brown hair lay softly on her shoulders, with lovely waves adorning her temples and complementing her prominent cheekbones.

To afford Hannah as much relief as possible, Sylvia worked extra fast to handle most of the customers. It was especially busy on Saturdays, when many farmers and ranchers came to town to stock up. But everyone was patient as they waited in line, while others milled around them, trying to get to the different shelves.

The aisles in the small sutler's building were crowded with boxes, crates, stacks of canned goods, and other paraphernalia necessary in stocking a general store, and the old building had a distinctive musty odor. No one mentioned it, but it bothered Hannah. She could hardly wait to get into her own building again, where the aisles were wide and there was plenty of room to arrange the wares for easy access and in a way more pleasing to the eye. She promised herself she would never let her new store smell musty, no matter how old it became.

When Heidi Lindgren stepped up to the counter and laid her goods down for tallying, she said, "Hannah, dear, Rebecca Kelly and Mandy Carver were in my store yesterday afternoon. They were telling me that Glenda was recruiting ladies to help you in the store when your time for delivery draws near, and for a couple of months after the baby is born."

"Yes," said Hannah, "Glenda told me she was going to do that."

"Well, I just want you to know that I'm signing up."

Hannah shook her head no. "Heidi, you have a store of your own to run. You can't close yours to help me in mine."

Heidi smiled. "I suppose that's why Glenda hasn't asked me yet. She figures the same thing. Well, if Glenda can find a lady who will take a half-day each week, I'll close the store for the other half and help you in your store."

Hannah smiled in wonderment. "I don't know what to say, Heidi. It would really bother me if I knew you were losing business."

"I won't lose business. I'll just put up a sign to explain why the store is closed that half-day. My customers will understand."

"Well, I'll pay you for your time."

"No you won't," Heidi said firmly.

The little bell above the door jingled often as people came and went. When the bell rang this time, Heidi looked up and noticed her sister enter the store with a woman she didn't know.

Sundi smiled as she drew up beside her sister and introduced her to Alice Barker. After exchanging pleasantries with Heidi, Alice smiled at Hannah. "Hello, again, Mrs. Cooper."

"Nice to see you, Mrs. Barker," said Hannah. "We sure are looking forward to having you and your family in church services tomorrow."

"And we're looking forward to being there," said Alice. She excused herself and went to look for the items she'd come to purchase.

Sundi stepped closer to the counter and helped Hannah and her sister place Heidi's goods in paper bags. While she was stuffing a bag, Sundi said, "I just came in to tell you how happy I am about the baby, Hannah. I haven't had a chance to see you since Mary Beth told me about it yesterday. I'm so glad for you."

"Thank you, Sundi. I'm very happy about it."

"The Lord was so good to let you have this baby, knowing that He was going to take your beloved husband the way He did."

Hannah's eyes misted with tears. When Sundi saw it, she laid a hand on Hannah's wrist. "Oh, I'm so sorry. I didn't realize—"

"No, no. It's all right," Hannah said quickly. She took hold of Sundi's hand and squeezed it. "It's all right. Really. You're right. I've thanked the Lord many times for letting me have this baby. It's just that...well, right now I'm a bit more emotional than usual. Sometimes my loss becomes a little overwhelming. Please don't feel bad."

Sundi leaned over the counter, hugged her neck, and said, "I know this baby will be such a blessing. See you in church tomorrow."

The Lindgren sisters left together, and within another hour, business had slowed quite a bit. Sylvia Bateman was busy tallying a bill for a rancher's wife while Hannah sat down on a stool to rest for a moment. The bell jingled again and Hannah saw Betsy Fordham enter with her youngest child, Belinda.

Betsy, the wife of Captain John Fordham, was an attractive, wholesome looking young woman in her late twenties. She wore her shiny black hair up on the sides with combs. Her eyes were hazel and fringed with long, thick lashes.

Betsy had proven to be a good friend to Hannah. Every Tuesday and Thursday she took Patty Ruth for the entire day to her house inside the fort to play with Belinda and get away from the store. Belinda and Patty Ruth were now best friends.

Betsy's gaze found Hannah's, and she hurried to the counter. "Oh, I just heard about your coming blessed event! I'm so happy for you, Hannah!"

"Me, too, Mrs. Cooper," said little Belinda, her eyes dancing. "Your new baby can come to our house when she gets old enough...just like Patty Ruth does!"

"Why, thank you, Belinda," Hannah said and smiled at the little girl.

Betsy's eyes misted over as she said, "Hannah, I know this baby will help ease the pain of your loss."

Hannah nodded. "The Lord has been so good to me. My four precious children have been such a blessing, but this little one will be extra special because of the Lord's timing."

Belinda looked around for her friend, and not seeing her, said, "Where's Patty Ruth, Mrs. Cooper?"

"She's at the Patterson place. In fact, all four of my children are there right now. They're getting acquainted with the Patterson children."

Betsy arched her eyebrows. "They haven't gotten to know the Patterson children yet? Your older three go to school with them."

"Yes," said Hannah, "but until Alex became a Christian, he wouldn't allow his children to socialize with my children. He was afraid they'd cause his children to become 'religious fanat-ics.'"

"I see," said Betsy.

"Of course, now that Alex is saved, it's all different."

Betsy rubbed her ear, and said, "Have you seen Dr. O'Brien about the baby?"

"Yes. Just this morning before coming to open the store."

"And everything is all right?"

"Mm-hmm. He says I'm doing fine, in spite of morning sickness."

Betsy chuckled. "We both know about that!"

"We *all* do!" said the rancher's wife, who was being waited on by Sylvia.

The door opened and two men in uniform entered. One was Sergeant Barry Wilkins, the other was Sergeant Del Frayne. Hannah noticed their wan faces as they approached the counter.

"Something wrong, gentlemen?" she asked.

Frayne glanced at Sylvia and then back to Hannah as he said, "Word just came to Colonel Bateman about a Blackfoot uprising."

Sylvia's face turned to stone. "Go on."

"Well, ladies, the Blackfoot have gone on the warpath far-ther north in Wyoming. They're attacking white settlements at random and leaving bodies strewn everywhere, and burning the buildings. The colonel just called a meeting of all troops in the fort and told us that starting tomorrow morning, he's going to keep twice as many units on patrol."

The bell over the door jingled, and three army women came in. They were discussing the Blackfoot uprising. When they noticed the sergeants and the wives of the commandant and Captain Fordham standing together, they rushed over.

"Oh, Sylvia! Betsy!" said Nadine Sellers, wife of Lieutenant Ken Sellers. "Have you heard about the Blackfoot uprising?"

"They have, ma'am," Wilkins said. "Sergeant Frayne just told them."

"Just horrible!" said Janet Diedrich, wife of Lieutenant Creighton Diedrich. "I hate the thought of my husband facing those red savages in battle!"

"Me too," said the third woman, who was married to a captain.

"How close are the savages to us?" asked Betsy.

"Colonel Bateman isn't sure, Mrs. Fordham," said Sergeant Frayne. "The report wasn't detailed. But he feels they're close enough to double up on patrols."

Betsy thought of John, who was leading a patrol at that very moment. Her hands trembled, and she bit her lip.

This time when the bell jingled, everyone started and glanced toward the door as Glenda Williams entered. "Hello, everyone," she said with a tremor in her voice. "Sounds like there's trouble with the Blackfoot."

"There sure is, Mrs. Williams," said the rancher's wife. "I just hope they leave our ranch alone."

"Right now, it's mainly settlements where white folks are collected, ma'am," said Wilkins. "Of course, that doesn't mean they won't take to attacking ranches. You folks need to keep a sharp eye."

"We will," said the rancher's wife as she gathered up her paper bags.

"Here, ma'am," said Frayne, "let me help you with those."

"Me too," said Wilkins.

"Why, thank you, gentlemen. My wagon is parked right out front."

As the soldiers and the rancher's wife left, Glenda moved close to the army wives and said, "My heart goes out to you ladies. I know it has to be extremely difficult to watch your husbands ride out on patrol and wonder if an Indian arrow or bullet will find them."

Nadine Sellers pressed her fingers to her temples as tears filmed her eyes. "You can't really know, Glenda," she said, "unless you wear our shoes."

Betsy Fordham turned her back on the small group, covered her face, and started weeping.

"Mommy," said little Belinda, wrapping her arms around her mother's waist, "don't cry. Daddy will be all right."

Hannah rounded the end of the counter, and Sylvia followed as the other women drew close around Betsy. Sylvia, who was in her mid-fifties and had been an army wife longer than the others, folded Betsy in her arms and said softly, "I know what you're going through, honey. When Ross was fighting in the Mexican War and in the Civil War, I thought I would die, just from the constant, aching fear I carried in my heart. And even though he doesn't go on patrol, I still live with the fear that an all-out attack will come against the fort, and he will have to use a gun once again."

Little Belinda clung to her mother as Betsy said, "Oh, Sylvia, sometimes I think I'm just not cut out to be a soldier's wife."

"We've all had those thoughts, dear," Sylvia replied.

The other army wives nodded their heads and murmured agreement.

Hannah touched Betsy's shoulder. "How about if you and I take a little walk together? I was an army wife, myself. Maybe we can just talk for a while."

Janet Diedrich reached for Betsy's little girl. "I'll take Belinda to my house. You two take your walk. Betsy, you can come by and get Belinda when you're ready."

Betsy nodded shakily and pulled a hankie from her dress pocket. She dabbed at her eyes and looked at Hannah, and said, "I'd like that."

Belinda hugged her mother's waist. "I'll be good at Mrs. Diedrich's house, Mommy."

"And I'll stay here at the store in case Sylvia needs help

while you're gone, Hannah," said Glenda.

Hannah nodded her thanks and guided Betsy out the door. Neither spoke until they had passed through the gate of the fort and onto Main Street.

"How well I remember," said Hannah, "when Sol was off in the war and going into battle after battle. I felt so hollow inside…and so helpless. All I could do was pray. But God gave me peace."

Betsy was silent a moment, then said, "It was tough on me, too, when John fought in the war. I…I remember some of the young women who were being courted by soldiers. They worried about them, but it wasn't the same as the wives. It's very different when you're married."

"A beau is one thing, but when the man facing a deadly enemy is one flesh with you, as the Bible says, it's altogether different."

"Yes," said Betsy, "but in this situation, it's even worse than having another white man as your enemy. It's these horrible Indians. I worry for John more than ever because those filthy savages are so…so cruel, so heartless…so inhuman."

"They're not all that way," said Hannah. "They—"

"I don't trust any of them! I read what the Sauk and Fox tribes did to white people during the Black Hawk War forty years ago. It was horrible! They're worse than animals! I also read about the Seminole wars in Florida, and the awful torture of white men when they captured them. And…and the Pawnees in Nebraska, and the Comanches in Texas. Nothing but brute beasts.

"Hannah, I've had a fear of Indians ever since I was a little girl. But it became more than fear when we were coming across Nebraska last year. We came upon a white settlement that had been attacked by Cheyenne and Arapaho. It was— Oh, I can't even describe it! Those loathsome, despicable beasts! I hate them!"

"Betsy," Hannah said, touching her friend's arm, "you can't let yourself hate them. They are human beings. They—"

"No, Hannah!" Betsy cut across her words. "They are *not* human! They're devils, I tell you! Devils! And here we are surrounded by them! Not only the evil, disgusting Cheyenne and Arapaho, but the Sioux, Snake, Shoshone, Crow, and these bloody Blackfoot breathing down our necks. Hannah, they're devils! They don't even have a soul!"

People on the street were beginning to gawk, and Hannah took Betsy's arm and led her down a side street. "Betsy," she said, trying to hold her voice level, "you have to understand something."

"Understand what?" Betsy's fear was written all over her face and showed vividly in her eyes.

"The American Indians have pagan religions. They fight their enemies the only way they know how, which has been handed down from their pagan ancestors. In their minds, it is right to make their enemies suffer. It's ingrained in them. Certainly I can't commend them for it, but neither can I hate them for it."

"But…they shouldn't be torturing and killing white people! We didn't come here with killing Indians on our minds. We came to start a new life."

"I know," said Hannah, "but we came as trespassers on their land. White men have killed their buffalo and other game. We've run wagon trains across their property—and now railroads—and we've built towns and villages where they've roamed unhindered for centuries. Betsy, how can we blame them for fighting us to defend their land?"

They were now walking on the bank of Black's Fork Creek, which meandered across the rolling hills and through the fort and town. Betsy bit her lip. "Well, I guess I can't blame them for putting up a fight, but religion or no religion, they shouldn't be so savage. It frightens me to death, thinking what they might do to John if they ever capture him. I hate them, Hannah. I just can't help it. I hate every last Indian."

"But your hatred certainly can't extend to the Crow, Betsy. Or even to the many Shoshone who have been friendly to us. Two Moons and his Crow people have been especially warm toward us."

Betsy was staring into the sun-dappled water of the creek and didn't reply.

Hannah continued to speak. "And then there are the Crow who serve as scouts for the forts all over Wyoming and into Montana. Though I haven't met them, I've heard much about the Crow who scout for Colonel Bateman—Gray Fox, Little Bull, Running Antelope, Tall Bird, and others. They've all proven their loyalty to the 'white man's' army, Betsy. You know that."

"Yes, but I don't trust them, Hannah. They're Indians. I still cringe whenever one of them comes near me. I wish Colonel Bateman would send them away and not use them." She stopped on the creek bank and turned her dark flashing eyes on Hannah. "This Blackfoot thing. Maybe when the Crows see the soldiers killing red men, they will turn on them."

"It's not like they've never seen such before," said Hannah. "The Crow scouts *have* seen the Fort Bridger soldiers killing red men, on several occasions. I've heard the soldiers talking about battles here in days gone by. And the Crow have still remained true and faithful to the army."

Betsy kicked a stone into the water, watched it splash and sink, then said, "Have you met this new major in the fort?"

"Major Clint Barker? Yes."

"No, not him. The one who came a couple of weeks before the Barkers arrived. Blaine Garland."

"Oh, yes. I've met both the major and Flora. Seem like nice people."

"They are. I was talking to Flora just yesterday. She told

me that her husband also hates Indians, and that's because he's seen their atrocities against white people all over the West. They came here from Fort Bowie in Arizona, and she was telling me some horror stories about the Apaches. Flora said her husband hated Indians before they were assigned to Fort Bowie, but now he hates them with a vengeance."

Hannah sighed. "I hope Major Garland can keep a cool head if he gets into battle with the Blackfoot. Sometimes a burning hatred for the enemy can take control of a soldier and make him vulnerable. I remember Sol telling me many tales of such hatred he had seen in the war…of men who got themselves killed because their hatred toward the Rebels marred their good sense in battle."

Betsy's hands were trembling, and fear showed in her eyes again. "Oh, Hannah, why does there have to be war and killing? Why does there have to be any fighting at all? Why can't people just live peaceably with each other?"

"I guess it boils down to the sin nature we inherited from Adam," said Hannah. "Goes back to Satan. The very first human being ever born into this world after Adam and Eve fell into sin, declared war on his own brother and murdered him."

"That was Cain, right?"

"Yes. And 1 John 3:12 says Cain was of 'that wicked one'…the devil. Behind all the greed and hatred and killing among human beings is Satan."

Betsy grew quiet and leaned down to pick up a fist-sized rock. She tossed it into the creek, then turned to Hannah and said, "I'm so afraid for John. I live with fear day in and day out, just knowing that at any time some Indians might decide to attack his patrol. But now, with this Blackfoot thing—" Betsy suddenly burst into tears and sobbed, "Oh, Hannah! I'm so afraid! So terribly afraid!"

Hannah took her in her arms and held her, stroking her head until she gained control of her emotions. When the sobbing subsided, Hannah said, "Betsy, I can tell you how to have the torment of your fears relieved."

"You can?"

"I just quoted from 1 John 3. In chapter 4, verse 16, it says, 'God is love; and he that dwelleth in love dwelleth in God, and God in him.' In verse 18, it says, 'There is no fear in love; but perfect love casteth out fear: because fear hath torment. He that feareth is not made perfect in love.'"

Betsy was standing like a statue, gazing into the water, but Hannah could tell she was listening.

"Betsy, just think of it. He that dwelleth in love dwelleth in God, because God *is* love. Your home is your dwelling place, isn't it?"

"Yes," Betsy said without looking up.

"Well, to dwell in love is to dwell in a home of love. God Himself is that person's home. Do you understand?"

"I think so." Betsy's head came up. "And you're going to tell me that only those who have repented and received Jesus into their hearts are in God. At least, that's what you said before when we talked about going to heaven and all."

"That's right. Betsy, you can't have the Father unless you're willing to turn to Jesus for salvation and open your heart to Him. You can be a good person in the eyes of man. You can be religious. You can be baptized and do all the things churches tell you to do to get to heaven, but Jesus said, 'No man cometh unto the Father but by me.' No one else. Nothing else. Just Him."

Betsy continued to watch the ripples on the surface of the water.

Hannah waited a moment and then continued, "Once you open your heart to Jesus, Betsy, and are born into God's family, you dwell in God, because the Son dwells in the Father. When you're in Christ, you're in God. Then you're in that sweet home, which is God Himself, and God is love. As I already told you, the Bible says there is no fear in love. In God's love there is no place for fear, for perfect love casteth out fear.

"Betsy, this world we live in is a fearful place, but genuine Christians do not have to be tormented with fears. Dwelling in God and His love puts you in a position where the torment of fear can't get to you. If you will open your heart to Jesus, the fear that brings anguish whenever your John rides out on patrol will subside, and the Lord will not let it torment you. You'll feel concern, of course. It's only natural. But with anything in life here on earth that has tormenting fear connected to it, the Lord is able to cast it out so the child of God isn't tormented by it."

Betsy turned and looked at Hannah. For the first time that morning, since hearing the news about the uprising, a faint smile touched her lips. "I'll think about it, Hannah. Thank you. I—I just have a hard time believing about all this concentration on Jesus Christ. It just seems to me—as with my husband— that as long as we live clean and decent lives, God will take us to heaven when we die."

"Not so, honey. Jesus went to the cross for you, shed His precious blood, died, and raised Himself out of the grave. He is alive to save you if you'll open your heart to Him. To refuse is to deny Him, and nobody in that condition is going to heaven."

Betsy sighed. "I guess we'd better get back now." She wrapped her arms around her friend and squeezed her tight, then said, "I love you, Hannah Cooper. Thank you for talking to me. I do feel better now."

CHAPTER FOUR

On Sunday morning, dawn came with pinks and pale purples coating the sky. A cold breeze swept in from the north.

Inside the stockade fence, Colonel Bateman stood facing the seventeen patrol units lined up in distinct ranks on the parade ground. The men stood beside their saddled horses, holding the reins and standing at attention. The hard ground was scarred with deep ruts cut by the iron-shod wheels of the supply wagons that crossed the compound almost daily.

The units ranged from twelve to sixteen men apiece. Each trooper held a .44 caliber Springfield carbine in his free hand. The officers wore .45 caliber sidearms and had identical carbines in their saddle scabbards to those held by the enlisted men. Some of the units had Crow scouts.

The soldiers who would remain behind, as well as the families of the men going on patrol, were collected in various places to look on. Some stood at the stable. Others were in front of the smithy shed, at the barracks doors, on the quartermaster's porch, at the door of the mess hall, and on the boardwalk that ran in front of the single officers' quarters. All were dressed warmly to ward off the chill.

Pastor Andrew Kelly, who pastored the only church in town, was also chaplain of the fort. With his wife, Rebecca, he stood on the porch in front of the commandant's office, looking past Bateman at the stolid faces of the men who would no doubt soon engage the hostiles in battle.

"Men," Bateman said loudly and clearly, "just after midnight last night, I received word from two of our Crow scouts that the Blackfoot attacked a small white settlement on Muddy Creek yesterday, about thirty miles northeast of here, leaving over a hundred and fifty men, women, and children dead. The Crow scouts, who returned to Two Moons's village after making their report last night, said the Blackfoot war party that attacked the settlement are camped close by it.

"Therefore, I am sending two patrols that direction and will spread the others out in all other directions so that if the war party decides to head elsewhere, or if there are others roving about looking for settlements to attack, they can be intercepted."

Bateman ran his gaze to Major Blaine Garland, who stood beside his horse, his stern jaw set. "Major Garland, you will take your unit toward the Muddy Creek settlement."

Garland nodded. "Yes, sir."

Next, Bateman's eyes met those of Captain John Fordham. "Captain Fordham, your unit will accompany Major Garland and his men."

"Yes, sir," responded Fordham in military fashion.

On the boardwalk in front of the single officers' quarters, Betsy Fordham stood with her three children: Ryan, eleven; Will, nine; and little Belinda. The boys looked up into their mother's face, knowing that their father would lead his men into what might be the teeth of a Blackfoot war party. Though little Belinda didn't understand it all, she knew it was bad by the way her brothers reacted.

Betsy steeled herself and forced a look of confidence on her features. As she returned her children's searching looks, she was even able to give them a grim smile.

The colonel cleared his throat and said, "I will allow a

brief moment for you married men to speak to your families before you mount up; but first, I want Chaplain Kelly to lead us in prayer, asking God to protect all of you as you ride forth to do your bounded duty."

Andy Kelly stepped off the porch and drew up beside Bateman. There was a hush as he prayed earnestly for the protective hand of the Lord on each and every man, asking God to bring them all back safely.

When Kelly finished, Colonel Bateman ran his gaze over the ranks of cavalrymen and said, "Five minutes, men. You will be given the command to mount up in five minutes."

Like a swarm of locusts, wives and children rushed to their men to kiss and embrace them, and to wish them well.

John Fordham smiled as Betsy and the children dashed to him. Fordham was a tall man with dark hair and mustache. He had a finely chiseled face with square features. He managed a smile as he hugged his children, starting with Belinda, and working his way up, according to age.

He then turned to his wife of nearly thirteen years and grasped both of her hands. He could feel her trembling. John's love for Betsy warmed his blood. He looked into her deep, expressive eyes, the kind a man could drown in. He looked at her wonderful coal-black hair. The graceful lines of her throat. The laugh lines at the corners of her mouth, which only added to her beauty.

Only Betsy wasn't laughing now. She wasn't even smiling. As she gripped his hands, her shoulders slumped, and her face seemed to cave in. An icy coldness had formed in her chest, restricting her breathing.

As John held her close, he said, "Betsy, you've got to keep a grip on yourself, honey. Our kids need you to be strong."

She drew in a shuddering breath as she clung to him. "I...I know, darling. I'm trying so hard."

"You did all right when I went off to fight the Rebels."

"That was different. You were at least fighting civilized men. Not heartless savages like the Blackfoot."

John relaxed his arms and let her slip back enough that he could look into her eyes. Tears were coursing down her cheeks. He cupped her face in his hands and used his thumbs to brush away the tears. "Honey, fighting the Blackfoot is no different than fighting Rebels. Both are human beings."

"No, John!" she said, choking slightly on her words. "Those Indians are nothing but devils with no conscience! They—"

"Betsy, listen to me. I'll be all right. You must believe that."

"How can I?" she asked, lips quivering. "If you're captured, they'll torture you, and—"

The blast of a bugle interrupted Betsy's words. John kissed his wife tenderly and told her he loved her, then spoke to his children one more time before taking his horse's reins and turning to prepare to mount.

As wives and children retreated to their former spots, Colonel Bateman stood before his cavalry and commanded, "Rifles in place!"

Almost as one man, the troopers slid their carbines into their saddle scabbards. When that was done, the colonel called, "Mount up!"

The first unit to move out was led by Major Clint Barker, who rode in front of his men as he shouted, "Company-y-y-y, ho-o-o-o!"

One by one, the patrol leaders led their men through the gate while those who stayed behind looked on with interest to the sound of creaking saddles, the jingle of bridle bits, and the soft pounding of hooves.

Betsy pulled her children close and held them tightly until John passed from view, then forced her voice to remain steady as she said, "Let's go get some breakfast in your stomachs."

As they walked together toward their house, which stood

under the towering pines next to Black's Fork Creek, Betsy knew it was going to be a long, difficult day. The better occupied she and the children were, the faster it would seem to pass.

"Tell you what," she said to her offspring, "I think it would be good for us to go to church today."

The boys agreed, saying they always enjoyed going to church and hearing Pastor Kelly preach.

Belinda jostled her mother excitedly. "Oh, boy, Mommy! I can sit by Patty Ruth in our Sunday school class! And…and could I sit by her in preachin' too?"

"You sure can, honey," said Betsy. "We'll just make it a point to sit by the Coopers in the service."

Hannah Cooper was gathered outside the gate with the rest of the townspeople to watch the cavalrymen ride out.

Captain John Fordham had a special liking for Chris Cooper, who had a military career in mind for himself. On several occasions, the boy had been privileged to visit the fort as a guest of Colonel Bateman, Major Crawley, and Captain Fordham. Each time, Chris had learned more about the army, fort life, and military procedure. On his last visit, only a few days earlier, he had found a new friend, Lieutenant Dobie Carlin.

Hannah smiled when she saw Captain Fordham salute Chris and Chris snap a return salute. In Fordham's unit, riding two rows behind him, was Lieutenant Carlin, who also smiled at Hannah's oldest son and saluted him. Again, Chris snapped a salute.

Hannah leaned close to her son and said, "Who is that lieutenant who saluted you, son?"

"That's Dobie Carlin, Mama," replied the fourteen-year-old.

"Remember, I told you I met him when I visited the fort on Tuesday?"

"Oh, yes. I recall you mentioning you'd made friends with a lieutenant in the fort. I'd forgotten his name. He just came here, didn't he?"

"Uh-huh. 'Bout two weeks ago, he told me. I really like him."

Even as she spoke, Hannah's gaze remained fastened on Lieutenant Dobie Carlin's face. There was something wistful about the look in Carlin's eyes, but she didn't mention it to Chris, who was now enthralled with the sight of the cavalrymen sitting tall and straight in their saddles, the metal of their rifles and sabers shining brilliantly in the morning sun.

Patty Ruth took her older brother by the hand, looked up at him as she squinted against the sunlight, and said, "You're gonna be a so'jer when you grow up, aren't ya, Chris? Jus' like Papa was."

"That's right, Patty Ruth," said Chris, squeezing the chubby little hand. "I sure am."

Later that morning, as Hannah and her children drew near the town hall where the church services were held, they caught sight of Betsy, Ryan, Will, and Belinda already standing in front, talking to Dr. and Mrs. Frank O'Brien.

Belinda ran to Patty Ruth, her eyes sparkling. "Hi, Patty Ruth!"

"Hi," said the little redhead, who held her stuffed bear in one arm.

"I'm gonna sit by you in Sunday school, and Mommy said I could sit by you in church, too!"

Hannah greeted the O'Briens and gave Betsy a hug as the older children greeted each other and went inside the building together. She was pleased to see Betsy and her children at church. The more gospel they heard, the sooner they would come to the Lord.

In the morning service, Pastor Kelly announced that their new church building would be ready for occupancy within two weeks. He then introduced a new family who had just moved to the area from the territory of New Mexico. David Morley, his wife Leah, and their two children—Keith, twelve, and Ellen, ten—had just bought a ranch a few miles east of town. Kelly asked the people to make them feel welcome when the service was over.

Before preaching his sermon, the pastor had a special time of prayer for the cavalrymen who were on patrol. Hannah had made a point of sitting next to Betsy and held her hand during the prayer. As the pastor delivered the message, Hannah prayed in her heart that the Lord would drive home the gospel to Betsy, Ryan, and Will.

When the service was over, the people indeed made the Morleys feel welcome. David and Leah were a handsome couple in their early thirties. David was an inch or two under six feet and was quite muscular, with a thick head of sand-colored hair. Leah was very blonde and had a scrubbed farm-girl look, with naturally rosy cheeks. Both Keith and Ellen had the sandy hair of their father.

When the Morleys learned that Betsy's husband was leading one of the patrols, Leah put her arm around Betsy and said, "Mrs. Fordham, I'll be praying very hard today for the captain, that the Lord will bring him home safely to you."

"So will I, ma'am," said David.

Betsy fought back her tears. "Thank you both. I appreciate it very much."

Moments later, the Morleys turned to receive the greetings of other church members, and Betsy and her children began walking with the O'Briens, the Williamses, and the Coopers.

"Hannah," said Edie O'Brien, "we got a letter yesterday from Michael. He's planning to come sometime in December, or maybe just after the first of the year. Depends on when they can get a replacement for him at the clinic where he's on the medical staff."

"Oh, that'll be wonderful," said Hannah. "I'm sure you'll be glad to see him."

"We sure will," said Doc, his blue eyes beaming. "I want him to get under Pastor Kelly's preaching. Edie and I have no doubt that Michael is saved, but he's just grown cold toward the Lord. His letters make this quite evident. He just doesn't have the old bubble in his life anymore. Doing fine in his medical practice, but not so fine in his walk with the Lord."

"Well, I'm sure when he gets under the right kind of preaching, the Lord will work in his life," Hannah said.

"I agree with that," said Gary Williams. "And Pastor Kelly's preaching is the right kind."

Glenda chuckled. "It sure straightened *you* out, husband of mine."

Gary elbowed her playfully, and said, "Seems *you've* made some changes, too, wife o' mine."

"Not as many as you," Glenda said.

"I know," said Gary with a sly grin. "There's plenty of room for more repenting from you!"

Glenda gave him a mock scowl. "Men!" she said.

Gary laughed and gave her a quick affectionate squeeze.

"Dr. and Mrs. O'Brien, why is your son coming to Fort Bridger?" Betsy asked.

"He's going to work with Doc, then eventually take the practice," said Edie. "Doc's going to retire."

"Not that I've got so many years on me, Betsy," said Doc, clearing his throat. "It's just the miles."

Betsy laughed. "Oh. All right. I understand."

Hannah was glad to hear Betsy laugh. Just being at church

and around Christians had seemingly helped her.

"Look, Mama!" Chris said, pointing up the street. "It's Chief Two Moons! He's got some of his braves with him!"

Two Moons and his small band of braves were stopped in front of the new general store building. The chief had dismounted and was looking through the windows.

Betsy took hold of Hannah's hand, squeezing it hard. Her skin had prickled in sudden fear, and her heart was thudding against her ribs. Hannah could feel her anxiety, and said, "Betsy, it's only Two Moons and some of his men. You don't have to be afraid of them."

The Coopers and the O'Briens kept walking, and Betsy went along reluctantly, her children following. Her face was a mask of fear mixed with contempt as they drew up to Two Moons.

The chief did not miss the look on Betsy's face, but he ignored it and greeted the group. Hannah was still holding Betsy's hand as Two Moons, wearing his full headdress, said, "We come town...see if store finished."

"Not quite," Hannah said, smiling warmly. "It will be ready to use in about three weeks."

"Mmm," said the dark-skinned chief, nodding.

"Two Moons, did you actually came all the way here just to see about my store?"

The chief smiled and snorted. "Two Moons not speak clear. We come to *fort* for one thing, then come into *town* to see about store."

"Oh, I see."

"We come to fort, bring two braves who wish to work as army scouts. Two Moons tell Colonel Ross Bateman they good men. Can be trusted. They with him now, talk business. Rest of us come to look at store."

Hannah could feel the tension in Betsy as she continued to hold her hand. Yet Ryan, Will, and Belinda didn't seem frightened of the Indians at all. Hannah was glad they had met up with Two Moons this way.

"Chief Two Moons," she said, "you already know Dr. and Mrs. O'Brien."

"Mmm," nodded the chief, smiling at the Irish pair.

"Hello, Chief," said Doc.

"It is nice to see you," said Two Moons, letting his dark gaze run to Betsy and her children.

"And Chief," said Hannah, "this is Betsy Fordham. Her husband is Captain John Fordham. And these are her children, Ryan, Will, and Belinda."

"Belinda's my best frien'," piped up Patty Ruth.

"That nice," said Two Moons. "Good to have friend. Like Chris is Broken Wing best friend."

"Yeah, like that," said Chris. "How is my best friend doing, sir?"

"He fine. Busy making new bow for arrows today."

"Oh. Maybe he and I will get to go squirrel hunting together?"

"Mmm. That be good."

Two Moons smiled at Betsy and said, "Glad make your acquaintance, Mrs. Betsy Fordham. And Ryan Fordham, Will Fordham, and Belinda Fordham."

The children nodded at him and smiled slightly. Hannah nudged Betsy.

With an audible swallow, Betsy managed the words, "You too, Chief."

"And how is my friend, Sweet Blossom?" asked Hannah.

"Sweet Blossom do fine. She looking for Hannah Cooper to visit again."

"I'll have to do that, Chief. I'm not sure just when I can come. I am carrying my husband's baby, which will be born in the springtime."

"Mmm," Two Moons said, letting his line of sight drop to

her slightly swollen midsection. "Maybe Sweet Blossom come see Hannah Cooper."

"That would be wonderful," said Hannah. "Bring her any time you wish."

Two Moons nodded, then bid them good-bye, mounted his horse, and rode away leading his braves.

When the Indians were a half-block away, Betsy put a shaky hand to her mouth and took a deep breath.

Hannah laid a hand on her arm. "Betsy, believe me. You don't have to be afraid of the Crows."

Betsy's chest moved in a quick, shallow rhythm as she gasped for air and said shakily, "I'm sorry, Hannah. I just can't help it. They frighten me. *All* Indians frighten me."

Glenda took a step toward Betsy. "I've already invited everyone else here to dinner at our house. Will you please accept an invitation to come eat with us?"

Betsy licked dry lips as little Patty Ruth and Belinda looked at each other and waited, hoping the answer would be yes. "Why, I...I really don't want to barge in on you, Glenda. I mean, four additional mouths means more food than you had planned, and more work."

"Oh, pshaw! It won't be a problem at all. Please? We'll help keep your mind off John's present situation."

"Please, Mommy," spoke up Belinda, who stood shoulder-to-shoulder with her best friend.

Betsy looked at Glenda. "You're sure this isn't going to be too much?"

"Absolutely."

"Keerect!" said Gary.

"All right. We'll take you up on it."

Patty Ruth and Belinda jumped up and down for joy.

Glenda Williams was an excellent cook and had plenty of experience cooking at Glenda's Place. As everyone took their places around a large round oak table covered with a snowy white cloth, Hannah made sure she sat next to Betsy.

Gary carved a succulent, golden brown turkey served with cornbread dressing, mounds of whipped potatoes, rich gravy, stewed tomatoes canned from their own garden, and thick slices of hot homemade bread. There was milk for the children and steaming hot coffee for the grown-ups.

During the meal, Hannah watched Betsy slowly grow calmer and actually begin to enjoy herself. Doc O'Brien told stories of his experiences as an army doctor in the war. Most of his tales were humorous, and even Betsy laughed.

They were just finishing dessert—black walnut cake— when the grandfather clock in the hall pealed four chimes.

Suddenly there were loud voices in the street. Gary jumped up from the table to see what was happening. Doc went with him.

It was some seven or eight minutes before the two men came back to the dining room, concern written on their faces.

"What is it, Gary?" asked Glenda.

"One of the…ah…patrols just came in. What was left of it, that is."

"What do you mean?" Betsy said, panic rising within her as she got up from the table.

"The patrol got into a battle with a Blackfoot war party. Half of the patrol was killed, and others were wounded."

Hannah laid a steady hand on Betsy's arm. "What patrol was it?" she asked.

"Those folks out there don't know, Hannah," said Doc.

"Their information was secondhand."

Betsy let out a tiny squeal, and her features went chalk white. There was a desperate note in her voice as she said, "You men don't have to tell me! I know by the way you're acting…it was John's patrol. Wasn't it? It was John's patrol! Tell me the truth!"

Doc moved toward Betsy and took hold of her shoulders. He looked her square in the eye and said, "Mrs. Fordham, Gary and I *are* telling you the truth. Those people out there honestly don't know whose patrol came in all shot up. We wouldn't hold anything back from you."

Betsy shook her head and screamed, "It was John's patrol! I know it! He's dead! He's dead!"

Belinda ran to her mother, crying, "Daddy's not dead, Mommy! He's not!"

Ryan and Will put their arms around their weeping, terrified mother and tried to comfort her.

Betsy was still weeping when Doc said, "Mrs. Fordham, someone told me that your husband's unit was riding with that new major's unit. What's his name?"

"Major…Blaine Garland." Betsy could barely choke out the words.

"Yes, Garland," said Doc. "So actually, there were *two* patrols together. But everybody in the street kept saying *the* patrol. It couldn't be your husband's, ma'am."

Betsy turned toward Glenda and stammered, "I—is it all right if I leave the children here till I can go to the fort and find out?"

Glenda scooted her chair back and stood up. "I'll keep the children, Betsy, but I don't want you to go alone."

"I'll go with her," said Hannah.

"I'll go, too," said Gary and the doctor in unison.

"I'll help Glenda with the children," Edie said.

When Betsy, Hannah, Doc, and Gary approached the fort, two sentries looked down from the platform on the stockade wall above them. "Can we help you folks?" asked one of them.

"We need to know about the patrol that just came in," said Doc. "Understand it was pretty bad."

"Yes, sir, Dr. O'Brien. Pretty bad. They ran into that Blackfoot war party that did the massacre on Muddy Creek yesterday. Only they were about ten miles south of there."

"Oh, so it wasn't Major Garland and Captain Fordham's doubled-up unit?"

"No, sir. It was Captain Darrell Brown's unit. Twelve men. Six were killed. Three wounded. Dr. Blayney is working on them now. Captain Brown was killed."

Betsy's instant relief turned to fresh horror. She knew Captain Brown and his wife, Roberta, well.

Turning to Hannah, she said, "I must go see Roberta and try to comfort her. Would you bring Ryan, Will, and Belinda to my house? I want to be here when John's patrol arrives."

"I'll be happy to, honey," said Hannah.

An hour and a half later, Betsy and her children were at the fort's gate when the patrols began arriving. The columns of blue-clad riders were coming in from every direction.

Suddenly Ryan pointed to the northeast. "Mom! It's Dad and Major Garland! They're coming in together. I don't see any riderless horses, or horses with men draped over their backs."

The words, "Praise God!" slipped from Betsy's lips.

When Captain Fordham dismounted to greet his family, Belinda leaped into his arms, and Betsy dashed to him. The boys closed in tight, welcoming their father home.

As they stood holding on to each other, Betsy said, "Oh, darling, we've been so afraid for you."

"Well, as you can see, I'm unscathed," he said.

"Did you run into any bad Indians, Dad?" asked Will.

"No, son. Didn't see a one. We found out the war party we were after had gone south. But we never saw them."

"Darrell Brown and his men ran into them, John," said Betsy.

"Oh?"

"Six men in the unit were killed, including Darrell."

"Oh, no!"

"Three others wounded, too. Looks like they'll be all right, according to Dr. Blayney."

"I'm glad to hear that."

"I...ah...I spent about a half hour with Roberta. Several other women were there, along with Pastor Kelly."

John nodded. "I'm glad you went to her, honey."

Betsy began to tremble. "She would have done the same for me it if had been you."

The Fordham family stayed in a close knot as John tried to encourage them and calm Betsy's weeping. "We'll get this Blackfoot thing under control, sweet ones, then the fighting will stop. At least for a while."

"I wish it would stop forever," said Ryan.

"Can't give you that kind of hope, son. We'll just have to take it one day at a time."

"One day at a time," echoed Betsy, trying to raise her own spirits while wiping her tears. "That's what we'll have to do. Take it one day at a time."

CHAPTER FIVE

Early on Monday morning, the soldiers who were killed the day before were buried in a solemn service conducted by Chaplain Andrew Kelly.

As soon as the bugler played taps, all patrols made ready to mount up. This time, Hannah Cooper remained close to the Fordhams. Betsy held up extremely well until her husband's patrol passed from view. At that point, she turned to Hannah and said, "I'm going to cry."

"No, you're not," Hannah said evenly. "You're going to hold your head up and take this one day at a time, as you told me a little while ago."

Betsy's features looked pinched. "I…I can't, Hannah. I can't."

"I'm here to see that you do," said Hannah. "But if you were in the place where fear cannot come, you'd find God's grace sufficient. He could do so much more for you than I can, if you would let Him."

Betsy pressed her lips tightly together, then said, "You really believe that, don't you?"

"With all my heart."

Betsy nodded, then drew in a deep breath and held it. She looked toward the gate where she had last seen her husband and let out the breath slowly. "I'll be fine, Hannah. Thank you for coming to be with me."

With that, Betsy turned toward her house, where Ryan, Will, and Belinda stood on the porch, waiting for her.

It was midmorning when Hannah sat on a stool behind the counter in the sutler's building, writing up an order to send to her supplier in Cheyenne City. Patty Ruth was playing next to her with Tony the Bear. She had Tony sitting on a chair and was feeding him breakfast.

Hannah smiled to herself when she heard her little daughter say, "There, Tony. That's a good boy. You ate all your oatmeal and you ate your fried eggs. Now, don't you burp. It isn't polite to burp at the table."

The door opened, letting in the cool fall air, and Hannah was pleased to see David and Leah Morley.

"Good morning, folks," she said, smiling broadly. "How are the Morleys today?"

"These two are just fine," replied Leah as they drew up to the counter. "And the other two are just fine because they're in school, and they love Miss Lindgren."

"All her students love her," said Hannah. "I know my children sure do."

More customers came in, and the Morleys began gathering groceries. Later, when they were ready for Hannah to total up the bill, they were the only customers in the store.

When Hannah had been paid, David said, "Mrs. Cooper, Leah and I would like to invite you and your children to have supper with us this Thursday evening. Could you come?"

"Why, that's awfully nice of you," Hannah responded warmly. "Of course we can."

"We're sort of making it a 'get acquainted' thing," said Leah. "We've already invited Pastor and Mrs. Kelly for the same time, and we're planning to invite the Fordhams. We really took to Betsy and the children, and we'd like to meet the captain."

"Sounds like a fun time," said Hannah. "Is there anything I can bring?"

"No, ma'am," said David. "All these groceries we just bought will more than take care of everything. Now, would you like me to come and pick you up? We understand you're living at the hotel at present."

"Yes. That would be nice. What time should we be ready?"

"Let's say…six-thirty?"

"Fine. The children and I will look forward to it. We'll be in the hotel lobby at six-thirty Thursday evening."

The door opened, and a small, pretty brunette came in. She recognized the Morleys and said, "Hello, David and Leah! Remember me? I'm Julie Powell. We met at church yesterday."

"Yes," said David. "Nice to see you again."

"Hello, Hannah," said Julie. "You ready to sit down and let me take over?"

"I think so." Then to the Morleys she said, "Some of the ladies from the town and fort have volunteered to help me run the store, since I have a baby on the way."

"We heard about it, Mrs. Cooper," said Leah. "And about the loss of your husband. I'm so sorry."

"Thank you."

"I'd like to volunteer to help," said Leah. "I suppose there's some kind of schedule set up."

"That's very kind of you," said Hannah. "You met Glenda Williams at church yesterday…"

"Yes."

"She's the schedule setter-upper."

"Then I'll see her about it."

"Thank you so much."

"Well," said David, hoisting his box of groceries, "we'll see you ladies Wednesday night at church, and I'll pick you and the children up at six-thirty on Thursday evening, Mrs. Cooper."

"I'd like it better if you'd both call me Hannah."

"Okay, Hannah," said David, and started toward the door.

Leah hurried ahead of him to open it, saying over her shoulder, "Bye, Hannah...Mrs. Powell."

"Julie," called the small brunette.

"'Bye, Julie!"

A red glow was just beginning to fade on the western horizon as Betsy Fordham paced back and forth at the fort's gate, wringing her hands. All the patrols had returned within the past half hour except her husband's. She looked out over the rolling hills surrounding Fort Bridger, where twilight was settling gray on the crests, and darkness in the hollows.

Betsy's children were in the tower with the sentries, looking out over the undulating land, hoping to catch a glimpse of their father's unit.

"Don't you fret, Mrs. Fordham," said one of the men in the tower. "They'll be along any minute now."

Betsy glanced up. "I sure hope you're right."

"Wait a minute!" shouted the other sentry. "Here they come now!"

"Yeah!" shouted Ryan, following the sentry's pointing finger. "It's them, Mom! It's them! I can make out Dad in the lead!"

The children stayed in the tower, watching the oncoming column of riders. When they were within fifty yards, Betsy lifted her skirts a few inches and ran as fast as she could toward them. John saw her coming and slid from the saddle. "You men go on in," he said to his unit, and took Betsy in his arms.

The weary cavalrymen moved on toward the gate as Betsy clung to her husband and said with a quaver in her voice, "I was so afraid you'd met up with a war party! I pictured you—"

"I'm all right, as you can see, honey," said John. "Are all the other patrols back?"

"Yes."

"Any of them meet up with hostiles?"

"No. Why are you so late?"

"Had to stop and help a rancher. His horse stepped into a hole and broke its leg, but when it went down, the rancher couldn't get out of the saddle fast enough. He was pinned beneath the horse. We got him out from under the horse. Had to shoot it. Then we took him to his house, which was quite some distance away. I'm sorry you were worried."

"No fault of yours, darling," said Betsy as they started toward the fort with John leading his horse. "You did the right thing to help that rancher."

In the gathering gloom, John saw his children waiting at the gate beside one of the sentries. When he and Betsy drew close, he called, "Hey, Belinda! Can you beat your brothers and hug Daddy's neck first?"

Belinda sprang forward, running for all she was worth. Ryan and Will were on her heels but purposely let her win the race. John hugged all three of his children. Then, as the family passed through the gate, he said, "Honey, you and the kids go on to the house. I'll put the horse in the corral, then make a brief stop at the colonel's house to give a report. Be home in about twenty minutes."

Betsy didn't want to let him out of her sight, but she nodded and took the children home.

As John led his horse toward the stables, he looked over his shoulder at Betsy and sighed. He wanted to calm her fears but felt powerless to help her.

Thursday night came, and when David Morley ushered Hannah and her children into his ranch house, Betsy and John Fordham had already arrived, as had Pastor Kelly and Rebecca. The pastor introduced John to David, and while Hannah and Mary Beth joined the women and young Ellen Morley in the kitchen, the men sat down in front of the fireplace in the parlor. Patty Ruth and Belinda were together in a corner, and Chris, B. J., Keith, Ryan, and Will were already sitting at the special table in the dining room where they would be eating. Chris was leading a discussion on military procedure.

Soon the meal was on the table, and everyone sat down at their places assigned by Leah. The house was filled with the delicious aromas of juicy baked ham spiked with cloves, glazed sweet potatoes, creamed baby peas, applesauce, and fluffy biscuits delicately browned on top.

Pastor Kelly offered thanks to the Lord for the food, and then everyone eagerly passed the plates.

As the meal progressed, the inevitable topic of discussion was the hostile Blackfoot war parties and the white people they were attacking. Two more settlements had been wiped out in southern Wyoming Territory within the past four days—both within fifty miles of Fort Bridger. Apparently the Blackfoot had waited till the army patrols had passed by the settlements, then attacked when the patrols were out of sight and earshot.

David changed the subject by turning to Hannah and saying, "I see your new store building is near completion."

"Yes, about two weeks, maybe a little more. It will be good to have my own building again."

"We've heard the story," said Leah. "How it was Alex Patterson who set the fire, and why…and that as a result of it, you were able to lead him to the Lord."

Hannah smiled. "Hard way to reach a man for Jesus, but it was worth it."

"It'll be worth it even more when you and Alex meet at heaven's gates, Hannah," said the preacher.

"I'm sure of that," she said, adjusting her position on the chair. Already the baby was beginning to make her feel somewhat uncomfortable.

"We've also heard that someone in the church gave you the money so you could rebuild it," said David. "I think it's marvelous. Whoever they are, it was a very generous thing to do."

"That it was," said Hannah, smiling at the Kellys. "It really is no secret who did it, David. You remember meeting Justin and Julie Powell at church…and you saw Julie in the store the other day."

"Yes?"

"They are the benefactors."

"Well, bless their hearts," said Leah. "What does Justin do for a living?"

"He works at Swensen's Hardware Store and Gun Shop."

David and Leah exchanged glances.

"And they were able to give you the kind of money it would take to rebuild your store?" said David.

Pastor Kelly spoke up. "Justin had a wealthy uncle who died and left him a substantial amount of money. He and Julie were kind enough to share a large portion of it with the Coopers."

"There was a reason behind it, which Hannah won't tell you," said Rebecca Kelly, "so I will. When Justin and Julie were destitute financially, Hannah gave them their groceries for several weeks. Later, when the unexpected inheritance came, the Lord timed it perfectly so they could help Hannah exactly when she needed it. Their gift to her came because of what she had done for them when they were in need."

"Now that Rebecca's told on me," said Hannah, "let me point out how good our God is. What little I gave the Powells, the Lord multiplied hundreds of times. Justin and Julie not only gave the children and me enough to rebuild the store and barn, they gave us enough to refurnish the new apartment upstairs and replace all the clothing and household articles we lost in the fire. And the Lord also touched contractor Clayton Farley's heart to rebuild the store for a special lower price. He's the one who built the first store building. The same God who provided for our salvation at Calvary is able to provide for our earthly needs."

"That's a marvelous story of God's grace and provision!" said David, smiling broadly. "Isn't Clayton Farley the man who's building your new church house, Pastor?"

"Yes," Kelly said. "Very conscientious man. Does a great job."

"Well!" said Leah, looking around the table and casting a glance at the nearby table where the boys sat. "Looks like everybody's about finished. Now it's dessert time!"

"Oh, boy!" said Keith Morley. "I know what it is! And is it ever good!"

The pastor gave the young boy a teasing smile. "Well, tell us, Keith!" he said.

"It's blackberry cobbler with real rich cream that Mom's got all whipped up!"

"Oh, no," said Hannah. "Blackberry cobbler! My favorite! Glenda is always making it at her house. I'm going to weigh a ton by the time this baby comes if I keep eating like this."

"You don't want any?" said Leah.

Hannah made a comical face. "Well…just a small piece. *Very* small, please."

After dessert, the men retired to the parlor while the women went to the kitchen. The women made Hannah sit while they and the girls washed and dried the dishes.

Keith took Ryan, Will, Chris, and B. J. upstairs to his room to show them his collection of painted wooden soldiers. Patty Ruth and Belinda played quietly on the hearth in the parlor—Belinda with her favorite doll, Betsy, and Patty Ruth with Tony the Bear.

In the kitchen, Mary Beth and Ellen paired off to dry dishes and talk about school. It wasn't long till Ellen knew that Mary Beth was planning one day to be a teacher like Miss Sundi Lindgren.

On the following Tuesday, late in the afternoon, Betsy Fordham and Belinda were taking Patty Ruth across the fort's compound to the sutler's building. It was almost closing time for the store, and Betsy wanted to have Patty Ruth there in time for Hannah to take her, along with the other children, to the hotel.

As Betsy and the girls drew near the store, they saw Leah Morley come out, buttoning her coat. Leah had helped Hannah at the store all day.

Just then, Chris rode through the gate on his horse, Buster, alongside Chief Two Moons's fifteen-year-old son, Broken Wing.

Patty Ruth ran ahead, calling, "Broken Wing! Hi!"

The teenage Crow slid off his pinto pony, smiling. "Hello, Patty Ruth!"

Betsy's whole body went rigid at sight of the Indian.

Belinda saw it and looked up at her. "Mommy, what's the matter?" she asked.

Betsy kept her voice low as she said, "It's that Indian with Chris. I wish they wouldn't let Indians inside the fort."

As she started walking toward the store again, she drew close to Broken Wing and glared at him, saying, "Come on, Patty Ruth. Let's take you to your mother inside the store."

"It's okay, ma'am," said the five-year-old. "I'll just stay out here with Chris and Broken Wing."

"You will not!" snapped Betsy, grabbing the child's hand. "I'm taking you inside!"

Patty Ruth bit her lip and glanced back at Chris as Betsy took her by the hand and pulled her through the door.

Hannah had just received payment from a rancher's wife at the counter when she looked up to see Betsy and the girls come in. She noticed that Betsy had a scowl on her face and was gripping Patty Ruth's hand. The little redhead looked dismayed. The rancher's wife thanked Hannah and walked out with her groceries.

Betsy dragged Patty Ruth to the counter and said sharply, "Hannah, this child was out there talking to that Indian boy who's with Chris! She wanted to stay out there with him, but I made her come in. They shouldn't let Indians inside the fort."

"There's no reason not to let friendly Indians in the fort," said Hannah. "And I don't mind Patty Ruth talking to Broken Wing."

"Well, you *should* mind! And you shouldn't let Chris run around with him! Don't you know what Indians are capable of?"

"I've told you before that the Crows are not like other Indians, Betsy," Hannah said. "Chris and Broken Wing are best friends. They ride and hunt small game together quite often. Right now, with the Blackfoot uprising going on, I only let Chris ride with him around the edge of town. I don't want him in the fields and forests where he would be vulnerable."

"Well, I think you'd better realize the kind of danger Chris is in, Hannah! That...that Broken Wing might just decide to put a knife in Chris's back!"

Hannah rounded the end of the counter and took Patty Ruth's hand. She shook her head and said, "Betsy, I trust Broken Wing implicitly. He's a very nice boy. I appreciate your concern, but Chris is in no danger from him."

Betsy's mouth pulled down in a hard, unrelenting line. "You're playing the fool, Hannah Cooper! When will you learn that you can't trust an Indian? *Any* Indian!" She grabbed Belinda's hand and said, "Come on, Belinda! We're going home!"

Hannah called after the angry woman. "Betsy! Don't leave like this! Come back and let's talk!"

"We've already talked about it!" Betsy said over her shoulder.

Suddenly the door came open, and Justin and Julie Powell came in with their children, Casey and Carrie. Their eyes popped as Betsy pushed past them and charged through the door, dragging a confused Belinda.

"Hi," said Hannah. "How are the Powells today?"

"The Powells are fine," said Justin, looking back over his shoulder, "but apparently Mrs. Fordham isn't."

"Betsy has some problems," said Hannah. "One of them is her fear of Indians. She's feared them for a long time—ever since she was a child. Now it has developed into a hatred, and she's upset because I let Chris be friends with Broken Wing."

"Doesn't she know the Crows aren't like other Indians?" asked Julie.

"I've tried to explain that, but it doesn't seem to help. It hurts me to see her so full of hatred."

"Maybe she'll get over it someday," said Justin.

"The main problem is her need to know the Lord," said Julie. "I pray for the Fordhams every day, that the Lord will bring them to Himself."

"Me too," said Hannah.

The three stood silently for a moment, then Justin said, "Well, guess what?"

"Okay, *what?*" said Hannah.

"This morning, Hans and Greta called me into the office

and offered to sell the store to me."

"Really?"

"Yes, ma'am! They want to move back East to be near their children and grandchildren."

"Well, it looks like my prayers have been answered. You know I've been praying for the Lord to lead you and Julie. This is really great! You already know the business."

"Right," said Justin. "We're thrilled, and we just wanted to come by and tell you about it."

"Well, I'm glad you did. Now I can change how I pray for you and ask the Lord to abundantly bless your business."

Julie gave Hannah a hug and said, "God knows how to abundantly bless, Hannah. He abundantly blessed us with a friend and sister in the Lord."

Hannah laughed. "The real blessing was when the Lord brought the Powells into my life!"

When they had gone, Hannah turned to Patty Ruth. "Well, we'd better head for the Williamses' house, or we'll miss supper!"

As they stepped outside and Hannah locked the door, Chris walked up, having put Buster in the army stable.

"Where are Mary Beth and B. J., Mama?" he asked.

"They're already at the Williamses'."

"Oh, Mama...let's go!" said Patty Ruth. "Or B. J. will eat it all!"

After supper, Hannah and her children walked through the hotel lobby on the way to their rooms. There were a few overstuffed chairs on one side of the lobby where people often gathered. Hannah saw Betsy Fordham, alone, sitting in one. She rose from her chair as the Coopers headed for the stairs.

Betsy's eyes were swollen and bloodshot as she drew up

and said, "Hannah, could I talk to you?"

"Certainly. Would you like to talk here or up in my room?"

"In your room, if it's all right."

"Of course."

Hannah told the children to go to their rooms; she would see them in a little while.

Betsy was quiet as they mounted the stairs and walked down the hall. When they entered Hannah's room, she began sniffling, and then threw her arms around Hannah and broke into sobs.

"Oh, Hannah, I'm so sorry for the way I talked to you! And...and for walking out on you like I did! Please! Can you find it in your heart to forgive me?"

Hannah hugged her tight. "Of course, honey. I forgive you. I know you've been under a lot of stress."

"That's no excuse. You've been such a good friend to me. You didn't deserve to be treated in such a rude and terrible manner. I'm sorry! Oh, I'm so sorry!"

Hannah pulled back and looked into Betsy's tear-dimmed eyes. "Betsy, I'm hoping that you'll learn to trust the Crows. I appreciate your concern for Chris being with Broken Wing, but I trust Two Moons and his people as much as I trust any white folks."

"I...I just don't think I could ever trust any Indian, Hannah. But I'll keep my mouth shut about how you feel toward them. I had no right to get angry at you."

"We'll consider it a closed issue," said Hannah. "Let's not ever allow anything to come between us."

"We won't, I'm sure. I'm so sorry."

"Don't punish yourself. It's over and forgotten, okay?"

Betsy looked her straight in the eye. "You mean like when a person asks Jesus to forgive them for all their sins...it's over with and forgotten by Him?"

"Yes. Like that. Only Jesus forgives and forgets better than any of us could."

CHAPTER SIX

Saturday arrived, bringing with it a heavily clouded sky and a cold wind that loosened and scattered the orange and yellow leaves from birch, aspen, and cottonwood. To the southwest, the ragged peaks of the Uintah Mountains were erased from view by low scudding clouds as dark as gunmetal.

Wind tugged at the feathers worn by Two Moons and his braves as they rode into town. The Crows had brought a wagon and team to transport Sundi Lindgren and Mary Beth Cooper to the Crow village. The two young women held regular Saturday classes for the Indian children.

The Crows were dressed warmly in furs, and the women wore coats and scarves to ward off the cold.

Hannah Cooper and Heidi Lindgren were there to see the teacher and her assistant off. Mary Beth's countenance made Hannah's heart glad. Mary Beth was born to be a teacher, and she was learning so much from Sundi, who delighted in using her as a student teacher.

The brave who drove the wagon helped Sundi and Mary Beth onto the wagon seat before climbing up himself.

"See you this evening, honey," Hannah said to her daughter as the wagon pulled away.

"Bye, Mama."

Two Moons took a moment to thank Hannah for allowing

her daughter to teach the Crow children, then trotted away with his braves following.

Just before the wagon passed from view, both Sundi and Mary Beth looked back and waved.

Heidi and Hannah waved in return. "Two happy girls," said Heidi.

Hannah nodded her agreement. "Especially Mary Beth. When she's teaching with Sundi, her feet are in the clouds."

Heidi looked up at the overcast sky. "Speaking of clouds, looks like we're about to get our first snow of the season."

"It's going to miss a good chance if it doesn't snow on us," said Hannah. "Well, Heidi, it's off to work for me."

"Where are your other children?"

"Glenda is taking care of B. J. and Patty Ruth for the day. Chris is already at the store to sweep up and dust the place for me. He and Broken Wing are going riding together this afternoon."

"And who's helping you in the store today?"

"Mandy Carver. She's got Grandma Yeggie taking care of her children so she can help me."

Heidi knew Myrtle Yeggie, who had been a part of Fort Bridger since Jim Bridger first established it as a trading post in 1843. Her husband had been a close friend of Bridger's in the fur trading business before his death in 1846. She was a dedicated Christian, and though her eighty years hindered her from doing all the things she would like to do for people, she did what she could. She loved the Carvers' three children and was happy to look after them so Mandy could help Hannah at the store.

"That's sweet of Grandma to help you indirectly this way," said Heidi. "And it's sweet of Mandy to pitch in."

"It sure is," agreed Hannah, pulling her coat collar tighter around her neck. "And it's mighty sweet of a certain Heidi Lindgren to close her shop a half-day a week to help me."

Heidi patted Hannah's shoulder. "We love you, Hannah. That's why we pitch in."

"I know that." Hannah took hold of the hand on her shoulder. "And I love all of you, too."

Heidi's attention was drawn down the street to Mandy Carver, who was hurrying toward them. "Here she comes now," Heidi said.

As Mandy drew near, her smile revealed her beautiful snow-white teeth. "'Mo'nin', Miz Hannah, an' you too, Miz Heidi," she said with a lilt in her voice. "Beautiful day, isn't it?"

Hannah and Heidi looked at each other.

Mandy laughed. "Don' let those clouds up there fool you! The sun is a-shinin' above 'em! It really is a beautiful day because the Lord done made it! Psalm a hundred eighteen and verse twenty-fo': 'This is the day which the Lord hath made; we will rejoice an' be glad in it'!"

"Can't argue with that," Heidi said, and laughed.

Mandy grinned. "'Bout time fo' us to be openin' the store, Miz Hannah."

"You're right. So long, Heidi."

Late in the afternoon, the wind was still blowing, and the clouds continued to hang low.

At the north edge of town, Chris Cooper and Broken Wing finished their ride and reined in.

Chris smiled at his friend. "Thanks for riding with me, Broken Wing. See you on Monday after school?"

"We will ride again on Monday," Broken Wing replied, leaning from his pinto to shake hands with Chris Indian style.

"Maybe someday your father will allow you to come on a Sunday and visit our church."

Broken Wing smiled. "Maybe someday."

Chris sat his horse and watched Broken Wing gallop northward. When the Indian boy was about a hundred yards out, he reined to a halt, turned around on the pinto's back, and waved before heading northward again. Soon he disappeared among the forested hills.

Chris caught movement from the corner of his eye and turned his head to see an army patrol coming in from the northwest. He could tell something was wrong. They were moving slower than normal. He could see two men draped over their horses' backs, and three of the riders were slumped in the saddle. He held Buster in place as the horse began to toss his head at the smell of blood on the wind.

It was Major Darrell Crawley's patrol. Chris was glad to see that the major was all right. Crawley had fought alongside Solomon Cooper in the Civil War and had a special place in Chris's heart.

As the unit drew near, the gate of the fort swung open. Chris waited for the bedraggled troopers to enter the fort and was about to follow when he saw another patrol coming in at a trot from the southwest. He recognized Captain John Fordham riding in the lead. At the same time, another patrol came in from due east, splashing through Black's Fork Creek.

He touched heels to Buster's side and rode up to Captain Fordham's patrol and swung alongside Lieutenant Dobie Carlin, who was riding next to the captain.

Before Carlin could greet the boy, Fordham said, "Chris, the patrol just ahead of us…had they been shot up?"

"Some of them, sir. It was Major Crawley's unit. The major is all right, though."

"Could you tell how many men were shot up?"

"It looked like two were dead, sir. They were draped over their saddles. And there were three men hunched over who looked to be wounded."

"You taking Buster into the fort now, Chris?" asked Dobie.

"Yes, sir. Broken Wing and I had a good ride around the edges of the fort today. He just headed for home. Figured I'd ride through the gate with you, then put Buster in the corral."

"Buster'll be lonely when you put him in his own barn and corral behind the store."

"Probably will, sir. He's had lots of company here in the fort."

When they arrived at the stables and corral, Chris noticed Betsy Fordham and her children, who rushed toward the captain. Other wives and children were there to meet returning cavalrymen, too.

Chris heard the Fordhams talking about Major Crawley's patrol, and the captain told Betsy he would be home in a little while. He wanted to go to the infirmary and check on Crawley's unit.

Chris slid from Buster's back and watched Lieutenant Carlin wearily dismount. While both loosened their saddle cinches, Chris studied the lieutenant's melancholic features. Though Dobie was always warm and friendly to him, Chris wondered why he often seemed so sad.

As they placed their saddles on the corral fence, Dobie glanced toward the infirmary where the wounded troopers were being carried through the door. "I sure hope we can get the Blackfoot under control soon."

"Me too," said Chris.

The wind howled through the fort and whined around the eaves of the buildings, flapping at their hat brims and snatching at their upturned coat collars with icy fingers. The smell of snow was in the air.

When the bridles were hung on pegs, Dobie said, "Looks like we're going to get some snow out of this one."

"Mm-hmm," said Chris. "You...ah...have to be somewhere special?"

"Not till suppertime. Something you wanted to do?"

"Oh…just talk, maybe."

Dobie widened his eyes in mock dismay. "You mean share some deep, dark secrets?"

"Well…sort of. Maybe."

"Well, let's go inside the barracks. I see they've got the fireplace burning good."

The lieutenant and Chris stopped just inside the door of the barracks where a group of soldiers was discussing the battle Major Crawley's patrol had fought that day with a Blackfoot war party. Carlin was glad to learn the war party was almost annihilated, but was saddened to learn the names of the two troopers who had been killed. Word was that the three wounded men were in bad shape, but Dr. Robert Blayney was hopeful he could pull them through.

Dobie led Chris to the fireplace at the end of the barracks building. Two corporals sitting in front of the fire greeted Carlin as he and the boy drew near. As Dobie and Chris sat down facing each other on wooden benches close to the fire, the corporals rose and walked slowly away.

The warmth felt good, and Chris loved the sound of the fire crackling and the intermittent popping of the wood.

"Well," said the lieutenant, "what was it you wanted to talk about, my young friend?"

There was a slight smile on Dobie's lips, which Chris was glad to see. He adjusted himself uneasily on the bench, letting his gaze swing to the soldiers who clustered in other parts of the barracks, then met Dobie's gaze. "I…ah…we're good friends, aren't we, sir?"

"The best. And I've told you, you can call me Dobie."

"Yes, sir. I…I mean, Dobie." Chris hesitated, trying to come up with the right words.

"Well, go ahead," said Dobie. "I promise not to bite you."

A grin spread over the boy's lips. "Yes, sir. I mean, Dobie." He cleared his throat. "Dobie, you seem so sad much of the time. Because I'm your friend, it bothers me. Is…is there anything I can do to help make things better for you?"

"Well, Chris, since you and I are friends, I'm going to tell you why you notice me with a sad face so much." Tears filmed Dobie's eyes. "You see, Chris, I have a son exactly your age—fourteen, going on fifteen."

Chris's eyes widened. "You *do?* I didn't know you were married, sir! I mean, Dobie. What's your son's name?"

The lieutenant's lips quivered as he said, "Travis."

"Travis. I like that name."

Dobie thumbed at the tears as they spilled onto his cheeks. "Have you heard of Fort Auger?"

"It's up north of here, isn't it?"

"Northeast about a hundred and fifty miles. Near Lander, Wyoming."

"Yes, sir."

"I was stationed there until the time I transferred down here to Fort Bridger. My wife—" Dobie choked up, cleared his throat. "My wife, Donna, met me at the door of our apartment when I came home from battling Cheyenne one day and told me she couldn't stand army life any longer—especially with the unceasing threat of hostile Indians. She said she was leaving, and taking Travis with her. If I wanted to be with them, I would have to get out of the army.

"I tried to reason with her, Chris. I explained that I had signed up for five years and had an obligation to fulfill my term. She seemed to understand, and Travis was happy to see it. He didn't want to leave Fort Auger. Like you, he dreams of one day being in the army."

Chris nodded. "I'm sure Travis and I would get along well."

"No doubt about it," said Dobie, thumbing away another tear. "You two are so much alike. You even look like him."

"Really?"

"Being around you is almost like being around Travis. It's more the color of your hair and eyes than your facial features. But you're built alike and just about the same height. Well, anyway, a couple of days after we seemed to get it settled, I came in from patrol duty and found that Donna had taken Travis and left for Denver that morning on a stagecoach. Denver's where Donna's parents live. She left me a note saying she was going to divorce me."

"Has she done that yet?"

"I haven't had any notice of it. Donna knows where I am. I've written several letters, both to her and Travis—at Donna's parents' house. But I've heard absolutely nothing.

"The reason I'm at Fort Bridger," said Dobie, "is because I asked for a transfer. Too many memories of Donna and Travis were connected with Fort Auger. I miss them both so much. I've talked to Colonel Bateman about it and asked if I could get time off to go to Denver. He said he just can't spare me as long as the Blackfoot are on the warpath. So all I can do is keep sending letters and hope to hear back. I know Travis would write to me if his mother would let him."

"I'm sure he would," said Chris. "Dobie..."

Carlin sniffed, blinking at his tears. "Yes?"

"Does it help being around me? I mean, since I remind you of Travis?"

"It does. I love my son very much, and it really is a help to be with you."

"Remember, I told you about my dad being killed by a rattler on the journey to Fort Bridger?"

"Of course."

"Well...you remind me of *him*."

Dobie smiled through his tears. "Really?"

"Uh-huh. Not that you look like Papa, but your voice sounds a whole lot like his, and your personality is a whole lot like his. I…I sort of…well—"

It was Chris's turn to choke up and shed tears.

Dobie left the bench and put his arm around the boy's shoulder. Still weeping himself, he said, "Chris, if there's any way I can be like a dad to you, it would make me very happy. I know no one could ever take your father's place. And I wouldn't even try. But if maybe I can help fill that empty spot just a little, I'd sure be glad."

Chris nodded and let the tears slip down his cheek. He couldn't say anything for a long moment. Then he straightened and said, "Guess I'd better be going. Supper will be on at the Williamses' pretty soon."

"Chris," Dobie said, "I appreciate that you cared enough about my sadness to ask about it. I know you really meant it when you said you wanted to help if you could. Believe me, just the fact that you've made me your friend has helped more than you know. But this little talk has been a tremendous boon on top of that."

"I'm glad," Chris said softly. "Could I ask you something else?"

"Of course."

"Dobie, are you a Christian?"

"Well, I guess so, Chris. I went to Sunday school as a boy. I believe in God."

"Do you believe Jesus Christ is the Son of God?"

"I do."

"Have you ever trusted Him as your personal Saviour?"

"Well, I…ah…I've sure asked Him to forgive me of my sins a lot."

"That's not the same as opening your heart to Him and asking Him to be your Saviour and wash away all your sins in His blood. It's believing in Jesus and His death on the cross that makes you a Christian."

Dobie looked at him blankly. "Well, if that's what the Bible says, I guess I'm *not* a Christian, Chris. Looks like I need to learn more about it."

Chris's eyes lit up. "You know that Colonel Bateman delays the patrols on Sundays till after church."

"Yeah. I've just been too busy to attend, but—"

"Will you come tomorrow with me? As my guest?"

"Okay. I will."

"Great! I've got to get to the store to walk with Mama to the Williamses' before she comes in here and drags me out by my ear! See you tomorrow at church, okay?"

Carlin saluted him. "Yes, sir, General Cooper!"

It had been the usual busy Saturday at Cooper's General Store, and as Hannah was about to close up, Mandy hugged her and said, "You go get off yo' feet, Miz Hannah. In spite of my bein' here, you jis' worked yo'self too hard."

Hannah chuckled. "Honey, I never would have made it through this day without your help. Thank you so much."

Glenda Williams had come in for groceries earlier and had brought Patty Ruth with her. The child asked to stay so she could walk back to the Williamses' house with her mother, and Hannah had granted her request.

Now Patty Ruth looked up at Mandy and said, "I'll make her rest this evening, Mrs. Carver. Even if I have to spank her!"

Hannah laughed. "Sure, Patty Ruth, *you* are going to spank *me*?"

"Mm-hmm," said the little redhead, putting hands on hips as she had seen her mother do. "You've been spankin' me long as I remember. If you don't rest like Mrs. Carver tol' you, I'm gonna spank you!"

Mandy laughed as she headed for the door. "You jis' do

that, sweetheart. Make yo' mama take care o' herself and that li'l baby she's carryin'. An' if'n you don' mind yo' little girl, Miz Hannah, *I* will spank you!"

Hannah lifted both hands in the air. "I promise, Mrs. Carver! I'll rest real good this evening."

Just as Mandy reached the door, it opened for her and Chris came in. She spoke to him briefly, then left.

Patty Ruth saw her big brother and ran to meet him, whooping with delight. He picked her up and swung her around, saying, "Hi, baby sister! You miss me today?"

"Sure did! Did you have a good time with Broken Wing?"

"Yes!" He held her chin and shook her head affectionately. Then, turning to Hannah, he said, "You look tired, Mama."

Hannah sighed as her oldest son gave her a hug. "Just a typical Saturday, honey," she said.

"I saw Mary Beth and Miss Lindgren come in just a moment ago, Mama. Mary Beth said she would meet us at Miss Glenda's house in a few minutes."

"Okay. Let's close the place up and head for Glenda's kitchen. I'm looking forward to a hot meal and getting to sit down for a while."

As Hannah closed the door and locked it, a pang of loneliness stabbed her heart. She thought of Sol and of all the times they had closed the store together in Independence. She missed him terribly. Now, having all the responsibility on her weary shoulders, she spoke to the Lord silently in her heart, asking Him for strength, as she and two of her children headed toward the fort's gate. She straightened her shoulders, took son and daughter by the hand, and led them to Main Street. The wind was still biting, and now flakes of falling snow showed under the glowing lamps along the boardwalk.

As they walked Chris said, "Mama, I had a talk today with Lieutenant Dobie Carlin."

"Oh? What about?"

"Well, I've been noticing that he looks so unhappy most of the time. We talked about how we're good friends, so I just came out and asked him about looking sad so much of the time and said I wanted to help him if I could. I didn't know he was married. But the whole thing is, his wife left him and took their son, Travis, who is my age."

"Oh, I'm so sorry," said Hannah, brushing snowflakes from her eyelashes.

Chris quickly explained about the Carlins, then said, "I asked Dobie if he's a Christian, Mama. At first he said he thought so because he went to Sunday school as a boy and believes in God. When I explained about receiving Jesus into your heart to be a real Christian, he said he must not be one, then, and needs to learn more about it. He promised me he'd come to church tomorrow."

"That's good," said Hannah. "We must remember to pray for him tonight, and to pray that his wife and son will come back to him." Hannah paused, then said, "Chris, you shouldn't speak of him as *Dobie*. You should call him Lieutenant Carlin."

"But he told me he wanted me to call him Dobie because we're good friends."

"Oh. Well, all right. As long as he did that, it's all right. But if you speak of him to any army personnel, or you speak to him in front of army personnel, you still call him Lieutenant Carlin."

"Yes, ma'am."

"Mama?" said Patty Ruth, who was having to take fast steps to keep up with her mother and brother.

"Yes, honey?"

"When Chris grows up and becomes a gen'ral in the army, will I have to call him *Gen'ral Cooper?*"

"No, sweetheart. Since he's your brother, you can still call him Chris."

"Even when I'm around army presnal?"

"It's *personnel,* honey."

"Pres—presnal."

"Personnel."

"Yeah, that."

"No, honey. Even in front of army people, you'll still be able to call him Chris."

"Good," said the little redhead, satisfied.

Hannah and her children had to walk past the Uintah Hotel, then turn down the side street to the Williamses' house. As they approached the front of the hotel, they saw Clayton Farley standing on the porch, talking to two well-dressed men.

Farley interrupted his conversation with the men. "Ah, Mrs. Cooper. How are you this evening?"

Hannah guided Chris and Patty Ruth to a halt. "A little weary after a busy day, Mr. Farley."

"That's understandable. I want you to meet these gentlemen. Mr. Winn Haltom and Mr. Stanley Mills, this is Mrs. Hannah Cooper, proprietor of Cooper's General Store. I showed you the nearly finished structure a little while ago."

Both men tipped their hats to Hannah, then Farley introduced them to Chris and Patty Ruth. To Hannah, Farley said, "These gentlemen are executives with the Wells Fargo Company. One of the army patrols escorted them their last fifty miles or so. In case of trouble from the Blackfoot, you understand. They're here to inspect the new Wells Fargo stage station, now that we've got it finished."

"Oh, yes. We're very glad your company's bringing stagecoach service through here, gentlemen," said Hannah, tugging at her coat collar as the wind whipped a gust along the street. "How soon will it begin?"

"We're looking at the last few days of this month."

"Oh, that soon?"

"Yes. We have a husband-and-wife team coming from California to serve as agents. They've been running a stage station on Luther Pass in the Sierra Nevadas for some time. Along with a general store, in fact. But they're getting up in years a bit and are glad they'll only be taking care of the stagecoach business. They'll be arriving at our office in Cheyenne City by rail shortly. Then we'll transport them on over here."

Another gust of wind whipped along the street, speckling everything with snow.

"It's been a pleasure meeting you, gentlemen," said Hannah. "We've got to keep moving. Good-bye, Mr. Farley."

The children said good-bye to the Wells Fargo executives and to Clayton Farley, and Hannah rushed them around the corner toward the Williamses' house.

On Sunday morning, sunshine welcomed the people of Fort Bridger as they left their homes to attend church services. A dusting of snow lay on the ground, sparkling like millions of diamonds and causing everyone to squint against the brilliance.

As the Coopers and the Williamses walked toward the town hall, B. J. bent over and began scraping snow into a snowball. Hannah said, "B. J.! Ah-ah-ah! Don't you do it!"

The eight-year-old paused, then said, "Aw, Mama. I wasn't gonna throw it at nobody. I—"

"B. J.," Mary Beth said, "that's a double negative, which produces a positive. If you are not going to throw a snowball at *nobody*, that means you *are* going to throw it at *somebody*."

"Yeah, B. J.," said Patty Ruth, who clutched Tony the Bear to her chest. "Don't you know nothin'?"

"Patty Ruth," said Mary Beth, "you just did the same thing. You used a double negative. You said—"

"Mary Beth," said Hannah, "she won't understand, even if you explain it."

"Well, B. J. should understand it. Miss Lindgren is teaching him English grammar in school."

Gary Williams laughed. "You mean she's *trying* to teach him English grammar, Mary Beth!"

B. J. dropped what snow he had collected, brushed the remaining particles onto his coat, and said, "It doesn't bother me, Miss Lindgren teaching me English, Uncle Gary. What bothers me is Mary Beth thinkin' that 'cause she's gonna be a teacher, she knows as much as Miss Lindgren does."

"I don't think I know as much as Miss Lindgren does, but—"

"Mary Beth, let it drop," said Hannah. "Let's not argue. We're about to enter Sunday school and church."

"Yes, ma'am," said Mary Beth.

Hannah looked at her youngest son. "B. J.?"

"Yes, ma'am," said B. J., giving his mother a sheepish look.

Glenda smiled at the boy, laid a hand on his shoulder, and asked, "What *were* you going to throw the snowball at, B. J.?"

"I don't know. One of them birds up in the tree, maybe."

"Well, he wouldn't have thrown it at *me*," said Chris. "He knows that if he did, I'd wash his face with snow."

Hannah smiled to herself as they drew near the town hall. She felt a new wave of love for her children wash over her and gently patted the wee one still growing within.

Her head jerked up as Chris blurted, "Oh, look! It's Dob—it's Lieutenant Carlin coming with those other soldiers!"

CHAPTER SEVEN

A big smile spread over Lieutenant Carlin's face when he saw Chris Cooper running toward him. The soldiers looked on with pleasure as the boy hugged the lieutenant. It seemed to them that Carlin smiled only when he was around the Cooper boy.

"Come on, Dob...er, ah...Lieutenant," said Chris. "I want you to meet my family."

Dobie Carlin liked the entire Cooper family immediately. He was especially charmed by Patty Ruth, who called him "Mr. Lieutenant Dobie Carlin."

When they stepped inside Chris introduced his friend to the Williamses and to Dr. and Mrs. Frank O'Brien, then to Pastor Kelly and Rebecca. Gary Williams invited Dobie to sit with them in the Sunday school class. Chris told him he would see him after Sunday school and hurried off to his own class.

Later, when the preaching service was about to begin, the O'Briens and the Williamses sat with Hannah, Mary Beth, B. J., and Patty Ruth. The latter was gladly sandwiched between her adoptive grandparents. In her arms, of course, was Tony the Bear.

Chris guided the lieutenant to the row of chairs just in front of Hannah. Some other soldiers sat with them.

Hannah looked across the aisle and saw the Alex Patterson family sitting together and smiled at them. And she was pleased to see the Fordham family enter and sit on the same row as the Pattersons. Silently she prayed, *Lord, please speak to Betsy and John today as the pastor preaches...and to Ryan and Will. They all need You so desperately. And please speak to Lieutenant Carlin. Having You in his heart would help to ease his pain.*

The church organist, Lila Sparrow, was pumping and playing as people filed in. Lila's husband, Captain Derk Sparrow, was the song leader. He and Pastor Kelly were on the platform, talking.

Captain Sparrow stepped to the pulpit promptly at eleven o'clock and started the song service. Hannah watched Dobie Carlin. She was surprised that he was able to sing the words of the first stanza without looking at the songbook.

As the service progressed, Pastor Kelly made announcements and recognized the first-timers. The offering was taken, the congregation stood and sang one more song, then the Lindgren sisters stepped to the platform. Lila Sparrow played the introduction to "Amazing Grace," and the sisters sang it beautifully.

Mary Beth Cooper decided she should learn to sing as well as her teacher.

"Amens" echoed through the town hall when the song was finished. As the Lindgren sisters left the platform, Pastor Kelly stepped to the pulpit and opened his Bible.

Chris moved his Bible so that Dobie could look on.

As the sermon progressed, Hannah studied Dobie from where she sat at an angle behind him. The only time his eyes left the preacher was when there was another Scripture passage to follow in Chris's Bible. Hannah prayed for the Holy Spirit to work on the lieutenant's heart.

Pastor Kelly closed his sermon with a heart-touching story that capped off the clear gospel message. The crowd stood to their feet, and Captain Sparrow led them while they sang the invitation song.

Dobie was visibly shaken. He continued singing, along with everyone else, but there were tears in his eyes, and his lips were quivering.

Pretty soon, two of the soldiers who sat on the same row stepped out to the pastor, saying they wanted to be saved. Kelly turned them over to two of the men from the church, who took them to a side room, Bibles in hand.

A moment later, a teenage girl who had been brought from her father's ranch by a neighbor, stepped forward to receive the Lord. Rebecca Kelly took her to another side room.

Dobie Carlin stood on one foot, then the other, but he didn't take a step forward. Chris looked over his shoulder at his mother, and Hannah nodded at him and smiled.

When Chris leaned close to the lieutenant and said just loud enough for him to hear, "Dobie, if you'd like to go and be saved, I'll walk with you," that was all it took. Dobie moved out, leaving Chris behind, and approached the pastor, wiping tears from his cheeks. Kelly motioned to Doc O'Brien, and the town's physician took Dobie out to counsel him.

Chris turned around and smiled at his mother, shaking both fists in jubilance, and Hannah mouthed, *Praise the Lord!* The rest of the row joined in the quiet celebration.

While this rejoicing was going on, Hannah saw Ryan and Will Fordham move past the Pattersons to the aisle and step to the pastor. She looked at John and Betsy out of the corner of her eye and saw that they were singing the invitation song along with everyone else, but showing no reaction to their sons' decisions.

Abe Carver took Ryan aside, and Justin Powell took Will.

Soon the invitation was brought to a close, and there was much rejoicing in the congregation as the pastor had those who had come to receive Christ make their public profession of faith in Him. There would be a baptismal service at Black Fork's Creek that afternoon for those who could make it, no matter how cold the water might be. Another time would be set for the soldiers, since they had to ride out on patrol shortly.

At the door, Pastor Kelly asked the Fordhams if it was all right for him to baptize the boys that afternoon. The boys were standing there and told their parents this was their desire. John and Betsy gave their permission, saying that if the boys wanted to do this, they would not stand in the way.

At the same time this conversation was going on, Dobie Carlin was thanking Chris for talking to him about the Lord and for inviting him to church. Hannah and her other children were standing close by.

To Chris, Dobie said, "I'm concerned for Donna and Travis now. I want them to be saved."

Hannah took a step closer. "Lieutenant, I'm very glad to hear you say that. Chris told us your story, and I'm pleased you're concerned about the souls of your wife and son. This is one of the signs of a true conversion, when you're immediately burdened for lost people."

"I know what Jesus did for me just now, Mrs. Cooper. I'm saved. I'm going to heaven, and I want Donna and Travis in heaven with me."

"We have a great and mighty God, Lieutenant, who works in accordance with how we pray. By earnest prayer, we can see God work and reach Donna and Travis. Believe me, He can do it."

Dobie smiled. "Ma'am, if He can reach me, I know He can reach my wife and son. I'm going to pray hard for their salvation."

"Our family will be praying too," Hannah assured him.

At that moment, David and Leah Morley stepped up,

introduced themselves to Carlin, and told him how glad they were that he was now a child of God. Many others were forming a line to do the same.

By one o'clock, Colonel Bateman had his cavalrymen mounted and ready to ride. Each unit had at least one Crow scout riding beside its leader. Some units had two.

Hannah stood with some of the army wives who had just kissed their husbands good-bye. Betsy Fordham stood on one side of Hannah, and Flora Garland on the other. Betsy was trembling. When Hannah took her hand, Betsy smiled at her and said, "Thank you for being here."

"Glad to do it."

Colonel Bateman had assigned Crow scouts Tall Bird and Little Bull to ride with Captain Fordham. Gray Fox and Running Antelope were with Garland.

As the patrols began riding out, Betsy said, "I wish Colonel Garland would quit using those Indian scouts. I don't trust them. John would be better off without them."

"Not so," said Flora Garland. "Those scouts are there for a reason. In fact, many reasons. They know how the hostile tribes think. They also know the land much better than any white man does, and they can spot the hostiles who have set up an ambush when no white soldier can see them. Betsy, you should be glad that Little Bull and Tall Bird are with your husband."

Betsy, who was chewing her lower lip, replied, "It all sounds good, Flora, but what if Little Bull and Tall Bird decide to join their blood brothers and lead my husband and his men into an ambush?"

Flora glanced at Hannah, who could only shrug.

Major Blaine Garland's patrol unit had been assigned by Colonel Bateman to ride due west of Fort Bridger toward the Utah border. Some twenty miles west of the fort was a small town known as Buffalo Lodge.

The sun had warmed up the air since the early morning, and except for shadowed places, the snow had melted.

Major Garland rode erect in the saddle, alert and ready for whatever might come his way. He scanned the land before him with eyes that were quick and darting. He had a stern look about him that was emphasized by his square jaw and steel-gray eyes—the kind of eyes that could look right through you. His thick, muscular body added to his "tough man" military mien.

Garland had served on the Union side of the Civil War as a lieutenant first, then captain, and finally as a major. His last two years were spent under the command of Major General Ulysses S. Grant, who now occupied the White House in Washington. Garland's no-nonsense philosophy when it came to handling the enemy had built him a reputation that few army leaders carried. If not admired by all, he was certainly respected.

Garland was at peace with himself as he rode, the two Crow scouts beside him and the column of men in blue following. This was what his life was all about—hunting Indians. He found solace in his mission and in the sounds that surrounded him: the jangle of bridles and cavalry equipment, the snort of horses, the sound of pounding hooves. He was proud to be a leader of soldiers.

It was midafternoon when Gray Fox pointed toward the uneven outline of rooftops a couple of miles ahead and said, "Major...Buffalo Lodge."

"Yes," Garland said, and nodded.

"Something wrong."

"What's that?"

"No smoke from the chimneys."

"You're right," said the major. Looking over his shoulder, he said to the bugler, "Sound double time, Corporal Smith. We need to get to Buffalo Lodge in a hurry!"

The horses were puffing hard and blowing when the soldiers slowed them from a full gallop a few minutes later as they entered the town. Garland signaled for the column to halt.

Buffalo Lodge was like a ghost town. The only sound other than from the cavalry was the wind whistling among the buildings and a banging shutter or door somewhere.

Buffalo Lodge's main street was lined on both sides by frame, false-fronted buildings. There was a small bank, a mercantile store, a saddlemaker's shop, gunsmith shop, a few other shops and stores of various kinds, a boarding house, and a livery stable.

Garland led his column further into the town, then halted them about midway and told them to do a search. He assigned half of the men to look through the business district and the other half to check out the residential area. They were to call out if they found anyone.

Within an hour, the search was complete. They could find no sign of human life. There were a few dogs in yards and inside houses, but that was all. The entire town was deserted, yet there was no indication of a struggle anywhere, and no blood.

Major Garland gathered his men in the center of the town and stood before them. As the wind toyed with his hat brim, he said, "Men, I haven't voiced it until this minute, but

I'm convinced this is the work of the Blackfoot. They've taken the people somewhere and killed them, I'm sure."

"Major Blaine Garland is no doubt correct," said Gray Fox.

Garland pulled at his heavy mustache. "All right, men, let's spread out and search the surrounding area. See if we can find anything."

Less than a quarter-hour later, Lieutenant Creighton Diedrich and three men topped a rise south of the town and froze in their tracks. What they saw turned their blood cold. The bodies of men, women, and children were scattered about in a meadow like broken dolls.

Diedrich shook his head. "Looks like we've got the whole town right here."

"Probably so, sir," said Sergeant Del Frayne. "I'll go get the major."

Moments later, Garland stood on the crest of the rise and let his eyes take in the carnage. He swore under his breath and said, "How can the Blackfoot be so brutal?"

It took only moments for the rest of the unit to gallop up and dismount, their eyes not believing what they saw. Some of the soldiers immediately turned away; others studied the scene, boiling inside toward the hostiles.

Suddenly, Sergeant Frayne pointed to a clump of bushes at the edge of the meadow. "Major, look!"

Three Blackfoot warriors were rushing from the bushes toward their pintos, which could barely be seen in a low area at the far edge of the meadow.

"Get 'em!" yelled Garland.

Several of the men yanked their carbines from their saddle boots. There was a volley of gunfire, and the darting, zigzagging Blackfoot went down with bullets chewing sod all around them.

The entire patrol unit and its two Crow scouts dashed to

the spot where the Blackfoot warriors had fallen. One was dead, the other two were wounded but conscious. They stared up at the men in blue who surrounded them.

Major Garland stood over them, his eyes burning with a bleak savagery. Then he gave a swift kick, driving his boot into one Indian's bleeding side. The Blackfoot cried out, and his face twisted in pain.

The other Indian spoke to Gray Fox and Running Antelope in his native language. Garland cursed him and kicked him savagely in the lower back. The Indian sucked air through his teeth and howled.

Lieutenant Diedrich eased up beside the major and said in a low tone, "Sir, pardon my intrusion, but this conduct is not becoming to an officer of the United States Army."

Garland whirled, eyes blazing. "You keep your comments to yourself, Lieutenant! These so-called braves took part in the slaughter of Buffalo Lodge! Don't tell me what's becoming to an officer of this army!"

He gestured to the wounded Indians and said, "I want you and Sergeant Frayne to drag these two vermin among the dead people over in the meadow. Let 'em take a look at what they did."

For a moment it looked as if Diedrich and Frayne were going to refuse, but finally they took hold of the Indians' arms and dragged them toward the meadow.

Garland stood with the other men and watched, saying, "I know some of you men don't like what's being done, but you'd best learn that these savages only understand one thing—brute force. So we'll give it to 'em!"

As Gray Fox and Running Antelope looked on, they could see that the two Blackfoot were in horrible pain. Gray Fox turned to Garland. "Major, Gray Fox pleads with you not to do this."

"He's right, sir," Sergeant Barry Wilkins said. "There's no

need for dragging those wounded men all over the meadow. I don't wish to antagonize you, sir, but I must say that this act makes us no better than these savages."

There was a rumble of assenting voices.

Garland raked the men with his steely eyes. "What's the matter with you men? Take a look around you! Can't you see what these barbarians did to your white brothers and sisters? They deserve what they're getting! And if any of you try to stop it, or tell this to Colonel Bateman, you'll be sorry! Got that? I'll make you wish you'd never been born!"

The cavalrymen looked at each other with a feeling of helplessness, but no more was said. Both Crow scouts stared at Garland in silent aversion.

Garland looked across the meadow to see that Lieutenant Diedrich had stopped amid the bodies.

"What are you stopping for, Lieutenant?" Garland demanded.

"The man's dead, sir."

"This one's dead too, Major," said Frayne.

Garland let out a snort. "All right. Couple of you men go bring their horses up here. I want them tied on the backs of their horses. We'll let the pintos carry them back to wherever they came from. It'll be good for their leaders to see what happens to filthy savages who massacre white people."

Lieutenant Greg Sullivan, who had been silent up till now, stepped close to Garland and said, "Sir, please don't do this. Just leave the bodies here. Don't antagonize the Blackfoot by sending them home tied to their horses' backs."

Garland's angular jaw jutted. "What is it with you, Sullivan? Don't you understand the Blackfoot are our enemies? Why do you think I had those two dragged among the people they killed? They are our *enemies!*"

Sullivan stood a little straighter as he said, "A wounded enemy who cannot fight back is no longer considered an enemy, according to army code of conduct, sir. You know that."

"You're out of order, Lieutenant!" snapped Garland. "I'm the major here. You're the lieutenant."

Gray Fox stepped up beside Sullivan, met Garland's piercing gaze with an unreadable expression, and said, "Gray Fox is in agreement with Lieutenant Greg Sullivan, Major. Such a deed will serve to irritate Blackfoot and cause white people somewhere else to suffer for it."

Giving the Indian a stern look, Garland said, "You have no rank at all here. Keep your comments to yourself."

Garland repeated his command, and soon the two pintos were moving away to the north with the bodies on their backs.

"All right, men," said Garland to his patrol, "let's mount up. We'll come back tomorrow under Colonel Bateman's orders, I'm sure, and bury all these people."

Sergeant Wilkins's horse was standing near a huge stand of bushes. As he started to mount, he heard a whimper and froze. The sound came again. Dropping the reins, he pushed his way into the heavy brush, and there on the ground lay a teenage girl. Her dress was torn and her blonde hair was tangled and matted.

Her eyes had a vacant look as she gazed up at Wilkins, then they focused slightly, and she ejected a low cry. She tried to get to her feet, but stumbled and fell into the bushes that surrounded her.

"Wait, little lady," said Barry gently. "I'm your friend. I won't hurt you."

Her eyes went wild as she screamed and tried again to escape him.

The scream caught the attention of the others, and they came running with Major Garland among them. As they drew up at the edge of the heavy stand of brush, Garland said, "Is that a girl in there, Sergeant?"

The terrified girl was still on the ground, breathing hard,

and looking up at Barry fearfully.

"Yes, sir," replied Wilkins, turning to face the major and the others. "She's probably about thirteen or fourteen, sir. She's in a state of shock."

"Can you get her out of there?"

"She's afraid of me, but let me see if I can calm her down enough to bring her out."

Barry knelt down and looked the frightened girl in the eye. "Listen to me, child. My name is Barry Wilkins. Sergeant Barry Wilkins. I'm from Fort Bridger, and there's a whole patrol unit from the fort right outside these bushes. I know you've been through a horrible experience, and I want to help you. Do you understand?"

The girl blinked and studied his face. She worked her jaw, trying to speak. Only a guttural sound came out. Slowly, Barry reached toward her and took hold of her hand. "See? I'm not going to hurt you. I only want to help you. If you'll let me, I'll take you to Fort Bridger where the doctor can look at you."

The girl stared vacantly toward him, moving her lips again. A breathy sound came with slurred words. "You…friend?"

"Yes. Can I take you to the fort? You need to have a doctor check you."

"Doc-tor-r-r."

"Yes. Doctor. Will you come? You can ride on my horse with me."

The fear in her eyes subsided, and she nodded. "Go…doc-tor-r-r."

Barry took both her hands and raised her to her feet, but her legs refused to hold her. He supported her so she wouldn't fall, and said, "Miss, may I carry you?"

She nodded slowly.

The young sergeant lifted her in his arms, cradling her as he would a small child, and moved toward the waiting men.

He talked to her as he threaded through the brush, telling her that all these men were her friends. She clung tightly to Barry's neck as he moved toward his horse. "Don't anybody make a sudden move," he warned. "She's been through a lot, and she's still frightened."

Barry talked to her some more as he hoisted her up and placed her in his saddle. Then he swung aboard behind her. He reached around her with one arm and took the reins, then looked around. The rest of the men were mounted and ready to go.

"All right, men," said Garland, sitting straight-backed in the saddle, "let's get this poor girl to Fort Bridger. Maybe some of you can see why I was rough on those Blackfoot. Just take a look at this pitiful little thing. They killed her family and friends before her very eyes. She'll be a long time getting over this, I guarantee you."

CHAPTER EIGHT

At Fort Bridger, Betsy Fordham and her children, along with Flora Garland, were waiting at the gate as the sun lowered behind the western horizon. All the patrols had come in except John Fordham's and Blaine Garland's.

Corporals Eddie Watson and Cliff Beemer were in the tower, scanning the land in all directions as the red-white-and-blue flag above them snapped in the wind.

As the two women trained their eyes on the rolling country before them, Flora said, "You're getting fearful, aren't you?"

Betsy drew in a deep breath, let it out slowly, and said, "Yes, Flora, I'm getting fearful. I can't help it. The fear just lives here, down deep inside."

Suddenly they heard pounding hooves and the rattle of a wagon. As the sound grew louder, the wagon came around the corner of the stockade from the direction of town. David Morley saw the women and children standing there, looking across the prairie, and pulled his wagon to a halt. "Evening, ladies," he said. "Hi, kids."

The Fordham children responded, addressing him as "Mr. Morley."

"Sure glad to see you boys open your hearts to Jesus this morning," said Morley. "And it was good to see you go ahead and get baptized this afternoon. Bet that water was pretty cold, wasn't it?"

"Sure was," Ryan said.

"Made my teeth chatter," said Will.

"I didn't get baptized," said Belinda. "I'm too little. Patty Ruth hasn't been baptized, neither, 'cause she's too little, too."

Morley smiled at her, then said, "Mrs. Fordham, I haven't met this nice lady yet."

"Oh! Mr. David Morley, this is Flora Garland. Her husband is Major Blaine Garland."

"Nice to meet you, ma'am," said David. "My family and I just moved here from New Mexico. We've got a ranch east of here a few miles."

"I see," said Flora. "Welcome to Wyoming, and welcome to Fort Bridger."

"Thank you, ma'am. You ladies waiting for your husbands' patrols?"

"Yes," said Betsy, "and it's getting a little late. All the other patrols are back."

Morley's glance swept over the prairie. "I suppose there are lots of things that can delay a patrol. Doesn't have to mean they've been in a battle."

A voice came from the tower. "That's what I was telling her, sir," said Corporal Beemer. "I'm sure they'll be along any minute."

"Hey!" said Eddie Watson, looking southwest toward the Uintah Mountains. "Here comes one now. Probably Captain Fordham's patrol since they're coming from the southwest."

"Yippie!" cried Belinda. "My daddy's back!"

"Well, I've got to head for home so I can get ready for church," said David. "I'm glad the captain's on his way in, Mrs. Fordham. I trust your husband and his unit will be along soon too, Mrs. Garland."

Flora nodded.

Betsy watched the Morley wagon bound away, then looked back toward the column of riders heading toward the fort. She could make out the shadowed figures of horses and riders against the glow of the setting sun. Two Crow scouts were flanking her husband.

Will I never have relief from this torment? she asked herself. Just then the Scripture passage Hannah had quoted to her came to mind: "There is no fear in love; but perfect love casteth out fear: because fear hath torment."

Betsy swallowed hard, pulled up her coat collar, and set her gaze on the incoming column of riders. She couldn't wait to be in John's arms once again.

The sun gave off its last fiery rays before slipping below the western horizon as Hannah Cooper and her three younger children were finishing up in the store. Chris had been helping until about twenty minutes earlier, when he heard the patrol units coming in. He happened to glance through the window when the unit Dobie Carlin was in passed by, and he asked his mother if he could go see Dobie and find out if he was coming to the church service tonight.

Hannah and the children were unpacking boxes and stocking shelves. She didn't usually work on Sunday, but she was trying to pace herself since she tired so easily of late. B. J. had taken over in Chris's place to handle the heavy boxes, although he needed a little help from Mary Beth to move a couple of them. The girls helped Hannah stock shelves while B. J. continued to bring boxes from the small storeroom at the rear of the sutler's building.

The task was relatively brief, but all the same, Hannah was more than ready to head for the Williamses' house for supper. She dusted off her hands and put on her coat as the children slipped into theirs. While she buttoned up, she ran her gaze around the crowded store, making sure all was in order for a new day of business tomorrow.

Mary Beth leaned over and tied Patty Ruth's knitted red cap under her chin, then clasped the little girl's hand as they went out the door, which B. J. held open for them. Just as Hannah finished locking the door, and they all moved toward the gate, Chris came running up.

"Get it all done, Mama?" he asked.

Hannah nodded. "Ready for morning. Lieutenant Carlin coming to church tonight?"

"Sure is. He's really got a different look."

"That's what Jesus can do, son, even when you're carrying a heartache like he is."

They were near the open gate when Hannah noticed Flora Garland standing just outside with Janet Diedrich. She ran her gaze from one to the other in the gathering twilight. "The patrol isn't in yet?"

"They're late," Flora said, "but they're coming in right now."

Hannah saw the column approaching from due west. Major Blaine Garland, as usual, was in the lead. But instead of both Crow scouts flanking him, Sergeant Barry Wilkins rode next to him. Running Antelope rode beside Wilkins, who had a teenage girl in his saddle and his coat wrapped around her. She was slumped against him, and only his arms around her kept her from falling.

"Look, Mama!" exclaimed Patty Ruth. "There's a girl on that horse with the so'jer!"

"I think she's hurt," said Mary Beth.

"I'd say so," Hannah said. "I don't think she's much older than you."

When the column came to a halt, Flora and Janet rushed to their husbands, and Hannah stepped up to Sergeant Wilkins.

"Is she hurt bad, Sergeant?"

"Not really hurt, ma'am. She's—"

"We found her at Buffalo Lodge, Hannah," said Major Garland, who was off his horse and moving toward her with an arm around his wife. "The whole town was massacred by the Blackfoot, except this girl. Sergeant Wilkins found her in some bushes near the town. Apparently she had hidden there to save her life and had watched the dirty Indians kill everybody else in the town. The slaughter took place in an open field."

"Do you know who she is, dear?" asked Flora.

"No. She's been mostly incoherent since we picked her up. A couple of times it seemed she might be able to tell us something. But for the past two hours, she's done nothing but stare into space and mumble words we can't understand."

Hannah looked closer and said, "The poor child is in shock."

"We'll take her to Dr. Blayney," said Garland.

"Maybe she ought to go to Dr. O'Brien, Major," said Hannah. "Since she's a civilian."

"I guess you're right."

"I'll go with you," said Hannah. Then to her oldest son, "Chris, you take your brother and sisters on to Aunt Glenda's for supper. You can walk to church with her and Uncle Gary if I don't make it back in time for the service."

As Chris and his siblings hurried off down Main Street, Hannah looked up at the girl, who was still slumped against Wilkins, then said to Garland, "You can come and check on her later if you want to, Major."

"Fine," said Garland. "Thank you, Mrs. Cooper."

"Would you like for me to come along, Hannah?" asked Flora.

"No, that's okay. Your husband has been out on patrol. You two need some time together. Sergeant Wilkins can return to the barracks as soon as we get this girl to the doctor's office."

Frank and Edie O'Brien were just finishing their supper when they heard a knock at the door of their apartment, which was above the office and clinic. The doctor hurried to the door and found a weary looking sergeant standing there.

"Dr. O'Brien," Wilkins said, "I'm Sergeant Barry Wilkins."

"Yes, Sergeant. I didn't know your name, but I've seen you around town. What can I do for you?"

Edie drew up beside her husband.

"I'll make a long story short, sir. Mrs. Cooper is down on the porch with a teenage girl our patrol found at Buffalo Lodge this afternoon. The whole town was massacred by the Blackfoot. The girl somehow managed to hide herself in some bushes and is the only survivor. She's in shock and has been that way since we found her."

"Is she hurt physically?" asked Doc, reaching for his coat and hat.

"Not that I can tell, sir. She's been on my horse with me all the way."

"I'll go with you, Frank," said Edie, taking her coat off a hook.

Moments later, Barry Wilkins carried the girl into the clinic, and Hannah followed. When Barry started to lay the girl on the examining table, she whined and clung to him.

"It's all right," he said. "These people are friends, just like me. I need to put you down on the table. This man is a doctor. He wants to help you."

The girl's half-vacant eyes told Dr. O'Brien that she indeed was in severe shock. She tried to focus on O'Brien as Barry sat her on the table. When he tried to move away, she held on to him with a death grip.

"Here, now," he said, gently prying her fingers loose from

his shirt. "I can't get my coat off you if you hang on to me. Let go, now, so the doctor can take a look at you."

The girl obeyed, and soon Barry had his coat in hand. When Doc stepped close, with Edie at his side, fear registered in the girl's sky-blue eyes, and she pulled her legs up, curling into a ball. She looked fearfully at Doc, shaking her head and whimpering.

Her dull eyes ran from Doc to Edie to Barry to Hannah. When she saw Hannah, she made a slight attempt to reach for her.

Doc took a half-step back, nodding for Hannah to move in.

Hannah moved close and gently took the girl's hand. The girl's fingers tightened on her own till they hurt, but Hannah didn't flinch. She brushed the girl's tousled blond hair from her eyes and spoke softly. "We're here to help you, sweetheart. Don't be afraid."

The girl's eyes took in the faces of the others quickly, then she looked back to Hannah and her lips began moving wordlessly.

Hannah moved closer. "Can you speak slow, honey? I'm listening."

The girl tried to speak, and finally succeeded, but all she could do was make a grunting sound. Deep lines creased her brow and tears filmed her eyes.

"You poor little thing," said Hannah, folding her in her arms.

The girl wrapped her arms around Hannah, holding her tight, and continued to whimper.

"It'll be good if she can break down and cry," said Doc quietly.

Hannah patted the girl's back and spoke softly in her ear, "I know it's been a terrible ordeal for you. But we're here to help you."

The whimpering stopped, and as tears filled her eyes, the

girl found her voice and said, "Mo-ther…"

"Yes, honey. You need your mother. I…I love you. I love you."

The girl burst into heavy sobs and heartrending wailing. Her body shook and tears spilled down her cheeks.

Hannah held her, speaking softly in her ear that she was loved and that they were there to help her. After almost five minutes, the girl began to grow calmer, and her sobbing stopped. Her body trembled some, and her lips were quivering. Edie rushed to a cupboard and returned with a heavy blanket.

"Now, honey," said Hannah, "Dr. O'Brien wants to examine you. He's your friend, too. He won't hurt you. All right?"

She focused on Hannah, looked at the doctor, then back at Hannah and nodded.

"I need you to lie down on your back," said Doc. "I want to look into your eyes."

The girl obeyed. When she was flat, Edie laid the blanket over her, then took her hand, patting it and cooing to her in a grandmotherly fashion.

Doc lowered the lantern that hung overheard, and examined her eyes. He then felt the skin on her arms under the blanket as she continued to shake. "It's deep shock, all right," he told the others. "Weakness, pallor, and cold, moist skin. She's shaking as if she were freezing. What she needs now is water. Lots of water."

As he spoke, Doc went to a water pail and took a dipper from a drawer. He filled the dipper and returned to the girl. "Can you sit up for me now? I want you to drink all the water in this dipper."

Edie and Hannah helped her up and stood on either side of her as Doc held the dipper to her lips.

Sergeant Wilkins had been standing there all along, watching. Moving closer, he asked, "Is she going to be all right, Doctor?"

"I'm sure she will. But we're not out of the woods yet. Sometime—it could be tonight, it could be a week or more—when her memory starts functioning properly, what she saw at Buffalo Lodge is going to come flooding back. It's going to hit her hard." He paused. "But we'll be here to help when the time comes. She may carry some emotional scars for the rest of her life, but for the most part, I think she'll be okay."

"Bless her heart," said Barry, moving closer. He looked down at the girl and stroked her cheek. "I have to go now, but I'll see you soon. These people love you, and they'll take good care of you."

The girl focused on his face and nodded as if she understood.

Barry Wilkins had been gone only a few minutes when Major Garland and Flora came in. When they learned that the girl would eventually be all right, they thanked Doc, Edie, and Hannah for what they were doing, then Garland said he had to go see the colonel.

Colonel Bateman entered his office, fired a lantern, and sat down at his desk. Almost immediately, footsteps sounded outside and there was a light tap on his door.

"Come in," said Bateman.

Major Garland entered first, followed by Lieutenants Sullivan and Diedrich. All three stepped before the desk and saluted as Garland said, "Major Garland and Lieutenants Diedrich and Sullivan reporting in, sir."

Bateman returned the salute. "Sit down, gentlemen." He indicated three straight-backed chairs standing close by. The officers placed the chairs before the colonel's desk and sat down.

"I've already heard a great deal about it, gentlemen, but let me hear it from you. Major?"

Blaine Garland gave his report, telling the colonel every sordid detail of the massacre. He then told how Sergeant Wilkins had found the girl in the bushes, and he gave a vivid description of what kind of condition she was in.

"Dr. O'Brien has the girl at the clinic, sir," Garland explained. "He says she will eventually be all right, but she might carry some emotional scars for the rest of her life."

"You don't know her name?"

"No, sir. She just hasn't been able to talk yet."

"I see." Bateman thought a moment, then said, "You didn't catch sight of any Blackfoot who did this?"

"No, sir."

"But you're sure it was Blackfoot, and not someone else. Not Cheyenne, Snake, Shoshone, Arapaho, or Sioux who decided to shed some white man's blood?"

Garland cleared his throat, adjusting his position on the chair.

"Well, sir, I just assumed it was Blackfoot because they're the ones who are on the warpath."

"Our Crow scouts have taught us how to know which tribe has committed carnage by how they do it," said Bateman. "What would you say about that?"

"Well, sir, apparently the scouts gave those lessons before I arrived. I haven't been taught those things."

Bateman then said to the lieutenants, "You gentlemen have sat in on those lessons. What do you say?"

"All the earmarks of the Blackfoot, sir," said Sullivan.

"That's right, sir," said Diedrich.

A slight smile tugged at the corners of Garland's mouth. He wished he could be there to see the faces of the Blackfoot warriors when the three corpse-laden pintos showed up.

The Crow army scouts kept tepees just outside the stockade walls of the fort. Sometimes they returned to Two Moons's village for the night, and other times they stayed in the tepees at the fort. On this night, all ten scouts had stayed just outside the fort.

Gray Fox gathered the scouts in the largest tepee and told them what had happened at Buffalo Lodge that day. Though the Crow had no love for the Blackfoot, they were appalled at Major Garland's conduct.

A scout named Black Eye set his steady gaze on Gray Fox and said, "What are we going to do? It's not right that we allow such devil behavior, even against our enemies."

Gray Fox sighed. "We can do nothing against the white soldiers without making Two Moons angry. It would only bring us shame, for Two Moons has given a good word to Colonel Ross Bateman about us."

Gray Fox let those words sink in, then said, "I hope this kind of behavior never happens again. Major Blaine Garland was in a bad state of mind when he saw the evil way the white people were treated by Blackfoot at Buffalo Lodge. Perhaps it was too much for him, and he went a bit crazy."

"But what do we do if this behavior happens again?" Running Antelope asked.

Gray Fox pulled his mouth into a thin line and scrubbed a dark hand across it. "We do not cross that river until we come to it. If such behavior happens again, we make our decision then."

Word of the Buffalo Lodge massacre soon spread through the fort, and then through the town. Everyone knew about the girl who had been brought in in such a state of shock that she hadn't been able to talk.

At the church that evening, Pastor Kelly explained all he knew about the situation, which he had received from Chris and Mary Beth Cooper. He took time just before preaching the evening sermon to have special prayer for the girl.

Lieutenant Dobie Carlin drank in the sermon like a thirsty man on a hot day. He was eager to learn more of God's Word, and about Jesus Christ. Pastor Kelly had given him a brand-new Bible before the service, and during the sermon, Chris helped him find each Scripture passage.

After the service was over, and the Williamses were about to take the Cooper children home for a light snack, Mary Beth approached Glenda. "Aunt Glenda, I would like to go to Dr. O'Brien's office and see how the girl is doing. Would that be all right?"

Gary, who was standing near, said, "Glenda, you go with Mary Beth, and I'll take the other three home. They need to spend some time with Biggie anyway. You know how he whines when they eat supper and leave so soon."

Glenda smiled. "Yes, I know. And I know a husband of mine who's going to miss that little dog when the Coopers move back into their apartment and take him with them."

"Who, me?" Gary said, laying a hand on his chest. "Me? Miss that yappy little mutt? Hardly!"

Glenda laughed. "Come on, Mary Beth, let's go."

Before they could leave, the Morley family stepped close to Glenda, and David Morley said, "Mrs. Williams, would you tell Dr. O'Brien that if the girl needs a place to stay, we've got an extra bedroom. She's welcome to stay with us as long as she needs to."

"We'll be glad to feed her and buy her any clothing she needs," added Leah.

"And Ellen and I will do whatever we can to help her,

ma'am," said Keith. "Please tell Dr. O'Brien that."

Glenda rubbed her jaw. "I'm not sure, folks, whether the girl will be a ward of the army, or if Colonel Bateman will turn her over to whoever offers to take her in."

Gary was still standing there with Chris, B. J., and Patty Ruth, who looked as if she wanted to speak. Mary Beth beat her to it.

"For that matter," said Mary Beth, "the Coopers could take her in if it would be any kind of problem for you folks. We could make room for her at the hotel, and when we move back into our apartment, we could make room for her there, too."

Patty Ruth's big blue eyes shone. "The girl could have my bed at the hotel, and when we move back home, I could sleep on the floor."

Glenda leaned over and hugged the little girl. "Patty Ruth, that's a very generous offer, but I would imagine with your mother expecting the baby, she probably has her hands full already."

The child shrugged. "I'd still sleep on the floor if the girl needs a bed."

Glenda patted her little shoulder and said to the Morleys, "I'll let Dr. O'Brien know about your offer."

CHAPTER NINE

The girl was still wrapped in a blanket, and Edie was giving her water, which she was taking in small sips. Hannah held a cloth beneath her chin to catch any drips.

The girl's eyes were vacant again as she stared off into space, and there was still a pallor about her features. She hadn't spoken another word, nor responded when spoken to, other than to accept the water placed to her lips.

The outside office door opened. "I'll see who it is," said Hannah, laying the cloth on the table.

As she entered the office and waiting room, Hannah was surprised to see her oldest daughter and Glenda. "Hello, ladies," she said with a smile. "I thought you'd be having your Sunday evening snack about now."

"Mary Beth wanted to come see about the girl," Glenda said, closing the outer door. "How's she doing?"

"Still about the same as when we brought her in. She broke down and cried, and we thought that would help bring her out of it, but she's slipped back into her shell. She barely focuses on us now. Just stares into nothingness. She's only spoken one word. *Mother.* So we still don't know her name. We don't know her exact age, or any more about her than that she was at Buffalo Lodge when the massacre took place."

There were footsteps outside, and the door opened to

admit Pastor and Mrs. Kelly.

"Hello," said the preacher. "Rebecca and I wanted to see about the girl."

"Well, she responded to us a little for a few minutes, then she slipped back into her shell," Hannah said.

Just then Dr. O'Brien came through the clinic door. "Hello, everybody," he said. "Sorry Edie and I missed church tonight, Pastor, but—"

"You don't have to apologize, Doc," said Kelly. "The Lord understands that your first duty was to see to the girl. Hannah was telling us that she responded for a little while, then drew back."

The doctor nodded. "With this kind of shock, it's hard to predict just how soon she might come out of it and be responsive."

"But you do think she's going to be all right?"

"Oh, yes. Maybe never quite the same, but she'll be able to live a normal life."

"That's good. Well, I know you're busy, here, so Rebecca and I will remove ourselves. I'll check on her tomorrow."

"All right, Pastor. Thanks to both of you for coming by."

When the Kellys were gone, Doc turned to Hannah. "I want you to leave now, young lady, and get yourself to bed. It's quite obvious you're very tired."

Hannah smiled. "You're like an old grandma, Doctor, do you know that?"

"I may be, but I'm also your doctor. You do as I say. Edie and I are going to switch off staying with the girl tonight. I'm afraid to give her a sedative because of her condition, so she may not sleep. We sure can't leave her alone."

"It would be no problem for me to stay here and sleep on that cot," said Hannah. "You and Edie need your rest."

"No, Hannah. You're carrying a baby, and you should sleep in your own bed at the hotel tonight...all night. You wouldn't do that if you stayed here. You get your little self headed for the hotel."

"Could we see the girl, Grandpa?" asked Mary Beth. "Just for a minute? Then Aunt Glenda and I will get Mama to the hotel and to bed."

"Sure. Come on back."

As the women followed Doc into the clinic, Glenda said, "Tell you what, Doc. I'll stay with her. You and Edie need rest more than I do. I'm a little younger, you know."

The stubby Irishman gave her a mock scowl. "You don't have to remind ol' Methuselah of that, girl!"

Glenda laughed. "Anyway, I'll stay the night with her."

Doc didn't respond as he led them to the examining table, where Edie now had the girl lying on her back, covered with the blanket. The girl was staring blankly toward the ceiling.

Mary Beth swung a glance at her mother, then at O'Brien. "Could...could I move close and see her?"

"Sure," said Doc.

Mary Beth stepped to the side of the long table and looked down into the girl's eyes. Her hand on that side was partially uncovered. Mary Beth took it and squeezed slightly, saying, "Hello. My name is Mary Beth Cooper. What's your name?"

The girl turned her head slightly in response, looked up at Mary Beth, and blinked as if trying to focus on her face.

Mary Beth squeezed the girl's hand a little tighter and said, "Can you hear me?"

The girl blinked again, moving her lips soundlessly for a moment, then spoke weakly. "Wh-what...is...your name?"

Hannah's daughter leaned down and said, "My name is Mary Beth Cooper. Can you tell me your name?"

The girl worked her lips some, then said in a half whisper, "My name...my name is...Abby Turner. Abby Lynn...Turner."

Mary Beth held her hand tightly and looked at the adults. "Did you hear it? Her name is Abby Lynn Turner."

Edie and her husband were clinging to each other and looking at Abby with tears in their eyes.

Abby focused on Mary Beth and said in the same half whisper, "M-Mary Beth...where is my family?"

Earlier in the evening at the Fordham house, the family was eating supper as they discussed the sole survivor of the Buffalo Lodge massacre.

"It must have been a horrible thing for that poor girl to watch," said Ryan. "I'd sure hate to watch wild Indians killing you and Ma. And Will and Belinda."

"That would be terrible," said Will.

"Indians are bad, aren't they, Papa?" said Belinda.

"Not all of them, honey. They're just like white people. Some are good, and some are bad."

Betsy's hands began to shake. She laid her fork down and put her hands in her lap.

John noticed and said, "Let's talk about something else. We're upsetting your mother. Betsy, you all right?"

Betsy's entire body was rigid. She swallowed hard. "I...I'm sorry, darling. I just keep thinking what might happen to you if you come up against those—"

John set down his coffee cup and said, "It would be much different for me. I wouldn't be in the helpless position those poor people in Buffalo Lodge were in. I'm always with a well-armed, well-trained unit of soldiers."

"Fine, if you see them coming," she said, her voice breaking. "But what if you get ambushed? Somebody will get hit with those first shots. And who would they shoot at first but the man in the lead? And for that matter, even if you see them coming, what if there are a hundred of them? Can your little more than a dozen well-armed, well-trained soldiers fight off that many Indians?"

John sighed heavily. "Betsy, you've got to get hold of yourself over this fear you've developed."

"I've only developed it since we came out here to this wild, crazy West," she said shakily. "I didn't have this problem when you were fighting Rebels in the war. At least they were civilized. They didn't torture and mutilate their enemies! And I didn't hate Rebels like I do Indians."

John was at a loss for words. His children were looking to him for an answer to their mother's fears, but he was stumped.

Betsy brought her trembling hands from under the table and pressed her fingers to her temples, her eyes dark and tortured. She caught her breath in a little gasp, and said, "John, I don't know how much longer I can stand this. I just can't stand the thought of—" Her words broke off, and she shoved the chair back, knocking it over, and ran from the kitchen. Seconds later, they heard the bedroom door slam.

John saw the fear in his children's eyes and rose to his feet, saying, "I'm going to spend some time with your mother. Please, don't worry. Everything will be all right."

He found Betsy sprawled across the bed facedown. She was sobbing hard.

As he sat down on the side of the bed, he took hold of her arm and said, "Honey, let's talk about it."

It took Betsy a moment to catch her breath and stifle her sobs enough to say, "I can't go on like this, John. I know other army wives seem to take this Indian warfare in stride, but I can't do it. I don't mean to sound melodramatic, and I'm sorry to put you through this, but I just can't take it anymore."

"Then, like I said, let's talk about it. What do you want me to do?"

Betsy turned her tearstained face toward her husband, then sat up, wiping the back of her hand across her cheeks. She drew a shuddering breath, and said, "I know the army is your life, John. And I wouldn't ask you to find another profession. But I want to go back to Fort Wayne. You were training soldiers there before we came west. Couldn't you do it again? I know it wasn't as exciting as being here in Fort Bridger, but the young recruits always liked the way you dealt with them, and certainly your superiors felt that you did a good job in training those new men."

John took her in his arms. "I'll talk to Colonel Bateman in the morning...before I go on patrol. I'll tell him I want a transfer back to Fort Wayne."

"Will you really?"

"Yes. I can't have you falling apart, Betsy."

This time the tears that sprang from her eyes were tears of joy. "Oh, thank you, darling! Thank you!"

"You do understand that it will take several weeks to get this transfer approved, don't you? And until we leave here, I'll still have to lead my daily patrol."

"Yes, I understand. As long as I know this horror will only last a few more weeks, I can handle it better."

John's attention went to the open door, where Ryan, Will, and Belinda were standing. Betsy's head came around as he said, "You children heard what we said, I take it?"

Ryan nodded.

"It's okay with us to move back to Indiana, Pa," said Will. "Right, Ryan? Belinda?"

"Sure," said Ryan. "Leaving this Indian country won't bother me."

Belinda moved closer to the bed where her parents sat. Her little brow was deeply furrowed. "Mama...Papa, I don't want to leave Patty Ruth. She's my very bestest friend."

Betsy gently pulled away from John and opened her arms to Belinda. When the child was in her arms, Betsy laid her cheek against the top of Belinda's head and said, "You still have friends back at Fort Wayne, honey. Wouldn't you like to see them again? There's Sally Castleton and Ellie Tremaine and Cynthia Warren. They'd all love to have you back. They've probably grown like weeds, just like you have."

Belinda's lower lip quivered and pushed out. "But they're not my bestest friend. Patty Ruth is."

"We'll talk about it some more, Belinda," said John. Then to the boys, "Ryan and Will, I want you to clean up the kitchen and do the dishes. Your mother isn't up to it."

"Oh, I can do it," she said. "I feel worlds better knowing you'll put in for the transfer tomorrow."

"Well, let's all help her," said John. "Together we can have it done in no time."

Belinda's lower lip was still protruding as she followed the family into the kitchen.

Mary Beth turned and looked to her mother when Abby Turner asked about her family. Hannah moved closer, as did Doc and Edie.

Edie took Abby's hand and said, "Honey, you need to get some rest. A good night's sleep will help you. We'll talk about your family in the morning."

Suddenly Abby's back arched, and her head jerked up. Her delicate features went white, and her eyes squeezed shut. A wild scream came from deep within her. When the scream ended, she choked out, "They're dead! They're all dead! The Indians killed them!"

Hannah took hold of Abby's ice-cold hands. Before Hannah could speak, Abby screamed again. When she drew her breath, her voice came out high-pitched and frantic. "They killed Papa and Mama! Billy! Laura Jane! They killed everybody!"

Edie and Hannah wrapped their arms around the child,

trying to calm her with soothing words. Mary Beth moved close to Glenda, who put an arm around her, and said in a low tone, "Abby's been through a literal nightmare, honey. And now it's recurring in her mind."

Doc was at the cupboard, hurriedly mixing a sedative. She could have one now that she had come out of her shock.

Abby was shaking all over as the two women held her. Her words came out clear but disjointed as she told of hiding in the bushes when the Indians were killing all the people. She sobbed every few seconds as she described it.

After what seemed a long time, Abby went limp and laid her head against Edie's breast, weeping softly.

Doc moved in with a cup in his hand. "Here, Abby, I have something for you to drink. It'll make you feel better and help you go to sleep. You won't be alone."

"No, you won't, honey," said Glenda, drawing up close so Abby could see her. "I'm Glenda Williams, and I'm your friend. I'm going to stay right here with you all night. Don't be afraid."

Knowing that she was with people who cared about her seemed to calm Abby, and she nodded and stopped crying.

Doc gave her the sedative, pressing her to drain the contents of the cup. When it was all gone, he said, "That's a good girl. Now we'll get you over here on one of these cots, and you can get a good night's sleep."

Edie brought a pillow from a cabinet, and Doc guided Abby to the nearest cot. When she had laid down and was covered with blankets, Edie said, "Glenda, you don't really have to stay. Doc and I can—"

"No, you can't," Glenda said firmly. "Hannah will tell Gary what I'm doing. I'm staying with Abby, and that's that."

"You're a sweet thing," said Edie. "Even if you do have a stubborn streak."

Glenda smiled. "Sometimes poor Gary only sees the stubborn part."

Edie hugged her, then headed for the cabinet to get blankets and a pillow for her.

Mary Beth knelt beside the cot and said, "Abby, do you remember my name?"

Abby blinked and reached up to touch her new friend's cheek with her fingertips, then said, "Mary Beth. Your name is Mary Beth. I…I can't remember your last name."

"Cooper. How old are you, Abby?"

"Fourteen. I turned fourteen on September 30. How old are you?"

"Twelve. I'll be thirteen on November 25."

For the first time since they brought her in, Abby smiled. Then her eyelids began to droop.

"Mary Beth, we have to go now," said Hannah.

Mary Beth nodded, then leaned down and kissed Abby's forehead. "Good night, Abby. I'll see you soon."

Abby nodded and closed her eyes.

Edie put an arm around Mary Beth and whispered, "You have a real way about you, honey. Maybe you should consider being a nurse instead of a teacher."

Mary Beth shook her head. "Hmm-mm. I'm going to be a teacher so I can boss all those kids around!"

When Hannah and Mary Beth were gone, Frank and Edie thanked Glenda for what she was doing, reminding her they were just upstairs if she needed them. They left a lantern burning low on a table near the cots and told her they would see her in the morning.

Not yet ready to retire for the night, Glenda drew up a chair and sat down beside the sleeping girl. Her heart went out to her. There was plenty more heartache ahead for Abby Lynn Turner.

She leaned close and tenderly stroked the sleeping girl's

brow, pushing back the matted hair. Being close to Abby made Glenda miss her own daughters, who had grown up, married, and were living in different places. Sweet memories of her daughters when they were Abby's age flooded her mind, and tears filled her eyes.

Soon Glenda found herself praying for Abby. "Dear Lord, this is a sweet and precious girl. I don't know if she's saved, but I pray that if she isn't, You will soon draw her to Yourself. I know when her mind comes totally clear that all of this is going to hit her harder than ever. She's going to need plenty of love and attention."

Glenda paused a moment to place both of Abby's hands under the covers, then said, "Lord, will You touch Colonel Bateman's heart so he won't make Abby a ward of the army? I'm sure Gary would go along with taking her into our home and caring for her. Maybe she has relatives somewhere else who would want her, but if not, we'd sure take her, Lord."

At the hotel, Hannah put on a robe and slippers, then left her room to check on the children. She could hear Patty Ruth's voice as she approached the door of the girls' room and tapped on it lightly.

"Who is it, please?" called Mary Beth.

"It's your mother."

Patty Ruth was sitting up on her bed in her red-and-white flannel nightgown. As Hannah stepped inside and closed the door behind her, she said, "Patty Ruth, isn't it time you were under the covers and ready to go to sleep?"

"She's in one of her chatty moods tonight, Mama," said Mary Beth, returning to the dresser to finish brushing her hair in front of the mirror.

Hannah moved purposefully toward Patty Ruth's bed. "All

right, Miss Chatty Patty, time to lie down."

Patty Ruth bounced on the bed then did as she was told. Hannah adjusted the covers over her youngest daughter while Patty Ruth asked, "Is that girl gonna be all right, Mama?"

"Yes, honey. It'll take some time and lots of love, but she'll be fine."

"Did her Mommy and Daddy go to heaven?"

"I hope so, honey."

"My Papa is in heaven, and someday we'll all go there and see him. I'm gonna hug his neck and tell him all the stuff I did down here after he went to be with Jesus. An'…an' I'm gonna tell him 'bout Grandma and Grandpa O'Brien. An' I'm gonna tell him about Aunt Glenda and Uncle Gary an'…"

Patty Ruth chattered on while Hannah left her for a moment to help Mary Beth with her hair.

"An' Biggie's sure gonna be glad to see Papa when he gets to heaven. Biggie's a Christian dog, isn't he? Of course. An' when we get to heaven, me an' Biggie are gonna get a drink at the big river up there. An' we're gonna go to church an' hear Jesus preach. Biggie can go to church in heaven. An' we're gonna look at all the gold, an' all the mansions, an' the shiny gates. An' me an' Biggie are gonna—"

Hannah and Mary Beth looked at Patty Ruth, wondering what had cut her off in midsentence. It was the sandman. Patty Ruth Cooper had fallen asleep to the sound of her own voice.

Hannah and Mary Beth smiled at each other. "That child is going to make the history books," whispered Hannah.

"Well, if anybody in this family is capable," Mary Beth said, "it'll be her!"

While Mary Beth climbed into bed, Hannah went to Patty Ruth's bed and readjusted the covers. She bent down and kissed the girl's chubby cheek and said in a light whisper, "Mama loves her baby girl, even if sometimes she is Miss Chatty Patty."

As she stepped back, she noticed a pair of little shoes on

the floor at the foot of the bed. She picked them up and placed them on the floor of the closet. While there, she saw that the child had used a chair so she could hang up her coat. The chair was still in the closet. Hannah set it against the wall in its usual place, then straightened the little coat on its hanger.

Sighing, she turned and headed for Mary Beth's bed, saying in a low tone, "That child. If she isn't a case. I'm telling you, Mary Beth, your little sister is—"

Hannah drew up to the bed and found that Mary Beth was already asleep. She shook her head with a smile and bent down to kiss her daughter's cheek. She stood there for a moment, watching Mary Beth's even breathing, then tightened the covers under her chin and said in a half whisper, "Thank You, Lord. You have given me quite a young lady here. Thank You that she could be such a help to Abby."

Moments later, Hannah entered the boys' room, and by the light that flowed through the windows from the street lanterns below, she could tell they were already sleeping.

She kissed them both, pulled the quilts up around their necks, and tiptoed toward the door. As she turned the knob, she heard a whispered, "I love you, Mama."

She stopped, looked back, and tried to see movement. There was none. She didn't know which boy had spoken, but responded, "I love you too, son. Good night."

There was no reply. Whichever one had spoken was already fast asleep. She smiled to herself as she closed the door quietly behind her.

Back in her own room, Hannah was feeling weary, but she sat down at the small desk and took out paper, envelope, and pen. Uncapping the bottle in the inkwell, she dipped the pen in the ink and began writing.

The letter was to her parents, Ben and Esther Singleton, in Independence, Missouri. She had written them after arriving in Fort Bridger almost two months ago, but had not received a reply. That letter told them of Solomon's death, and how he gave his life to protect his family.

As she wrote, Hannah recalled how her father had angrily told Solomon and her that they were making the biggest mistake of their lives moving to Wyoming. It was not easy for Hannah to write that first letter, for she knew the report of Solomon's death would confirm in her parents' minds that they had been right.

Had her parents not written back because they didn't receive her letter? Or had they responded, but the letter never arrived at Fort Bridger? Hannah knew it took about two weeks for the mail to get to Missouri; it had to go by military wagon train to Cheyenne City, then by rail the rest of the way.

Or was it possible the Singletons were so put out with Hannah and Sol that they were willing to just turn their backs? Could they just forget her? And their grandchildren? Could they actually ignore the letter that had been stained with tears?

And then there was the letter she had sent to Solomon's brother and sister-in-law in Cincinnati, which she had mailed at the same time she sent the letter to her parents. Why hadn't she heard from Adam and Theresa? Certainly they would respond to a letter telling of Solomon's death. Had Ben and Esther turned them against the Coopers because they had gone off to Wyoming and left them?

Hannah paused in her writing. "Lots of questions," she said audibly, "and no way to get them answered. It must be that the mail has been extra slow…or they never got the letters at all."

She finished the letter, telling herself she would write another one to Adam and Theresa soon, then folded it and sealed it in the envelope.

As she climbed into bed, Hannah prayed again for the salvation of John and Betsy Fordham. She also prayed for poor Abby Turner. She prayed about her parents and Solomon's brother and sister-in-law. She brought her children before the

Lord, including the one in her womb, and thanked the Lord for all her blessings.

Hannah lay awake for a while, missing Solomon, and letting her thoughts go to precious moments in their lives.

Hannah's mind went back to the moment each of her children was born—the happy days when she and her beloved husband waited eagerly for them to come into the world, and the joy she felt when each new little life was laid in her loving arms.

She smiled to herself as she remembered how she and Sol counted their fingers and toes to make sure there were ten each. Then they would unwrap the blankets and go over every inch of the precious baby. After satisfying themselves that all was well, they would wrap the wiggling infant in the warm, soft blanket, then hold each other, along with the baby, and gratefully thank the Lord. At the same time that they thanked the Lord for this wonderful new life, they dedicated the child to God for His service and committed him or her to His keeping.

A sad smile curved Hannah's mouth as she once again reached down and patted the little one she carried beneath her heart. She whispered to Sol as she often did in the lonely hours of the night. "Darling, this little child will be dedicated to the Lord and raised in His nurture and admonition...I promise."

Finally her thoughts quieted, and resting in the everlasting arms of her God, Hannah Marie Cooper fell into a peaceful and restful sleep.

CHAPTER TEN

The sun was just peeping over the eastern horizon, thrusting its early morning light into the office of Colonel Ross Bateman as he looked at Captain John Fordham with a stunned expression.

"Captain, with your record, I don't see any problem at all getting you transferred back to Fort Wayne, but isn't there some way you can calm Betsy's fears? You're a good man. I need you here. I'm thinking that it won't be too long till there's a promotion coming your way if you stay. I think Major John Fordham sounds real good. You might remain a captain for another ten years if all you're doing is training soldiers in Indiana."

Fordham was seated in front of the colonel's desk and held his campaign hat in his hands. "Sir, I really don't want to leave here, and I like that 'major' sound myself, but I can't let Betsy have a nervous breakdown. Or worse. She can't handle this Indian thing. It's something she just can't seem to help. I know other wives are handling it well, but Betsy's got some deep-seated fears that won't leave her alone. I really don't have a choice. I've got to get her out of here."

Bateman rubbed the bank of his neck and nodded. "I certainly wouldn't want to keep you here if it meant jeopardizing Betsy's mental health. I'll wire Washington today and request the transfer."

Betsy waited anxiously for John to return while she prepared breakfast for him and for the children. Ryan, Will, and Belinda were filing into the kitchen to the aroma of frying bacon and hot pancakes when they heard the front door open and close.

John took time to remove his hat and coat at the front of the house, then entered the kitchen. "Everything went fine," he announced. "Colonel Bateman will wire Washington today, requesting my transfer back to Fort Wayne."

Betsy dashed to him and threw her arms around him. "Oh, wonderful! We're going to get out of this wild country!"

The boys smiled, but Belinda's countenance fell.

Betsy went to her and said, "Honey, I know it's hard for you to leave Patty Ruth, but like I said, you have friends back at Fort Wayne."

The girl's lower lip protruded. She looked as if she were about to cry. "But Patty Ruth is my very bestest friend."

"Belinda, you know that Daddy's job here is very dangerous, don't you?"

"Yes, Mommy."

"Even if you have to leave Patty Ruth, isn't it best that our daddy be safer in his job?"

The child pondered her mother's words for a moment, then nodded. "Uh-huh. I want Daddy to be safe. I love Patty Ruth, but I love Daddy more."

John was fighting tears as he swept his little girl into his arms and hugged her. "You're Daddy's sweetheart, aren't you, punkin?"

"Yes. But I'll miss Patty Ruth."

"Of course you will, punkin. And I'm sure she'll miss you, too."

Betsy walked John to the stable and watched him saddle his horse. While he was doing so, they saw Major Garland's unit ride out for burial duty. A wagon followed, bearing picks and shovels.

"I wouldn't want their job," Betsy said.

"Neither would I," agreed John. "At least they'll bury all the bodies in a common grave. That's a lot easier than digging a separate grave for each person."

Moments later, after the colonel had addressed the patrol units, he gave the families time to tell their men good-bye. When Betsy embraced John, she said, "Thank you, darling, for requesting the transfer."

"I want what's best for my wife and children," John told her.

They kissed, and Betsy backed away toward the porch of the single officers' quarters as he mounted. When he led his unit toward the gate, he turned and waved. Betsy waved back but couldn't help the cold lance of fear that stabbed her heart when he passed from view.

Monday was Sylvia Bateman's day to work in the store with Hannah. The morning was busy, and when noon drew near, Hannah said, "Sylvia, you go on home and eat lunch. Patty Ruth and I can handle it till you get back. Then she and I will eat lunch with Glenda at the café and take this deposit to the bank and go by and see about Abby." As she spoke, Hannah placed an envelope with checks and currency from Saturday's business into her purse, which was under the counter.

"Tell you what, honey," said Sylvia, "I'll just skip lunch

today. Be good for my waistline. You two go on any time you want."

Hannah chuckled. "Well, whether I eat lunch or not, my waistline is disappearing."

"That's because you're carrying a baby," said Sylvia. "Mine's because I did that a couple of times myself, plus I'm on the down side of middle age."

"I think you look great," Hannah said.

"You mean, for my age," Sylvia said.

Hannah took off her apron. "If I can look half as good as you do in another twenty-five years, I'll be happy as a lark."

Since Hannah and Patty Ruth were off for lunch earlier than expected, Hannah decided to go to the clinic and see abut Abby Turner first. Glenda wasn't expecting them at the café until around one o'clock.

Edie O'Brien, who was sitting at the desk in the waiting room, looked up with a smile as Hannah and Patty Ruth entered. "There's Grandma's little sweet 'tater," she said, turning on the chair to open her arms to the little redhead.

"How's Abby?" Hannah asked.

"She's asleep right now," said Edie, after planting a kiss on a chubby cheek. "When Doc and I came into the clinic this morning, she was awake and in Glenda's arms. She was crying hard, making sense sometimes and incoherent the rest of the time. Doc gave her another sedative—a powerful one—and she's still asleep."

"Bless her heart," said Hannah. "Poor little thing. I can't even imagine what it must have been like for her."

"None of us can," said Edie with a sigh. "But at least things are looking up for her, even though she doesn't know it yet."

"Oh? How's that?"

"Well, Colonel Bateman came in right after he sent the patrols out this morning…about 8:15. Said that Gary and Glenda had visited his office just after he met on army business with one of the captains. Had to have been less than an hour after Glenda left here. She and Gary had talked it over and had come to the colonel to offer to take Abby into their home—providing she was willing—until her life was pieced back together."

"I knew Glenda would get right on this," said Hannah.

"Well, she did. She and Gary told the colonel they realized Abby might have relatives somewhere who'd want to give her a home, but if not, they'd adopt her and keep her for good."

"Oh, those generous people!"

"Yeah," chimed in Patty Ruth. "Uncle Gary wants to adopt Biggie, but we ain't gonna let him."

"Doesn't he already have a dog?" Edie asked.

"Mm-hmm. But Uncle Gary likes Biggie best."

"Oh. But you're not going to let him."

"We sure ain't."

"*Aren't,* Patty Ruth," said Hannah. "We *aren't* going to let him."

"That's right. We sure ain't."

Hannah rolled her eyes toward the ceiling.

Edie snickered, then said, "So now we'll have to wait till Abby can tell us what relatives she might have, and how to reach them. Glenda was really happy that at least Colonel Bateman wasn't going to make Abby a ward of the army."

"I'm glad, too," said Hannah. "It'll be best for Abby if she can stay with the Williamses, at least until any relatives she might have can come and get her."

After lunch at Glenda's Place, Hannah and Patty Ruth headed for the Fort Bridger bank. Upon entering, Hannah went directly to a teller's window to make her deposit. As she waited, bank owner and president Lloyd Dawson stepped up behind her.

"Good afternoon, Hannah."

"Hello," Hannah said, looking over her shoulder. Then to the teller, "Just a simple deposit, as you can see."

"Yes, Mrs. Cooper."

Dawson, a man in his late fifties with thick silver hair, patted Patty Ruth on the head. "Hello, Miss Patty Ruth Cooper."

The little girl was holding Tony the Bear as usual. "Hello, Mr. Dawson," she said, smiling.

Hannah finished her transaction and said, "So how's the banking business, Mr. Dawson?"

"Just fine. And by the looks of that deposit, I'd say the general store business is doing well."

"It'll do better when we get back in our new building."

"I'm sure of that. Lois tells me you can't carry near the stock that you did before."

"That's right. Simply too small."

"So what can you tell me about that little girl from Buffalo Lodge? I know you've been involved with her."

There were several customers in the bank, and most of them heard Dawson's question, as did some of the bank employees. All looked at Hannah, who explained Abby's condition as Edie had described it to her earlier. One woman asked what would happen to the girl if there were no relatives to take her in, and Hannah said nothing had been settled yet.

On their way back toward the fort, Hannah said, "Patty Ruth, let's stop in and say hello to Miss Heidi for a minute."

"Okay," said the little redhead. "I like Miss Heidi. She's my Sunday school teacher."

"Oh, really?" Hannah kidded her. "I thought B. J. Cooper was your Sunday school teacher."

"Aw, Mama, you did not. B. J. ain't smart enough to teach Sunday school."

"B. J. *isn't* smart enough to teach Sunday school honey. *Isn't.*"

"See, you know it. You were jis' kiddin' me, weren't you?"

Hannah laughed. "Patty Ruth, you're a mess, you know that?"

"No, I ain't. I ain't no mess. I took a bath this mornin'. Don' you 'member?"

When they came in sight of Heidi's Dress Shop, Patty Ruth ran ahead and opened the door.

Heidi Lindgren was putting a dress on a form behind the counter. She looked up as the bell above the door jingled. "Well, hello, Patty Ruth! And hello, Patty Ruth's mother! How are you ladies today?"

"We're jis' fine, Miss Heidi," said Patty Ruth. "An' how are you?"

"Well, I'm just fine too." Then to Hannah, "How's that little Abby Turner doing?"

Hannah went through the explanation again, and answered Heidi's questions as much as possible. Again she held back on the request the Williamses had made to the colonel about the girl.

"Well, I sure hope things turn out all right for her," said Heidi.

"Me, too," said Hannah. "She really seems to be a sweet girl. Well, we'll be moving on. We just wanted to stop and say hello."

"I'm glad you did," said Heidi, smiling impishly as she

moved toward a nearby clothes rack. "There's...ah...something here on the rack that belongs to you, Hannah."

Hannah noted the roguish smile and said, "What's this all about?"

Heidi took three dresses on hangers from the rack and held them up for her friend to see. "These are yours."

Hannah stared unbelievingly at the dresses. "Why, Heidi, those are maternity dresses! They're beautiful! You made them for me?"

"Yes, I did. I figured you'd be needing them pretty soon."

"Well, Heidi Lindgren! I was wondering when I would ever find the time and energy to make myself some maternity clothes. What are the prices on them?"

"Oh, about ten thousand dollars apiece," Heidi said.

Hannah dipped her head and looked at her friend from the tops of her eyes. "Now look, Heidi. I can't let you just make me dresses for free."

"I didn't. I told you they're ten thousand dollars each, and you can pay me the second Tuesday of next week."

"Oh-h-h, Heidi," said Hannah, moving close to examine them. "What can I say?"

"That's easy. Say you'll take them as my gift to you, and wear them."

"Those are pretty, Mama," said Patty Ruth.

"They sure are, honey," said Hannah, feeling the texture of each one.

"I was going to bring them to the store today," said Heidi. "There are two everyday ones, and one for Sunday."

One dress was a soft gray-and-white vertically striped cotton with a big bertha collar. Another was sprigged muslin with tiny pink roses on a cream background. The Sunday dress was dark blue gabardine with covered buttons down the back and white lace collar and cuffs.

"They are absolutely beautiful, Heidi," Hannah said with

feeling. "This is such a surprise. They're perfect. And your timing is perfect. I seem to be getting bigger earlier than I did with the other four."

She hugged Heidi gently and said, "Thank you so very much. It was so thoughtful of you. And I know you're so busy. How did you find time to do this?"

"Oh, I just squeezed a little time here and a little time there."

"But you should let me pay you for them."

"I'll do that when elephants climb trees!"

"Oh, you're impossible!"

Heidi looked down at the stuffed bear in Patty Ruth's arms. "So how's Tony the Bear today, Miss Patty Ruth?"

"He's jis' fine."

"I've had Tony in my Sunday school class for about two months now, but I've never asked where you got him."

"Tony Cuzak gived him to me. He was with us in the wagon train."

"Oh, I see. You named your bear after the man who gave him to you?"

"Uh-huh."

"The way it happened, Heidi," said Hannah, "was really special."

Hannah explained that Patty Ruth was given a stuffed bear by her grandmother Cooper, which she named Ulysses after the man her daddy had fought under in the war—General Ulysses S. Grant. Patty Ruth and Ulysses were inseparable. On the journey to Wyoming from Missouri, the wagon train stopped for water at a small farm in Nebraska. The farm was owned by a young widow named Amanda Kline, who was in dire financial straits. Amanda's youngest child, Matthew, was less than two years old. Matthew had no toys, and he became enamored with Ulysses. By her own choice, Patty Ruth gave the stuffed bear to little Matthew before the wagon train pulled out.

Hannah went on to explain how the Lord gave Patty Ruth a new stuffed bear through a man in the wagon train whose name was Tony Cuzak. Tony had been led to the Lord earlier on the trip by Solomon. After Tony had driven one of the Cooper supply wagons to Fort Bridger, he had gone back to court Matthew's pretty mother. Hannah said she expected to hear any day that Tony and Amanda were getting married.

Heidi smiled. "That's a beautiful story, Hannah." She patted the bear's head and said, "Tony, I'm glad to know how Patty Ruth got you."

Patty Ruth lowered her voice and wiggled Tony's head as if he were speaking. "Thank you, Miss Heidi. I really like you. You are a good Sunday school teacher."

Heidi patted the bear's head again and said, "You are quite the young man."

"Thank you," said Patty Ruth in the same deep voice.

"Well, daughter, we'd better get back to the store," said Hannah. "Miss Sylvia is going to be wondering what happened to us."

"Let me wrap up those dresses for you," said Heidi.

When it was done, Hannah hugged her again and thanked her.

Heidi gave the bear one last pat on the head and said, "Tony, you take good care of Patty Ruth."

The little girl wiggled the bear's head again and said, "I will take care of Patty Ruth, Miss Heidi, 'cause I love her. And 'cause she's the cutest little girl in the whole world."

Heidi and Hannah covered their mouths to stifle laughs, and the Cooper women left the store.

From there, Hannah and Patty Ruth walked toward the fort, but paused at the new general store when they saw Clayton Farley helping two of his men put the glass in the big front window. Farley said the new sign was ready to put up on the front of the store and asked Hannah if she had a few minutes to go through the building.

Hannah knew Sylvia could handle things at the store a little longer and gladly took the tour. The barn out back was finished, and the apartment upstairs was taking shape. The store itself would soon be ready for occupancy. Hannah was happy with the progress, and expressed her thanks to Farley. As she and Patty Ruth headed for the fort, Hannah thanked the Lord for Justin and Julie Powell, who made the rebuilding possible.

The patrol units returned to Fort Bridger that evening, and in the time between their arrival and supper, Lieutenant Dobie Carlin lay stretched out on his bed in the single officers' quarters.

As usual, Dobie was weary from the long day's ride and the mental strain of being on guard against Blackfoot ambush. He lay with his hands behind his head, fingers interlaced, and stared up at the ceiling. "Oh, Donna," he said in a whisper, "I miss you so much. And Travis, your ol' pa sure misses you, son."

He swallowed hard and said, "Lord Jesus, I'm asking you to—"

There was a knock at the door. A wide grin spread over his face when he saw who was outside. "Well, howdy, friend Chris. Come on in."

"Just wanted to see you for a few minutes," said Chris Cooper, moving past Dobie into the room. "See any Indians today?"

"Nary a one. Of course, that didn't make me mad."

"I'm sure of that."

Dobie had started to close the door when he heard footsteps in the hall. It was Andy Kelly with a Bible in his hand.

"Hey, Chris," said Dobie, "it's the preacher!"

"Whoops!" said Kelly. "I can see I've come at the wrong time. Don't want to interfere with Chris's visit."

"You're not interfering, Pastor," said Chris. "I just stopped by to see how Dob—how Lieutenant Carlin was doing after patrol duty today. If you need to see him, I'll be on my way."

"Just wanted to catch him before suppertime and spend a few minutes in the Word together."

"Well, I'll go on and get out of the way, Pastor, so you can do that."

"You're welcome to stay and listen if you want to."

"You sure are," said Dobie.

"Okay," Chris said, grinning. "I'll stay just in case the pastor should need my help in answering your questions."

Kelly laughed. "Who knows? I just might!"

For nearly half an hour, Kelly gave Dobie Scripture after Scripture, which Dobie marked in his own Bible, concerning such important doctrines as the deity of Jesus Christ, His sinlessness, and His virgin birth.

Finally, Kelly closed his Bible and said, "That'll do for this session, Lieutenant. Next time we'll cover some other important doctrines."

"One thing I want to learn more about is prayer," said Dobie. "I want Donna and Travis to be saved, and I want us back together. I know only God Himself can ever make it happen."

"You're right about that. We'll cover prayer next time. But let me say this: you keep your wife and son before the Lord every day. Rebecca and I sure do, and I'm sure the Coopers do too."

"That's right," said Chris. "We're praying that the Lord will somehow bring someone to give the gospel to Travis and Mrs. Carlin, and save them. After that, God will bring them back to Dob—back to Lieutenant Carlin."

Kelly smiled at the second near slip. "You two are pretty close friends, aren't you?"

"That we are, Pastor," said Dobie, laying a hand on Chris's shoulder. "It was this boy right here who made me see that I wasn't a Christian—that I was lost and headed for hell. Chris is the one who invited me to church so I could hear you preach."

"I know," said Kelly. "And the bond between you will always be a precious thing."

"For all eternity," said Dobie. "We'll have forever in heaven to make the bond stronger."

Chris smiled at his friend. "And your wife and son will be there with us because God is going to answer our prayers."

Tears misted Dobie's eyes. "I...I have to believe that, Chris."

"Do you have time for me to show you just one passage on prayer?" asked Kelly.

"Even if I didn't, I'd pass up supper at the mess hall to learn about it."

Kelly opened his Bible and started flipping pages. "Help him find 1 John 5, will you, Chris?"

"I know where it is," said Dobie. "Near the end of the Bible, right?"

"Right," said Chris. "Go ahead."

After a few seconds, Dobie had it.

"Okay, Lieutenant," said the pastor, "read verses 14 and 15 to us out loud."

Dobie set his eyes on the page. "'And this is the confidence we have in him—'"

"This is talking about God, Lieutenant," cut in Kelly. "And it's addressed to saved people. That's you, right?"

"It sure is, sir."

Kelly grinned. "You don't have to call me sir. You can call me pastor."

"All right, Pastor. And you don't have to call me lieutenant. You can call me Dobie...like Chris does when no one else is around."

Kelly chuckled. "Do tell. Go ahead."

"'And this is the confidence that we have in him, that if we ask anything according to his will, he heareth us. And if we know that he hear us, whatsoever we ask, we know that we have the petitions that we desired of him.' Pretty plain, isn't it?"

"God doesn't beat around the bush, Dobie. Now, please note it says 'if we ask anything according to His will.'"

"Mm-hmm."

"You can't pray outside of God's will when you ask Him to save a soul. Jesus shed His blood on the cross, died, and rose again so that sinners would have a way to be saved. Second Peter 3:9 says, 'The Lord is *not willing* that any should perish, but that all should come to repentance.' It is His will that souls be saved. You're asking within God's will when you ask Him to save your wife and son."

Dobie blinked against the tears that had formed in his eyes.

"Not only that, Dobie," the preacher said, "but God is the one who established marriage, and He never wants a marriage to break up. It happens, yes. Just like multitudes of people die lost and perish, but it isn't His will. So when you ask Him to bring your wife and son back to you, you are praying in His will."

Dobie looked at the verses again and said eagerly, "And it says right here that if we know he hears us, we know we have the petitions we desired of Him."

"Right. So many Christians don't get their prayers answered because they don't believe God is really listening to them. We are saved by faith, and we walk by faith, the Bible says. So we get our prayers answered by faith. Jesus said in

Matthew 21:22, 'And all things, whatsoever ye shall ask in prayer, *believing,* ye shall receive.'"

"Wait a minute," said Dobie, flipping pages. "I want to mark that one too!" When he had marked it, he said, "I've got to believe that the Lord is going to answer. And when I believe Him, He will do it, won't He, Pastor?"

"If you will trust the Lord to answer your prayer in His own time and His own way, it says right there, 'ye shall receive.'"

"Thank you, Pastor, for coming by," said Dobie. "The Lord is going to save Donna and Travis and bring them back to me...I just know it."

CHAPTER ELEVEN

I t was suppertime at the Williamses' house. As Gary and Glenda and the Coopers enjoyed the meal, Chris told them about the Bible lesson Pastor Kelly had given Dobie Carlin.

"And what was really neat was what Pastor Kelly showed Dobie about God's will and prayer being answered and all that. It was really good. After seeing that, Dobie's sure the Lord's going to give him his wife and son back, and they're going to get saved too."

"Well, let's hear about it," said Gary. "What Scripture did pastor show him?"

To the best of his recollection, Chris repeated the pastor's words about the passages in 1 John, 2 Peter, and Matthew 21. Gary opened his Bible, and between mouthfuls of food, he read the verses to everyone.

"We need to really pray for Dobie's family too," said Gary.

Hannah nodded, and said, "We have been praying, and we'll continue to do so."

Glenda brought a chocolate cake to the table, and while everyone enjoyed their dessert, she said, "Gary and I are excited about the prospect of keeping Abby Turner, even if it's just for a while."

"You two are really something," said Hannah, "especially when Gary hasn't even seen her yet."

"Don't need to," Gary said. "Glenda's told me enough that

I know she'd fit in fine around here. And if she doesn't know the Lord, it would be a blessed opportunity to bring her to Him."

"I sure hope Abby will want to stay with you, Aunt Glenda," said Mary Beth. "That way I could get to know her better."

"Yeah...I'd like to meet her," said Chris. "As soon as she's up to seeing and meeting people."

"Me too," said B. J.

Patty Ruth grinned mischievously at her oldest brother. "I know why Chris wants to meet her. 'Cause she's close to his age and she's pretty!"

Chris scowled at his little sister and took another bite of his cake.

"Abby can hold Tony if she wants to," she added.

"Boy, are you ever being nice, Patty Ruth," said Chris. "Not too many people get to hold Tony."

The little girl made sure her mother wasn't looking before she made a face at him.

Chris started to say something but was prevented by a knock at the front door. Gary shoved back his chair to go see who it was. A moment later, he called, "Glenda! It's the Morleys!"

Since everyone had finished eating, they all left the kitchen to greet David, Leah, Keith, and Ellen.

"We just stopped by to talk with Gary and Glenda about Abby Turner," said David.

"Sure," said Gary. "Let's go sit down in the parlor."

Chris, Mary Beth, and B. J. took the Morley children into another room, but Patty Ruth wanted to remain with her mother.

As everyone found a place to sit, David said, "We've been to the clinic. Dr. O'Brien told us Abby muttered some words to him and his wife, but that's about all."

"I was there just before I came home to start supper," said Glenda. "She put a few words together, but they didn't make much sense. Doc probably told you he expects her to say more soon. Especially since she spoke so clearly to Mary Beth before she retreated back into her shell."

Leah Morley nodded. "Yes. Dr. O'Brien says that to withdraw into herself is her only way of fending off the pain of her loss and the horror she saw from the bushes."

"Well, anyway," said David, "what we wanted to talk about was this. Dr. O'Brien told us that Colonel Bateman isn't going to make Abby a ward of the army, so she's free to be placed with civilians. He said you folks had offered to keep her for as long as needed."

Gary nodded.

"We made the offer too," David said, "and we wanted you to know it. Leah and I got to talking about it, and we're wondering if it wouldn't be too much for you, Glenda. You know, since you run the café and often help Gary at the hotel."

"I appreciate your thoughtfulness, but I have a man who not only cooks, he looks after the business. I have waitresses who also cashier, so I'm not tied to it. As for the hotel, the only time I have to give it attention is when I have to straighten up some mess in the books Gary has made."

Everyone laughed, and Gary made a face at his wife, then grinned and said, "I wish it weren't true."

"Seriously," Glenda said, "having a girl Abby's age in our home won't work a hardship on my time like a small child would. I appreciate you people being willing to take her in, but you do have Keith and Ellen to care for. All I have is Gary."

"I don't know how to take that, Glenda," Gary said.

Glenda grinned mischievously. "Oh, yes, you do."

"You mean like all men are just little boys in grown-up bodies," said Leah with a snicker.

Glenda winked at Leah. "That's exactly what I mean."

David snorted and looked up at the ceiling "Women!" he said. "They just don't understand, do they, Gary?"

"I'm afraid that's the problem, David. They *do* understand!"

Glenda gave out a delightful peal of laughter and said, "Let's get back to the subject…Abby Turner."

"Tell you what, David and Leah," said Gary. "We could let Abby choose which home she wants to stay in, once she's thinking clearly."

The Morleys looked at each other, then David said, "Might be best not to force her to make such a decision. As long as you folks can handle having her in your home, we'll just back off. If for some reason you come to the point where you feel you can't, then we'll sure take her."

"I think that's the best approach," Hannah said.

"I agree," said Leah.

Gary nodded. "All right, we'll leave it at that."

"Well, let's get the kids, Leah," said David. "I'm sure these folks have things to do."

When the Morleys were gone, Glenda said, "It's time to tie into those dirty dishes, then I'm off to the clinic. I'll be spending the night with Abby again."

"Would you mind if Mary Beth and I came along?" asked Hannah. "We'd like to look in on her."

"Of course not. Maybe it would help Abby to see Mary Beth again."

Glenda made Hannah sit down at the kitchen table, and with help from Gary and the Cooper children, the kitchen was soon cleaned up and the dishes washed, dried, and put away.

Gary said he would entertain Chris, B. J., and Patty Ruth until Hannah and Mary Beth returned.

The O'Briens were seated on opposite sides of the desk, doing some paperwork, when Hannah, Mary Beth, and Glenda entered the clinic office.

"Aren't you two working a bit late this evening?" asked Hannah.

"We've had a busy couple of days," said Edie, as she laid down her pencil. "But even if we didn't have Abby to care for, we'd still be doing these bills and making up the bank deposit at this hour."

"So how's Abby doing tonight?" asked Glenda.

"She's sitting in a chair back there in the clinic" said Doc. "She's even spoken a few words that make sense. She's definitely doing better. But you know what?" Doc's eyes swerved to Hannah's pretty blonde daughter. "She's been asking when Mary Beth was going to come back and see her."

Mary Beth's eyes lit up. "Really?"

"Sure enough. I told her we could get you here after school tomorrow, but I'm glad you came tonight. Come on; let's go see her."

Abby was sitting on a wooden chair next to her cot. A couple of lanterns were turned up, making the room bright. She turned her head at the sound of footsteps, and when she saw Mary Beth, a wide smile graced her lips. "Mary Beth!" she said, rising to her feet.

Abby was wearing a new dress Doc and Edie had bought at Bledsoe's Clothing Store, and Edie had washed and brushed her hair, which was almost the same shade of blonde as Mary Beth's.

Mary Beth rushed to her side. "Oh, Abby you look so pretty!"

The girls embraced for a long moment, then Mary Beth said, "You're doing better, aren't you?"

"A...little, Doctor says."

Hannah hugged her, and Glenda did the same.

Abby studied Glenda for a moment. "You...you are Mrs. Will— Will—"

"Williams, honey."

"Mm-hmm. You stayed with me last night."

"That's right."

"Thank you."

"It was my pleasure, and I'm staying with you tonight too."

Abby's eyes went to Mary Beth. "Is Mary Beth staying too?"

"She won't be able to do that, honey," spoke up Edie. "There's nothing for her to sleep on."

"Oh."

Abby then set her gaze on Hannah and studied her. "You...you are Mary Beth's mother."

"That's right," said Hannah.

"You...love me."

Hannah smiled. "You remember that I told you that, don't you?"

"Yes. I...love you too."

Abby's eyes were showing more life as she looked at Glenda and said, "I love Mrs. Williams too." Then to the O'Briens. "I love Doctor and Edie." But when she looked at Mary Beth again, the smile came back. "I love you, Mary Beth."

Doc chuckled happily. "I have to admit it. The best medicine Abby's got is *you*, Mary Beth."

Abby ran her gaze over all of them and said, "Thank you for being so kind to me. Can...can I talk about it? I need to talk about it."

"About what happened when the Indians came to your town?" asked Edie.

Abby bit her lower lip and nodded.

Doc moved close. "Maybe you shouldn't think about it right now. It might be best—"

"It would help me to tell you about it. I hurt so much down inside. It will make me feel better if I can tell you nice people what happened."

"You remember it clearly, do you?" asked Doc.

"Yes."

"All right, Abby. You sit back down on the chair and we'll listen. But if at any time it becomes too difficult for you to go on, please stop. Okay?"

"Yes, sir. Could Mary Beth sit beside me?"

Doc grabbed a nearby chair and placed it next to Abby. "Here, Mary Beth. You get the seat of honor."

The twelve-year-old blushed and quietly eased onto the chair. Abby took her hand and held it tight, then said to everyone, "We…we were all inside the house when Mr. Faulkner came to the door and knocked. Mr. Faulkner is—*was* the chairman of our town council. He told us that the Blackfoot had taken three children from their yard, where they were playing. The parents hadn't yet missed them.

"Chief Crooked Foot had come into town with three braves, carrying a white flag, and talked to Mr. Faulkner, who owned the mercantile store. He told him they had the children, and he said their names to prove he really had them. It was the three Patrick children."

"Crooked Foot," said Doc. "He's the worst of all the Blackfoot chiefs."

"That's what Papa said at the time, Doctor. Mr. Faulkner said Crooked Foot told him to round up all the people in the town and tell them to come to the south meadow. They were to bring no weapons. If they refused to do as he said, the children would be killed. Mr. and Mrs. Patrick were quite upset. They begged Mr. Faulkner to do as the chief said."

Tears filled Abby's eyes as she continued the story. "Everybody cooperated. None of us wanted anything bad to happen to those children. Papa and Mr. Faulkner talked about it for a few minutes, and they agreed that whatever the Indians wanted, they wouldn't harm the whole town." Abby's breath caught on a sob.

"You sure you want to go on?" Doc said.

Abby nodded, using her free hand to brush away tears. "I have to let this out of me, Doctor."

"All right. Go on."

Abby looked into Mary Beth's eyes, then scanned the other faces, and said, "When the crowd gathered at the meadow, Crooked Foot had his warriors check every building in town to make sure no one was hiding. When they came back and said they found no one, the chief spoke in his own language, and suddenly the warriors surrounded us and started shooting. They—"

Abby's features had gone a sickly gray. She looked at the floor and a muscle twitched in her right cheek.

Mary Beth squeezed Abby's hand. "Maybe you had better not talk about it any more."

"I *have* to," choked the girl. "I *have* to."

Doc sighed. "Go on, Abby."

"When…when the shooting started, the men put up a fight, even though they didn't have any weapons. They tried to overpower the Indians with their bare hands, but they couldn't. Papa—"

She choked up, closed her eyes, and took another deep breath. "Papa was one of the first to get shot. When the men began to fight back, and the guns were firing, there was a lot of smoke and dust. I couldn't even see Mama or Billy…or Laura

Jane. I saw a chance to run for the bushes. When I got there and ducked down, I saw Laura Jane lying on the ground. Then I saw Billy trying to fight off a warrior, and suddenly…he went down with a bullet in him. And then I saw Mama—" Abby lost control and broke into sobs.

Mary Beth took her in her arms, and Doc and the women drew close, speaking soft words to her. After a few minutes, Abby was in control of her emotions once more.

"Everybody didn't die from Blackfoot bullets. I won't describe what the Indians did, but they tortured many of the people to death. It was horrible."

"What are your parents' names, Abby?" Hannah asked.

"Wesley and Frances."

"How old were Laura Jane and Billy?"

"Billy was seventeen. Laura Jane was eleven."

"Do you know of any relatives who might want to take you into their home?" Glenda asked.

Abby's reddened eyes looked at Glenda. "I have an aunt, uncle, and some cousins on my father's side. They were living somewhere in New Jersey the last time we heard from them. That was probably five or six years ago. I don't even remember what city they lived in. I don't even know if they're still there. My papa and his brother weren't close at all. Even if I could find them, I don't think they would want me."

"And that's all? No other relatives?"

"Not that I know of. My grandparents on both sides are dead. Mama had one sister, but she died with cholera before she was old enough to be married. There really isn't anybody for me to go live with."

Glenda dropped to her knees in front of Abby and took hold of her hand. Her voice quavered as she said, "Abby, honey, you *do* have somebody who will take you into their home and raise you as their own daughter. That is, if you want to live with them."

Abby saw the love shining in Glenda's large blue eyes. "Are...are you talking about *you*, Mrs. Williams?"

"Yes. My husband, Gary, and I have talked to the commandant at the fort, and he's willing to let us take you into our home. That is, if you want us to."

"Do you have other children?"

"We have three daughters, but they're all married. Two of them live in Missouri, and one lives in California. We have two spare bedrooms in our house. You can pick whichever one you like the best to be your room."

Abby studied Glenda for a moment. "Your husband is willing to take me in, even though he hasn't met me?"

"Mm-hmm. I've told him enough about you that he feels he already knows you."

"You'll love Uncle Gary, Abby," Mary Beth said. "He's really a wonderful person."

"He's your uncle? Mrs. Williams is your aunt?"

"Well, not really. We just call them that. But I promise...if you live with them, you'll be treated wonderfully, and they'll show you lots of love."

"Let me explain about us, honey," said Glenda.

Abby listened closely as Glenda told her that she and Gary were owner of Fort Bridger's Uintah Hotel and the café next to it known as Glenda's Place. She made it plain they were not rich but were well off enough that they could take good care of her.

Abby began to sniffle.

Glenda looked dismayed. "What's the matter, honey?"

"I just can't believe that people like you—all of you—really exist. You've been so good to me. Dr. and Mrs. O'Brien...Mrs. Cooper...Mary Beth. And then, Mrs. Williams, to know that you and Mr. Williams are willing to let me live in your home— it's like a dream. What happened to my family and the other people of Buffalo Lodge was a nightmare, but this is all like a wonderful dream."

Glenda's eyes brimmed with tears. "Then you want to come live with us?"

"Oh, yes. Thank you."

Abby looked at Mary Beth. "Can we see each other a lot?"

"We sure can," said Mary Beth.

"Do you have any brothers or sisters? Will I get to meet your father?" Abby noticed the sad look that settled in Mary Beth's eyes. "Oh, I'm sorry. Did I say something wrong?"

"No, you didn't say anything wrong. But let me explain," Glenda said.

Hannah moved close to Mary Beth and laid a hand on her shoulder as Glenda told Abby about the heartaches the Coopers had suffered since leaving Independence, Missouri.

When Glenda had finished, Abby said, "Mrs. Cooper …Mary Beth, I am so sorry about Mr. Cooper. You've had your share of suffering too. I'm really looking forward to meeting the other children in your family."

"They will love you, I'm sure," said Hannah. "I'm so glad you've taken so well to Mary Beth, and I assure you that the two of you can spend a lot of time together."

"Even at school," said Mary Beth. "You'll love our schoolmarm, Miss Lindgren."

Abby thought of her own teacher and felt a pang in her heart. She forced a smile and said, "I'm sure I will, if you do, Mary Beth."

"Doc," Glenda said, "since Abby's thinking and speaking so clearly now, could I take her home tonight?"

Doc watched Abby perk up at Glenda's question. He looked at her and said, "What about it, Abby? Would you like to go tonight?"

"Oh, yes, sir! I sure would!"

"All right. Glenda, you take her home. I think she's over the hump on this. She no doubt will have moments when it all comes back again, but I don't think it will be as bad as it's been for the past couple of days. However, if she has any problems that you think demand my attention, I'll come at your call, or you can bring her to the office."

"We'll watch her close, Doc. Thank you." Glenda turned to the girl and said, "Well, Miss Abby, let's go meet Mr. Williams. Tomorrow I'll take you to the clothing store and buy you what you need. We also have a dressmaker here. We'll see about getting some dresses made for you."

"Oh, that will be wonderful, Mrs. Williams," said Abby. "I'll do all the housework I can to help pay for them. And since you told me that the Coopers eat their meals at your house, I'll do *all* the dishes by myself."

"You're not being hired as a housekeeper, honey," Glenda said with a chuckle. "You can help, sure, but you don't have to do it all."

Glenda draped her coat around Abby's shoulders and waited, smiling, while the girl hugged the O'Briens and thanked them for all they had done for her.

"Uncle" Gary Williams was playing dominoes at the kitchen table with Chris and B. J. while Patty Ruth entertained herself nearby playing "doctor" with Tony the Bear. Tony had a fever, and Doctor Patty Ruth Cooper was wiping away sweat with a cloth Uncle Gary had provided.

Chris shouted, "Domino!" at the same moment they heard the front door open and Glenda call out for everyone to come.

Glenda, who was standing with her arm around Abby's shoulders, said, "I want all of you to meet Abby Turner. She is now an honored guest in our home. Dr. O'Brien said she's doing well enough to move in right now."

Gary stepped forward, smiling. "Hello, Abby. I'm Gary Williams. Welcome to our home."

"Thank you, sir," said Abby, smiling. "I'm very happy to be here."

Gary leaned down, looked her in the eye, and said, "It is the custom in this household that when we take in an honored guest who's as pretty as you are...I get a hug."

Abby's face tinted slightly as she hugged the warm, gentle man. She liked him immediately.

Glenda then introduced Abby to Chris, B. J., and Patty Ruth. As they greeted her, Patty Ruth watched her oldest brother closely. She could tell he thought this girl was something special. Patty Ruth smiled to herself. Now she had something new to tease her big brother about.

"Well, Cooper clan," said Hannah, "it's time to get all of you in bed."

As Hannah and her brood turned to leave, Abby wrapped her arms around Mary Beth and said, "I don't want you to go. Couldn't you stay here with me...just for tonight?"

"She can if it's all right with her mother," Glenda said.

Hannah smiled, stroked Abby's face, and said, "You've had many sudden changes in your life. If it will help you to have Mary Beth stay with you, it's all right with me. What about it, Mary Beth?"

"Oh, I'd love to!"

"All right," said Gary. "It's settled."

"I'll see that Mary Beth has a nightgown, Hannah," said Glenda.

Moments later, when Hannah and her other three were gone, Glenda said, "Both the spare bedrooms have two single beds. Let's go upstairs, Abby, and see which one you want for your room."

One of the spare bedrooms was at the rear of the house,

and the other was at the front, overlooking the street. Abby chose the one at the front. She not only liked the view from the windows, she also liked the furnishings.

The front bedroom faced east and would have early morning sunshine through its sparkling windows. The room was cheerful and airy, and the windows were decorated with white ruffled crisscross tie-back curtains. Both of the single beds were piled high with feather mattresses and blue-and-white checked quilts. Blue area rugs lay on the hardwood floor beside each bed, and a glowing kerosene lamp sat on a table with an embroidered cloth between the two beds. Next to the lamp lay a Bible.

There was a dresser with plenty of drawers, and a large mirror above it. In one corner was a washstand with a pretty blue-and-white pitcher and bowl.

On the long outside wall was a grouping of four landscape paintings, one for each season of the year. Flanking each side of the groupings were crystal and brass candle sconces with hurricane chimneys. The candles cast a soft, mellow glow on the paintings.

A short time later, alone in the room and clad in flannel nightgowns, the girls turned down their beds. Abby slid between the clean sheets, sighed, and said, "I'm so glad you stayed with me tonight, Mary Beth."

Mary Beth sat down on her own bed and smiled. "It's my pleasure." She fell silent for a few seconds, then said, "Abby, I always pray before I go to sleep. Would you like to pray with me?"

"Pray?"

"Yes."

Suddenly Abby started to cry. Mary Beth left her bed and sat on the edge of Abby's.

"What is it, Abby? What's wrong?"

"God wouldn't listen if I prayed."

CHAPTER TWELVE

M ary Beth looked confused and laid her hand on Abby's shoulder. "Why wouldn't God hear you if you prayed?"

Abby sucked in a deep breath and choked out, "Because I'm an infidel."

"An infidel!" Mary Beth was shocked to hear such words coming from a girl who seemed so sweet. "What do you mean?"

Abby's lips quivered as she said, "Mary Beth, I've been around born-again Christians enough to know how they live. The real ones, I mean. I figured that your family and the Williams family are the born-again kind. I overheard Dr. and Mrs. O'Brien talking at the clinic, and I know they are too. They discussed whether to talk to me about Jesus Christ or not, and decided to wait till I was better."

Abby drew in a shuddering breath and let it out slowly. "You see, Mary Beth, Mama, Billy, and Laura Jane were Christians. The real kind, not hypocrites. But Papa—much to Mama's sorrow—was not. She became a Christian after they were married. I was closer to Papa than Billy and Laura Jane were, and he influenced me with his skepticism. Mama, Billy, and Laura Jane showed Papa and me lots of love, but we still didn't believe."

"So are you saying you're skeptical about the Bible being

the inspired Word of God…and Jesus Christ being the only begotten Son of God…and there being a heaven and a hell?"

Abby's cheeks flushed. "I…I've felt in my heart all along that Papa was wrong, Mary Beth. But his influence was so strong over me that I was afraid to go against him."

"Then if you actually didn't agree with your father on these matters, you really aren't an infidel."

"But I let him influence me to stay away from Jesus and the Bible. I figured that makes me like Papa."

"But Abby, you really do believe that the Bible is God's inspired Word, don't you?"

"Yes," Abby said, choking up again.

"And you believe it when it says Jesus is God's only begotten Son, and that He's the only way of salvation?"

"Yes. I know Mama, Billy, and Laura Jane went to heaven when the Indians killed them. And I know that unless I get saved, I'll go to hell when I die."

Mary Beth's heart was banging against her ribs. "Is that what you want, Abby?"

"No. I want to be saved."

"You can be saved right now, if you want to."

"I do. Will you help me?"

"I want to be sure it's done right," Mary Beth said. "I'll go get Aunt Glenda."

The lamps were out, and Gary was already snoring next to Glenda when she heard a light tap on the door and a whispered, "Aunt Glenda?"

Thirty minutes later, after Glenda had led Abby to the Lord, both she and Mary Beth held Abby as she sniffled and said shakily, "I know I'll see Mama, Billy, and Laura Jane in heaven. And that makes me so happy!"

"Don't ever lose sight of that," Glenda said. "You've had them taken from you as far as this brief life is concerned, but you'll be with them forever when this life is over."

Abby grimaced, as if in sudden agony.

"What's wrong?" asked Glenda.

"Papa. He's in hell. I'll never see him again!"

Glenda hugged her. "You must try not to think about your father, honey. Don't dwell on his whereabouts. Nothing can change for him. Just ask the Lord to help you keep your thoughts on your mother and siblings. They're up in heaven, waiting for you right now."

"And I'm going to be there one day!" Abby exclaimed. "Oh, praise the Lord! I'll see them again!"

The sun was just lifting above the horizon when a patrol unit of sixteen men left Fort Bridger, riding slowly toward the Uintah Mountains some twenty-five miles southwest of the fort.

Leading the patrol was Captain Leonard Brooks. Flanking him were Crow scouts Owl Eyes and Lame Elk. Just behind them were Lieutenants Dolph Jones and Alvin Meadows.

The troopers rode double file, carbines canted forward. The nippy morning air was filled with the sounds of tinkling metal, squeaking saddles, and blowing horses.

A defined trail ran through rock scattered along the edge of the foothills of the Uintahs, and to the column's right, the foothills gently rose to sharp slopes dotted with Douglas fir, birch, and aspen that swept upward to an altitude where no trees could grow, blending into jagged, rocky peaks.

Jones and Meadows were discussing the massacre at Buffalo Lodge two days before, agreeing that they would like to rid the earth of Crooked Foot.

Suddenly Owl Eyes pointed to a narrow opening in the

foothills. "Captain Leonard Brooks! Up there! I saw movement!"

Abruptly, a band of whooping Indians came charging through the opening on horses, rifles belching fire.

"Dismount, men!" Brooks shouted as bullets hissed and hummed through the air. "Fight them from behind the rocks!"

No sooner had the men started to leave their saddles when a volley of shots came from behind them. The Blackfoot were coming at them from both sides!

Lame Elk saw Owl Eyes take a slug in the chest just as his feet hit the ground. Lieutenant Meadows's horse screamed and fell with a thud. Guns roared, smoke rose, troopers shouted, and Indians whooped and barked like dogs. Soon all was bedlam.

Lame Elk dropped to his belly behind a huge rock and fired at a Blackfoot warrior, knocking him off his horse. Suddenly a shadow loomed over him as he jacked another cartridge into the magazine of his carbine. He turned just in time to see a muscular Blackfoot warrior swing a war club.

Lame Elk was first aware that he was still in the world when, from his pit of darkness, he heard male voices speaking the Blackfoot language.

His head was throbbing, and he felt as though he were whirling upward from a dark, mysterious vortex toward some kind of vague light. Suddenly the spinning stopped, and he felt the bright light of the sun trying to pierce his eyelids.

He grit his teeth against the pain in his head and let his eyes flutter open. At first the sunlight stabbed him with more pain, making him squeeze his eyes shut. Then a shadow covered his face, blocking the sun, and he opened his eyes again to see a stone-faced Indian looking down at him. The Indian wore the full headdress of a chief.

It had been more than a year since Lame Elk had seen Crooked Foot, but he instantly recognized the fierce fighter who showed no mercy for his enemies.

Crooked Foot's eyes were black pools of hatred as he grunted to two warriors who stood beside him and said, "Get him up."

Strong hands gripped Lame Elk by the arms and jerked him to his feet. The sudden movement made him feel as if he were riding the whirling vortex again. He closed his eyes and felt his knees give way. The warriors held him up, and the dizziness passed, but the throb in his head was still there.

He let his gaze take in the scene. All about him were the sprawled and crumpled bodies of Captain Brooks's patrol unit. A few lifeless horses lay among the bodies. He recalled shooting a warrior off his horse, but there were no dead or wounded Blackfoot to be seen.

Panic washed over Lame Elk, followed by a settled cold dread. His heart pounded in his breast as Crooked Foot stepped close, looked him square in the eye, and said, "Name?"

"Lame Elk," he said, struggling to keep the fear from his voice.

"Lame Elk," echoed the chief, nodding. "Lame Elk will take a message to Colonel Ross Bateman for Crooked Foot."

Lame Elk looked around and saw an Indian leading one of the army horses toward him.

"Lame Elk will take this message to Colonel Ross Bateman. What happened today is a taste of what will happen to every bluecoat before Crooked Foot is through. White men want Indian land. Good. Crooked Foot and his warriors will bury them in it."

Colonel Bateman rose to his feet as a corporal escorted Lame Elk into his office. He motioned for Lame Elk to be seated and eased back onto his own chair. "All I was told was that you returned alone, Lame Elk. I can see that you've come in early. What happened?"

The Crow scout looked at the floor for a moment, then met the colonel's gaze. "We were ambushed by Crooked Foot and many warriors at foothills of Uintah Mountains. All dead except Lame Elk."

Bateman's face looked like a statue carved out of stone. To Lame Elk, the silence in the room was almost a solid thing. When the colonel didn't respond, the scout said, "Lame Elk allowed by Crooked Foot to live for one reason."

"And what reason was that?"

"Crooked Foot give Lame Elk message to give you. He say tell Colonel Ross Bateman what happen today is taste of what will happen to every bluecoat before he is through. White men want Indian land. Good. Crooked Foot and his warriors will bury them in it."

Colonel Bateman rose slowly to his feet. "Lame Elk, I'm glad you're still alive. There will be a meeting of all soldiers and scouts this evening when all the patrols are back. Now, if you'll excuse me…"

The evening meal for soldiers and Crow scouts had to wait. As each patrol unit arrived at the gate, they were informed of the ambush and of the meeting that would take place as soon as the last patrol was in.

It was almost six-thirty when Fort Bridger's commandant

stood before his troops and scouts in the mess hall. His voice broke several times as he gave them details of the ambush as reported by Lame Elk, then had Lame Elk repeat Crooked Foot's message.

The words stirred the anger of the soldiers and other Indian scouts.

Major Garland could hardly contain himself. Fury edged his words as he said, "Crooked Foot must be defeated, men!"

A rousing cheer went up as men applauded his words, and Major Garland swung a fist through the air, cursing the Blackfoot chief.

Colonel Bateman motioned for the men to quiet down, then said, "I wish I had enough men in this fort to launch an assault against the entire Blackfoot tribe and wipe them out. But I don't. According to our scouts, the main problem is that the war parties stay scattered and only return to their main villages once in a while. There just aren't enough men in the fort to hunt them down. Assaulting their villages and killing women, children, and old men wouldn't stop the warriors. We can only hope to keep the hostiles from killing white people in the small towns and settlements by being at the right place at the right time. And while we're defending them, we can hope that in some battle somewhere, a bullet will find Crooked Foot. If he were dead, I believe they'd pull in their horns and go back to Montana and stay there."

Major Garland raised his hand.

"Yes, Major?" said Bateman.

Garland rose to his feet. "Colonel, what about sending a couple of men on a mission to find Crooked Foot and kill him?"

Bateman waited for Garland to sit down, then said, "I can't do that, Major. It would be nothing short of a suicide mission. It's next to impossible to sneak up on an Indian, unless another Indian does it."

"Well, how about sending one or two of these Crow scouts to do the job?"

The scouts looked at each other, shaking their heads.

"These men volunteered as scouts, Major," said Bateman, "not assassins."

Garland's face went crimson. "Those dirty Blackfoot savages have got to be stopped, Colonel! We need to give them what they deserve!"

Some of Garland's men exchanged furtive glances.

Bateman stroked his mustache and waited until the room was silent, then said, "Men, to prevent another slaughter like what happened today, I'm doubling up the patrols. From now on, two units will always go out together. We'll cover less ground, but the greater number in each patrol will force the Blackfoot leaders to think twice before attacking."

A general rumble of agreement went through the room.

Bateman added, "Until this Blackfoot thing is over, each patrol will pull two howitzers. I know it will slow you down some, but when you engage the hostiles, you can cut a big hole in their ranks with grapeshot and cannonballs."

A cheer went up.

Bateman smiled grimly and held up a sheet of paper. "I've teamed you up as listed on this sheet of paper. I'll leave it on this table so you'll know who's going with whom. You can assemble yourselves accordingly on the parade ground in the morning. I've assigned one double-up unit to go to the scene of today's ambush, in the morning, and bring back the bodies of our men and any horses the Indians didn't steal."

Bateman dismissed the men, and the unit leaders immediately huddled at the front table to learn who the colonel had paired them with.

When Captain John Fordham reached out to take the list in hand, Major Garland turned and smiled at him. "Looks like it's you and me, Captain," he said.

Fordham nodded at Garland, saying, "See you on the parade ground in the morning."

There was weeping and wailing in the fort that night. Chaplain Andy Kelly and Rebecca visited each widow and her children to comfort them as much as they could.

The next morning, after the doubled-up patrols had gone out and the doubled-up unit assigned to pick up the bodies had headed toward the ambush spot, several men were kept at the fort to dig graves.

All the units were back at the fort an hour before sunset to attend the burial service held at the cemetery just outside the walls. The town's stores and businesses were closed so that everyone could pay their respects.

When Chaplain Kelly finished the service, both civilians and army people gathered around the widows and their children to give their condolences.

John and Betsy Fordham were standing near the group when Betsy began to cry. As John took her in his arms, she said, "Oh, John, that could have been your patrol instead of Captain Brooks's! It could be you in one of those graves!"

Hannah, who was standing with the Williamses and the O'Briens, excused herself and moved up beside John and Betsy. John looked to Hannah for help, and she nodded and spoke softly into Betsy's ear as John continued to hold her. After a few minutes, Betsy began to calm down.

As Hannah headed back toward the O'Briens and the Williamses, she passed close by Dorothy Meadows, who was talking to Colonel and Mrs. Bateman. She heard Dorothy ask how long she would have before she had to move out of her small house inside the fort.

Bateman said it would take him a good six weeks to get

the replacements he needed. She was welcome to stay in the house until they arrived. If the lieutenant who was sent to replace her husband wasn't married, she could stay even longer. However, she needed to begin making plans about where she would go.

On Sunday the church members were elated to know this was their last Sunday in the town hall. Next week they would be in their brand-new building.

Abby Turner attended the service and sat between Glenda and Mary Beth. She found comfort in the pastor's sermon, which was on heaven, knowing that her mother and siblings were there, waiting for her.

When the invitation was given, Abby walked the aisle, made her public profession of faith in Christ, and presented herself for baptism. After the service, the people gathered around to welcome her and say what they could to console her over the deaths of her family members.

Gary and Glenda introduced Abby to the Morleys, letting her know that they, too, had offered to take her into their home. Abby thanked them with misty eyes.

When the Morleys moved on, Chris motioned to Dobie Carlin and said, "Lieutenant, come and meet Abby."

Dobie came toward the two young people with a smile as Chris said, "Abby, I want you to meet my very good friend, Lieutenant Dobie Carlin. He's only been saved a week."

Abby smiled back at the lieutenant. "Really?" she said. "So we're both just new at this."

"Yes," Dobie said, "and it's the most wonderful thing that's ever happened to me." He turned to Gary and Glenda. "You're doing a wonderful thing for Abby, taking her into your home. I commend you for it."

"It's our pleasure," said Glenda. "We're so glad she wants to stay with us."

Others joined the small group, and Dobie moved out of the way, pausing to say something to Chris before leaving.

Suddenly, Gary pulled Glenda a step away and whispered in her ear. She smiled and nodded, saying, "You go ahead."

Just as Dobie was about to leave, Gary stepped in front of him and said, "Dobie, could I talk you into coming home with us for dinner?"

"You mean, right now?"

"Yes. As usual, the Coopers will be eating with us and, of course, Abby will. We'd love to have you."

Dobie glanced at Glenda. "Is it all right with your wife? I mean…will an extra mouth to feed at the table be a problem?"

"I already checked with the cook," said Gary.

Glenda chuckled. "No, it won't be a problem. If I see we're running low on food, I'll simply tell my husband he can't have his usual fifth or sixth helping."

"Aw, Glenda," Gary said, shaking his head. "You make me sound like a hog."

"No, dear. You don't sound like a hog, you eat like one!"

Dobie laughed. "Well, I'll try to put away enough food to help him change his image!"

As usual, the Sunday dinner Glenda prepared was excellent. When Dobie Carlin sat down at the table, his mouth watered at the aroma. It was so different than army food.

His gaze roamed over the table, taking in the chicken and dumplings in creamy white sauce, black-eyed peas, green beans with crisp bacon and canned tomatoes, golden brown corn bread, and freshly churned butter. When he spotted the large three-layer black walnut cake on a small table in the dining room, he said, "Maybe I'll let you go ahead and have your fifth or sixth helping, Gary. I'll just fill up on that luscious cake!"

There was some argument from Chris and B. J. about that, then Gary said, "Let's thank the Lord for the food so we can get started!"

Heads were bowed and eyes were closed around the table. Abby was seated between Mary Beth and Chris. Chris had thought he'd positioned himself there in a nonchalant manner, but the move hadn't escaped anyone's eye, not even Patty Ruth's.

They had hardly begun eating when the little redhead looked across the table at her oldest brother and said, "Hey, Chris…"

Chris saw the impish look in her eyes and said, "Just eat your food, Patty Ruth."

"I will," she said, "but I need to ask you somethin'."

"Can't it keep till later?"

"No. I want to know now."

Chris sighed, laid his fork on the plate, and said, "All right. Get it over with."

Patty Ruth rocked back and forth sideways on her chair and said, "How come you're sittin' at that place? You never sat there before."

Chris's features tinted as he shot a glance at Abby from the corner of his eye. "I…uh…well, this place was vacant, so I took it."

Hannah covered her mouth to hide a grin, while Mary Beth and B. J. seemed to be holding their faces a bit too still.

"Well, it sure seems funny to me that you gave up the place you always fight for to sit by Abby!"

This time it was Abby who blushed, and B. J. and Mary Beth snickered.

Chris cleared his throat, turned to Abby, and said, "I'll have to ask you to overlook my little sister. She's got an ornery streak."

"Oh, I think she's adorable!"

Everyone burst into laughter.

When it died down, Patty Ruth looked at Abby and said, "Chris thinks you're adorable, Abby!"

While Chris's neck and face went crimson, Hannah said, "Okay, Miss Patty Ruth. That's enough."

Patty Ruth looked down at Biggie, who sat on the floor next to her chair. The little black-and-white rat terrier raised his ears and wagged his tail. Patty Ruth ran her gaze to her mother, who was saying something to Abby, then slipped a piece of buttered corn bread to him.

Gary asked Dobie if he'd heard anything from his wife and son.

Dobie quickly swallowed a mouthful of dumpling and said, "No, sir. I wrote them last Sunday night to tell them I'd become a Christian. I asked Donna to seek out a church that preaches the Word of God and to take Travis with her to Sunday school and church. She should be getting the letter within two or three days. Pastor Kelly told me to pray that the Lord would send someone to Donna and Travis to give them the gospel, but I didn't think it'd be wrong to just flat out ask her to find a good church where she and Travis can hear about how to be saved."

"Nothing wrong with that at all," said Gary. "When we're trying to reach souls for Jesus, we need to pray hard, but we also have to leave no stone unturned."

Dobie smiled. "Good. I thought I did right."

"Glenda and I will keep praying for Donna and Travis. And I know Hannah and her youngins will too."

"Most assuredly," said Hannah.

There was a brief silence, then Dobie said, "The thing that scares me most is that Donna will marry someone else as soon as the divorce is final, and I won't know about it until it's all done."

Hannah reached over and patted his hand. "The same

God you're trusting to bring your wife and son to salvation is the God who can also bring them back to you. He can keep your family intact."

Dobie grinned and said, "You'd make a good preacher, Hannah."

Gary laughed. "The only woman I know who'd make a better preacher than Hannah is the one who cooked this meal!"

A cloth napkin sailed across the table, striking Gary in the face.

CHAPTER THIRTEEN

F all's colors made California's Sierra Nevada Range a beautiful sight to behold as Judy Charley Wesson surveyed its grandeur. Farther to the west, the sun was just setting, and cold wind plucked at Judy's hat brim. To the south, a jagged peak lifted its magnificent head some thirteen thousand feet above sea level. High up, in the center of its northern face, the eternal snowpack sat in gouges left by an ancient glacier.

Judy turned her gaze to a U-shaped valley that began turning a darker purple as the sun dropped lower behind the distant peaks. One thousand feet above the valley, a broad expanse of rocky tundra swept downward, giving way to thick patches of alpine and balsam firs, and finally, forest moraine. A stream of foamy water cascaded its way down the western slope, where it would flow into the Sacramento River and eventually spill into the Pacific Ocean.

Judy knew it was God's will that she and her husband of less than two years leave Luther Pass and go to Fort Bridger, but this high country held many memories, and it was hard to leave it.

As she turned toward the store and stage office, fifty yards away, she saw the small, thin form of Curly climbing toward her. He wore a long-tailed overcoat, and the wind was whipping it about his legs. The temperature had fallen rapidly, and she could see Curly's breath as he hopped spryly from point to point on the uneven rocky surface that led to the high spot where she stood.

As he drew up, puffing, Curly said, "Honey pot…what in the world…are ya doin' up here…all by your lonesome?"

Judy wiped a tear from her cheek. "Well, since the Johnsons are here to take over the store and the stage office, and since you and me are leavin' in the mornin', I jist had to come up here an' look at my mountains one last time."

Curly took her in his arms, bumping against the Colt .45 on her slender hip, and said, "Let me catch…my breath."

When his labored breathing subsided, he said, "It ain't easy leavin', I admit. But we done prayed 'bout this move, and them there Wells Fargo fellers shore did give us a nice deal."

"Oh, it couldn't be no better," said Judy, squeezing his bony hand. "I'm plenty thankful we got the job at Fort Bridger, and I know we'll be happy as larks there, but it's jist tough on this ol' girl to uproot and plant elsewhere."

"I know. But your right. We're gonna be real happy at Fort Bridger, I jist know it. The winters there ain't no picnic, but they'll be a whole lot easier than up here on this pass."

Judy turned to look westward again and wiped away another tear. The sun was almost out of sight. "Okay, sweet 'tater," she said, her voice catching. "You can walk your ol' lady back down to the store."

"You ain't my ol' lady, Missus Wesson. You're my sweet lump o' sugar and spice and everthin' nice."

As they started down the rocky path, Judy took Curly's hand and said, "You are the most romantic hunk o' he-man I ever did see. I shore do love you."

"An' I shore do love *you,* honey bee. You sweeten everythin' up wherever you are. All I can say is look out, Fort Bridger, you ain't never gonna be the same after my li'l sweet thing moves in!"

Moments later, when they reached level ground, Judy

paused to look back at the sunset. Curly put an arm around her shoulder and they stood together, taking in God's marvelous handiwork.

David Morley and his family were eating breakfast at the same time the patrol units were leaving Fort Bridger for the day.

"I really feel sorry for Abby Turner," said Ellen. "Her whole family is dead, and worst of all, her father died lost. I'm sure glad we're all Christians. I know we'll be together in heaven."

Leah nodded. "Abby's going through a real rough time. Both of you kids should make it a point to be extra nice to her at school."

"We have been," said Keith. "Miss Lindgren really took her to heart too. She's helped her a lot with her lessons, knowing her mind has to be on her family much of the time."

"That's good," said Leah. "Both of those Lindgren sisters are such sweet Christians."

Keith swallowed a mouthful of oatmeal, took a drink of milk, and said, "If those Blackfoot hadn't been so mean, poor Abby would still be living a normal life with her family."

"At least she has a good home with the Williamses," said David.

"Will they adopt her, Daddy?" asked Ellen.

"Wouldn't surprise me."

"What if it didn't work out with the Williamses, and she wasn't happy there? If we took her in, and she liked it here, would you adopt her?"

David set down his coffee cup and glanced at Leah before answering his daughter. "Well, Ellen, it's hard to answer that question. Would you object if we did adopt Abby?"

"Oh, no! I really like her. It would be fun to have her as a sister.

David arched his eyebrows in a question. "What about you, Keith?"

"Wouldn't bother me if you adopted her. She's a nice girl. And now that she's saved, she'd fit in real good in this family."

"I doubt we'll be called on to make that decision," said Leah. "I have a feeling Abby's going to be very happy with the Williamses."

Keith shoved his empty cereal bowl toward the center of the table and said with an edge to his voice, "I sure wish I was old enough to join the army. I'd like to help fight those low-down Blackfoot."

Leah shook her head. "Honey, I hope that by the time you're old enough to join the army, the United States government and the Indians will have worked out a solid and lasting peace treaty."

"Me too," said David, twisting around in his chair to reach for his Bible. "Bible reading time."

After reading Scripture to his family and discussing it briefly, the Morleys prayed together. Then David shoved back his chair and rose to his feet. "I've got to ride out to the pasture at the rear of the property and check that fence. Keith, you go ahead and hitch the horses to the wagon. I'll be back in time to take you and Ellen to school."

"I can drive them if you need to work on the fence, honey," said Leah.

"If possible, I'll do a quick temporary job," he said, heading toward the door. "But if not, it'll wait till I can take the kids to school and get back. You have enough work to do today, Leah. See you shortly."

Morley bridled and saddled his horse, Brownie, swung into the saddle, and rode at a good clip toward the back side of his property, which was beyond a ridge in a shallow valley.

After a ten-minute ride amid his cattle herd, he found a small section of the split-rail fence down, just as his neighbor had said. It didn't look like any of the cattle had gotten out, so he propped the rails against the fence posts as a temporary measure until he could come back with the proper tools and make it permanent.

As he turned away from the fence, Brownie nickered and looked in the direction of the house. His ears pricked up and he worked them back and forth, nickering repeatedly.

David felt a coldness settle in his stomach. He vaulted into the saddle and headed for home, praying all the way.

The horse seemed glad to be put to a full gallop and eager to get over the ridge. Above the thunder of Brownie's hooves, David heard a volley of gunshots. His breath caught in his throat.

The gunfire continued as he topped the ridge and saw one of the cavalry units from the fort chasing a small band of Indians out of his yard. He was still several hundred yards from the house. As he bent low over the horse's neck, driving him hard, he watched the Blackfoot race in a northeasterly direction and splash across Black's Fork Creek. When they reached the far bank, with bullets chewing dirt all around them, one of the warriors took a slug and fell from his horse, rolling down the bank into the creek.

Seconds later, another warrior peeled off his horse just as his companions reached the nearby forest and plunged into its deep shadows with the cavalry right behind them.

David aimed Brownie toward the house and outbuildings, scanning the area for any sign of his family. "Dear God," he breathed, "let them be all right!"

He glanced toward the barn, where Keith was supposed to hitch the horses to the wagon. The wagon was there, but no horses. Then his eye caught sight of the team standing in a grove of trees some fifty yards away, the harness trailing behind them.

David could feel the pulse in his temples pounding as he

skidded Brownie to a halt at the back porch of the house, crying, "Leah! Keith! Ellen!"

Suddenly the back door flew open, and a terrified Leah rushed across the porch and lunged for him as he slid from the saddle. The children were right behind her.

"Oh, David!" she gasped, as he folded her in his arms. "Those awful Indians!"

Keith and Ellen joined their mother, and David held all three in his arms.

When their emotions settled down, David said, "Tell me what happened."

Keith's voice quavered slightly as he said, "I was backing the horses up to the wagon when I saw the band of Indians riding toward the front gate. Their faces were striped with war paint. I ran for the house, shouting to Mom and Ellen that Indians were coming."

"Ellen and I were in the kitchen," said Leah. "Keith had barely gotten inside when there was this sudden burst of gunfire. We thought the Indians were shooting at the house. Then we heard horses' hooves and ventured a look outside. A cavalry unit was galloping across the field from the back side of the house, shooting at the Indians."

"Yeah!" said Keith. "And when the Indians saw they were outnumbered, they took off like scared rabbits!"

They could still hear the sound of gunfire, popping like giant firecrackers.

David looked in the direction of the forest for a few seconds, then hugged his family tighter, and said, "Thank the Lord you're all right. Let's go in the house."

As they stepped onto the porch and entered the kitchen, Leah said, "Were you already headed this way when the firing started?"

"No. I had just finished propping up the rails when...well...it was very strange. Brownie whinnied and looked toward the ridge, flicking his ears nervously. At the same time, I had this unexplainable feeling that something was wrong. It was like the Holy Spirit was telling me my family was in danger. I instantly prayed for your protection, jumped on Brownie, and headed for the house. Minutes later, I heard the gunfire, and when I crested the ridge, I saw the cavalry chasing the Indians out of the yard."

"Isn't it wonderful how the Lord works?" said Leah, as the sounds of battle continued from the deep woods. "He chooses to work by prayer, and He spoke to your heart about us being in danger, and had you praying for our protection at the very moment we needed it."

David nodded. "Let's thank Him right now for the way He worked to protect you. Had He not sent the cavalry by here exactly when He did, all three of you would be dead by now."

The Morleys clung to each other as they bowed their heads and David led them in giving thanks to the Lord.

When the "Amen" was said, Keith said, "Listen…"

"To what?" asked Ellen.

"The silence. There are no gunshots coming from the woods. I hope the cavalry wiped out those Indians."

The Morleys stepped out on the back porch in time to see the army patrol splashing across the creek toward them. Soon the unit of thirty-two men pounded into the yard, led by four officers and two Crow scouts. The Morleys recognized Lieutenant Dobie Carlin and smiled at him as the column drew to a halt. Four officers, including Carlin, dismounted and walked toward the porch.

"You folks all right?" asked Major Crawley.

"Yes, thanks to you and your men," said David.

"Are you the Morleys?"

"Yes, sir. This is my wife, Leah; my son, Keith; and my daughter, Ellen. I'm David."

"I know you're already acquainted with Lieutenant Carlin,

here," said the major. "I'm Major Darrell Crawley. This is Captain Ron Phillips. And this is Lieutenant Wiley Hanks."

"We're very happy to meet you, gentlemen," said David. Then he raised his eyes to the entire column and added, "*All* of you!"

Some of the men nodded.

"What about the Indians, Major?" said David. "We heard a battle going on in the woods."

"None of them will see another sunset, sir," said Crawley.

"There's no way I can thank you enough for driving them away from my family, Major," said David. "I was beyond that ridge to the east, repairing a fence, when my horse looked in the direction of the house and whinnied. At the same time, a strange feeling came over me that my family was in danger. I mounted my horse and galloped for the house, praying the Lord's protection on them. It took probably three or four minutes to reach the ridge. Just before I got to it, I heard gunfire. When I topped the ridge, I saw you men chasing the Indians out of the yard."

Major Crawley, who made no pretense of being a Christian, turned to Lieutenant Carlin and said, "What do you think about that, Lieutenant?"

Dobie shook his head, smiling. "That just about beats all, Major."

"What do you mean?" asked David.

Crawley lifted his campaign hat, scratched his head, and said, "Tell him, Lieutenant."

Dobie pointed south and said, "The column was riding across your unfenced field back there, heading south. We had noticed your house and outbuildings as we passed within about five or six hundred yards. We were climbing over those hills out there when a strange feeling come over me. I didn't hear an audible sound, but a voice inside me seemed to say, 'Look back toward the house.' I looked over my shoulder just in time to see those Blackfoot warriors coming out of the forest from the north and heading straight for your place."

"If Lieutenant Carlin hadn't turned around and looked back when he did," Crawley said, "he wouldn't have seen the Indians. Another few seconds and we'd have been on the other side of the hill."

Leah's eyes shone. "Oh, can you see it? God's perfect timing?"

"There's no question about it," David said. "Do we have a great big almighty God or not?"

Dobie's eyes danced and he almost did a jig as he said, "Praise the Lord! He used *me* to spot the Indians! He used *me* to answer your prayer, David!"

Every man in the patrol unit looked on in wonder. Those who were Christians smiled at each other knowingly. The others would leave the Morley ranch with something to think about.

Leah could hardly contain her joy as she put her arms around her children and said, "The Lord be praised for His goodness! As King David said, 'The Lord is my light and my salvation; whom shall I fear? the Lord is the strength of my life; of whom shall I be afraid? When the wicked, even mine enemies and my foes, came upon me to eat up my flesh, they stumbled and fell'!"

It was just past noon when the combined patrol units led by Major Garland and Captain Fordham rode away from a small white settlement some thirty miles due east of Fort Bridger, pulling two howitzers. The sight they had just beheld left every man feeling nauseated.

Fordham looked at Garland out of the corner of his eye. The man was livid and ready to exact vengeance on every Blackfoot warrior who had committed the atrocities at the settlement.

"Somebody's gonna pay," Garland said. "I don't know if I'll be able to identify the animals who did it, but somebody's gonna pay."

Gray Fox and Running Antelope were on either side of Garland and Fordham. Behind them were Tall Bird and Little Bull. The latter two had ridden with Captain Fordham on many patrols.

As Garland spoke the bitter words, Running Antelope glanced over his shoulder at Little Bull and Tall Bird. What they had just found at the settlement, they were sure, was the work of Crooked Foot himself. His marks of brutality against whites were as recognizable as if he had signed his name.

Little Bull and Tall Bird knew exactly what Running Antelope was saying with his eyes. What would Gray Fox do if Major Blaine Garland was somehow able to capture Crooked Foot?

Garland's words had also started Gray Fox thinking about what he would do if he were thrust between the major and Crooked Foot. His mind slid back in time some seventeen years...

It was a bright, clear summer day in the forests of the Big Horn mountains in northern Wyoming Territory. Gray Fox, who was now fifteen grasses in age, rode out of his village and crossed a wide meadow carpeted with thick green grass and brightly colored wildflowers.

After riding for nearly an hour, he came to a dense forest and entered its sun-dappled shadows. Noting the landmarks, which were mostly giant rock formations, he came upon the familiar open area where he and his friend had met before.

He saw Crooked Foot's pinto first. Then his friend, who

was also fifteen grasses, stepped out of the shadows of the surrounding trees.

A slight breeze was blowing, carrying the pungent aroma
of pine with it. Birds twittered in the branches of the trees,
seeming to put their blessing on what was about to take place.

The friends gripped each other's forearms, then moved to
a secluded spot and sat down cross-legged, facing each other.
Crooked Foot pulled out his knife from its buffalo hide sheath,
and Gray Fox took the eagle feather from his headband and
placed it between his teeth.

Solemnly, Gray Fox offered his right arm to Crooked Foot
and turned his wrist skyward. The knife blade flashed in the
sun as Crooked Foot made an incision about an inch long in
Gray Fox's wrist.

While the blood welled up, Crooked Foot handed the
knife to Gray Fox, who made a similar cut in Crooked Foot's
wrist. Gray Fox then laid the knife on the ground and took the
eagle feather from his teeth, placing it on his bleeding wrist.
Crooked Foot pressed his wrist against the eagle feather so their
blood would mingle through the feather.

They then wrapped their wrists with cloth strips, dug in
the ground with their fingers, and buried the feather. They rose
together and looked at each other gravely as they gripped forearms again.

"Blood brothers forever," Crooked Foot said.

"Blood brothers forever," echoed Gray Fox. "Nothing will
ever change it."

Gray Fox felt an emptiness in his heart. Although the blood
brothers had been forced to fight on opposing sides less than a
year after the solemn ceremony, they had been able to see each

other on the sly a few times since then. Nearly two grasses had passed since they had met. Gray Fox missed his blood brother's companionship.

But there was more than emptiness in his heart; there was dread. If he should find himself in a conflict between the white man's army and Crooked Foot, he would have to refrain from firing his gun at his blood brother. Worse yet, if somehow Crooked Foot should fall into the hands of Major Blaine Garland, Gray Fox would be honor-bound to risk his life to save the life of his blood brother.

Suddenly, a large band of Blackfoot warriors came over a nearby hill at full charge, guns blazing. They were no doubt the very men—the savages Major Garland would love to punish—who had wiped out the white settlement less than an hour before.

And Crooked Foot was in the lead.

CHAPTER FOURTEEN

Major Garland shouted commands as he slid off his horse. "Fight 'em from the ground, men! Make a circle! Howitzers front and center!"

The bugler sounded the signal so that every man knew the orders. While the howitzers were being positioned against the charging Blackfoot, puffs of blue-white smoke filled the air as army carbines flared.

Blackfoot bullets struck sod all around the kneeling men in blue, while some bullets ricocheted off rocks, buzzing away like angry bees.

Suddenly, Major Garland heard one of the men shout, "It's Crooked Foot!"

Garland squinted at the leader of the thundering warriors. He swore through clenched teeth and drew his revolver. Already in a kneeling position, he dogged back the hammer and said to himself, "Come close enough, you filthy beast, and you'll taste some hot Garland lead! That is, unless the cannons get you first!"

He turned to check on the howitzers. The men were already blocking the wheels, and the sergeant in charge of the cannons was holding a sulphur match to his firing rod, preparing to light the fuses. "Blast 'em!" Garland commanded, then looked back toward the charging hostiles.

Crooked Foot, his eyes bulging, skidded his mount to a

halt and shouted for his warriors to turn about and ride for the hill.

"Fire!" shouted Garland. "Don't let 'em get away!"

The howitzers belched fire, their loud roars echoing across the hills. Two cannonballs struck ground in the midst of the fleeing Blackfoot and exploded, taking men and horses down in a rain of smoking shrapnel.

Garland swore when he saw Crooked Foot ride unscathed over the crest of the hill. He headed for his horse and called for his men to mount up. Fordham's unit and the Crow scouts were to stay and disarm the wounded Blackfoot.

Soon Garland and sixteen men had disappeared over the hill in pursuit of the Indians.

"All right, men," said Captain Fordham, "let's see about these wounded Indians."

Garland and his men pushed their horses as hard as they could. When they crested the hill, Crooked Foot and his warriors were nowhere in sight.

The major drew rein and darted his glance from side to side. "They couldn't have just disappeared. They—"

"Major! Out there!" shouted a trooper, pointing to the far side of a draw. The Indians were climbing out of the draw as fast as their horses would carry them.

The major gouged his horse's sides with his heels and took off after them.

Crooked Foot had started out with maybe twenty warriors. The big guns had cut down almost half of his band, and his only goal now was to elude the pursuing troops.

Garland kept sight of the Indians for several minutes, though it was hard to gain on them. Suddenly, they dipped into a deep ravine and vanished from view again. By the time the soldiers reached the ravine, there was no sign of the hostiles. Garland pulled rein and looked around to find a maze of rock-sided canyons going off in various directions. His men could feel the wrath vibrating through him as he sat in silence, breathing heavily.

Lieutenant Diedrich drew up alongside him. "You all right, Major?"

"Yeah." The major drew in a deep breath and let it out slowly.

"Should we try to find them?"

"No. This rocky ground will hide any trace of which way they went, Lieutenant. I hate it, but it looks like that snake has gotten away.

"We'll catch him one of these times, sir," said Diedrich. "At least we came close on this one."

"Close isn't good enough," said Garland in a clipped tone. "I want that filthy savage's neck in my hands."

"I understand, sir."

The major's eyes scanned the ravine in every direction. Finally, he said, "We might as well get back to Captain Fordham and the others. I want to see if any of the wounded warriors are still alive."

Captain Fordham and his men stood over the six wounded Indians. Four had taken shrapnel in the legs, and two had taken it in their torsos. After seizing their weapons, Fordham had removed what shrapnel he could from their bodies and bandaged them up with medical supplies he carried in his saddlebags.

Three Blackfoot lay dead where they had fallen. Two pintos lay dead nearby.

Fordham was kneeling between two Blackfoot, checking

their bandages, when Lieutenant Mack Stewart—one of two new lieutenants assigned to Fordham's unit—drew up and said, "Sir, the major and his men are back."

The captain rose to his feet and watched Garland and his unit trot down the gentle slope. The other men in Fordham's unit collected around him as Garland and his riders drew up.

Gray Fox and the other three scouts stood aloof in a little knot, looking on.

Garland's features were like stone when he looked down at the six wounded Indians. As he dismounted, he set steady eyes on Fordham. "What's this I see? Bandages on low-bellied savages?"

"Pardon me, sir?"

"Why have these filthy savages been bandaged?"

"Because they're wounded, sir. These two over here are in pretty bad shape."

"Because they're wounded? Are you aware, Captain, that they got themselves wounded while coming at us to kill us?"

"Yes, sir. But now they're our prisoners. I don't understand your questioning the fact that we've treated them as best we could."

"You don't coddle enemies, Captain! You kill 'em! But before you kill 'em, you give 'em a good dose of their own medicine!"

Fordham gave Garland a wary look and said, "What are you talking about?"

Garland arched his back and said stiffly, "Didn't we just ride away from a settlement where we found the results of what these animals did to our white brothers and sisters?"

"Yes, but—"

"But nothing, Captain! We're gonna show 'em what it feels like to be on the receiving end of what they did." He turned to speak to the entire unit. "All you men find yourselves sticks. That stand of trees right over there should supply everybody with one. I want those sticks red-hot. We're going to show these vile beasts what it feels like!"

Fordham stiffened and set his jaw. "Now, wait a minute, Major! You're not going to torture these wounded men!"

"Oh, yes, I am…and you and your men are going to join us. When the U.S. Army in Indian country stops coddling these beasts, maybe we can make some headway against 'em. Get those sticks, men, and heat 'em up!"

"You men under my command are not to take part in this atrocity!" Fordham said loudly. "That's an order!"

"You men will do as I say!" Garland said. "All of you! I am ranking officer here!"

Captain Fordham faced the major nose-to-nose and said, "Major, this is against military procedure! Civilized people do not torture their wounded enemies!"

"Then call me uncivilized, Captain, but you have your orders, and so do the rest of these men. I'm gonna teach you how to stop the kind of thing we saw back at that settlement. All this soft-handed military procedure hasn't made a dent in it, has it?"

Fordham's jaw muscles flexed as he continued to stare at Garland.

"Well, have they?" demanded Garland.

Gray Fox moved silently behind Captain Fordham.

"What you're doing won't make a dent in it either, Major," Fordham said. "First and foremost, it's wrong. Second, it's against army rules of warfare. And third, it will only make the hostiles more hostile. Other white people will suffer for it."

"I am asking Major Blaine Garland to remember something," Gray Fox said as he moved up beside Fordham.

Garland glared at him.

"Major Blaine Garland will remember that at Buffalo Lodge, the major make Lieutenant Creighton Diedrich and Sergeant Del Frayne drag wounded Blackfoot on ground till they die. Does the major remember?"

"Yes, of course."

Fordham blinked in disbelief at the news.

"Then Gray Fox begged Major Blaine Garland not to send bodies back to Blackfoot village on pintos. Gray Fox warn such deed would cause more white people to suffer. Does the major remember?"

"Yeah, I remember."

"Let Gray Fox ask the major…has he seen such horror done to whites as back there at the settlement a little while ago?"

"No."

"Then Gray Fox say horror was result of Major Blaine Garland sending dead, tortured Blackfoot warriors to village."

"You don't know that, Indian! Don't tell me I'm responsible for what happened to those people back there!"

"Major," said Fordham, "what I've just heard concerns me greatly. You know Colonel Bateman would never stand for such conduct."

Garland stared at Fordham and held his body rigid but didn't respond.

Fordham continued. "You so often refer to the Blackfoot as 'filthy savages' or 'dirty savages.' What makes you different if you torture these wounded warriors the way they tortured those white people back there? If you follow through with your order to use burning sticks on these warriors, that makes you a savage. Now, would that be 'filthy' or 'dirty'?"

"Have you forgotten who's the major here and who's the captain? You and your men will do as I say or suffer the consequences of insubordination!"

"You, Major," Fordham said, "are the one who will suffer consequences when Colonel Bateman learns of this."

"If you or any of your men blab a word of this to

Bateman, you'll be sorry you ever joined this army! Don't make me prove it! I'm high rank, here, and these filthy savages are going to suffer for what they did today!"

"I can't tell you what to do with your men, Major," Fordham said, "but my men have orders from me not to so much as pick up a stick."

Garland turned to the men and said, "As the major here, I'm commanding all of you to follow my command! Now !"

As Garland's men headed reluctantly toward the stand of trees, Gray Fox said, "Major Blaine Garland, Gray Fox begs you not to do this."

The soldiers stopped in their tracks and looked back, waiting for their major's response.

Garland's eyes flashed fire as he said to Gray Fox, "You keep your mouth shut! This is none of your affair!"

"But it is! It is Gray Fox's business, as well as his three Crow companions. We are U.S. Army scouts. We are observing the major directly disobeying U.S. Army rules. Captain John Fordham did right to give medical attention to wounded enemies."

"On with it, men!" said the major. "All of you!"

Fordham's men kept their eyes on their leader. Not one man moved.

Garland ejected a string of profanity, looked at his own men, and waved toward the trees. "Hurry up!"

As they obeyed, the major gave John Fordham a hateful stare, then started laughing and stepped up beside the Blackfoot warriors who lay on the ground. "You vermin are about to find out what a torture stick feels like!"

While Garland continued to taunt the wounded Indians, Gray Fox slipped up beside John Fordham and said in a low tone, "You must put your gun on Major Blaine Garland and stop this horrible thing, now!"

"I can't."

"I do not understand. The major is going against U.S. Army rules!"

"It would be worse for me to put a gun on a superior officer than to be guilty of allowing him to torture the wounded Blackfoot."

"But Captain John Fordham said what the major is doing is wrong! If Captain John Fordham is right kind of man and soldier, he will use his gun to stop wicked thing!"

"I can't do it."

Some of the men were returning from the stand of trees, already lighting the tips of the sticks.

Gray Fox returned to the other three scouts, who stood apart from the soldiers, and spoke so that only they could hear. Little Bull, Tall Bird, and Running Antelope nodded their heads in agreement.

"I don't care what kind of threat you make, Major, you will face a court martial for this," Fordham said. "You can talk tough all you want, but there are enough men here who will testify against you. Stop this thing now, and we'll forget all about it."

"You haven't fought these devil savages as long as I have, John. One day, after you've seen their heartless tactics repeated over and over until it wrenches your stomach, you'll realize that army procedures are written by big-shot brass in Washington who've never seen an Indian and think they're all like Hiawatha!"

"Devil savages, are they?" said Fordham.

"Yes!"

"Well, so are you!"

Garland turned his gaze to his men, who were letting the slight wind give life to the smoldering sticks, and without looking at Fordham, said, "You'll be sorry for—"

The major's words were cut off by the cold muzzle of a

gun shoved against the base of his skull. Gray Fox eased back the hammer, which gave off a dry double-clicking sound. "The major will command his men to throw down the sticks now or Gray Fox will kill him!"

"Gray Fox," Fordham said, "I understand what you are trying to do, but—"

Suddenly Fordham felt the pressure of a carbine against his backbone. His men looked on in astonishment. Little Bull, who was holding the gun, said, "Captain John Fordham will very carefully drop his gunbelt."

The other Crow scouts had their guns trained on the remaining officers. While Gray Fox relieved Major Garland of his gunbelt, he commanded all the soldiers to throw down their weapons, threatening to shoot the major if even one man disobeyed.

Within seconds, all guns were on the ground.

Gray Fox continued to hold the muzzle tight against the base of Garland's skull as he said, "All soldiers except officers stand in one place. Over here." He pointed with his free hand to a spot in front of Garland where he could see all of them.

The troopers quickly did as they were told and collected themselves into a tight bunch.

Gray Fox pressed his gun hard against Garland's skull and said, "Get down on knees."

The major dropped to his knees and looked at his men, who stood watching helplessly. He wanted to scream at them to do something. Instead, he rolled his eyes from side to side, as if doing so would finally bring Gray Fox into view.

The pressure of the Colt .45 against his skull was excruciating. In a low and steady voice, he said, "Gray Fox, call off whatever you've got planned and we'll forget the whole thing. We'll take these Blackfoot to the fort and give them proper medical attention. Nothing will ever be said about you and your friends putting guns on me and these other officers."

His words were met with stone-cold silence.

"How about it, Gray Fox?"

Silence.

Even though the air was cool, Garland's brow began to sweat. "Gray Fox...?"

Silence.

Garland spoke to Fordham, though he could not see him. "Captain Fordham, talk to this man!"

"I've got a gun muzzle against my spine, Major," Fordham said. "I'm in no better position to persuade him of anything than you are."

Garland's body began to tremble. "Gray Fox, listen to reason. I'm willing to forget this whole thing and go on like it never happened."

"I am not," Gray Fox said coldly. "And I do not believe you. Like so many white men, you speak with forked tongue."

The major blinked against the stinging sweat in his eyes and clenched his teeth, trying to force his body to stop shaking.

Suddenly Gray Fox said sharply, "All blue coats except officers mount up and ride to fort!"

The troopers looked at the Indian scout in astonishment.

"Gray Fox," said Sergeant Frayne, eyes bulging, "what are you going to do with the officers?"

Gray Fox said, "Mount up with the rest of them, Sergeant Del Frayne, or I will shoot the major!"

"They're going to kill us!" Lieutenant Anthony Udall cried. "That's what! They're going to kill us!"

"That'll be murder, Gray Fox!" Sergeant Barry Wilkins said. "Do you hear me? If you shoot them, you will be murderers!"

Gray Fox's eyes flashed fire as he pressed the muzzle against Garland's skull even harder. "Do as Gray Fox said! Now! Or I will shoot the major!"

Some of the soldiers began to move toward their horses while others hesitated.

Gray Fox's anger made his voice shake. "Do as Gray Fox says! If major dies, it is your fault! Go!"

To a man, the troopers headed for their horses.

"Go to the fort!" Gray Fox called after them.

Sergeant Frayne paused beside his horse. "Gray Fox! You can't send us out there without our weapons! If we run into a Blackfoot war party, they'll massacre us!"

Gray Fox thought a moment, then said, "All right. Pick up guns. But if bluecoats try to circle around and sneak up on us, every officer will die before bluecoats fire first shot!"

CHAPTER FIFTEEN

As the troopers shoved their carbines into the saddle scabbards and mounted their horses, Captain Fordham felt a tightening in his chest. Gray Fox and his comrades could kill the officers only when the bulk of the patrol unit was gone. Otherwise, the others could rush them and overpower them.

He felt a numbness settle over him. Though Little Bull still had the muzzle of the Remington .44 solid against his backbone, the captain had to try to save the lieutenants. He looked at Gray Fox, who stood with his gun pressed against the back of Major Garland's head. "Gray Fox…" he said.

The grim-faced Indian looked at him with passionless eyes.

"Gray Fox, listen. You should allow the lieutenants to leave too. Especially those under my command. They weren't going to torture and kill the wounded Blackfoot."

Gray Fox's dark countenance showed anger. "Captain John Fordham was not going to do it, either, but he did not have the courage to stop what was going to happen."

Major Garland pressed his palms against his aching thighs and said, "What happens now, Gray Fox?"

The Crow leader looked at the position of the sun in the sky and said, "You will know in about an hour. Major Blaine Garland will now sit on ground."

Glad for at least some relief to his legs, Garland eased onto the ground in a sitting position. It felt good to get the pressure of the gun muzzle off the back of his head.

While Gray Fox held his gun pointed at Garland's skull, he motioned with his free hand for Fordham to move beside the major. "Captain John Fordham sit here. There will be no talking between you."

Fordham eased down beside Garland. They exchanged glances, then looked at their captors.

"Lieutenants will now join them," said Gray Fox.

Gray Fox and Little Bull stood guard as Lieutenants Diedrich, Sullivan, Stewart, and Udall sat down beside Garland and Fordham.

Gray Fox nodded silently to Running Antelope and Tall Bird, who went to the wounded warriors and checked their wounds. Satisfied that Captain Fordham had done as much as he could for them, they gave the Indians water from their army issue canteens.

John Fordham had no doubt that Gray Fox was planning to kill them. He thought of Betsy and the children and felt a shrinking within himself. Poor Betsy. She'd know that all of her fears had been well founded, in spite of how he'd tried to persuade her otherwise. And what about her distrust of the Crow scouts? She might never know the whole story of what happened here, but the troopers would tell her as much as they knew. And that would be enough to convince her she'd been right about the Crows all the time.

Then, sooner or later, Betsy would receive official word from the army. Her husband had been murdered by the Crow scouts. Maybe…maybe Hannah Cooper would be there to help her and give her strength. Hannah. What a fine woman. She had proven herself a friend to the family, especially to Betsy, over and over again. The only fault she had— No, he shouldn't call it a fault. The only peculiarity Hannah had was being so forward and uninhibited in speaking about her faith and the realities of heaven and hell.

Heaven. He was about to be killed. Would he really go to heaven, as he had tried to convince himself for so many years?

John's chest felt heavy. His religious philosophy, he had often said, was good enough to live by. *But was it good enough to die by?*

Suddenly John's thoughts were interrupted by Gray Fox, who checked the position of the sun and said, "Hour is passed. Lieutenants may go now. Ride to fort."

Creighton Diedrich looked at the other three lieutenants, who seemed as shocked as he at Gray Fox's words. He set widened eyes on the Crow and said, "You mean we're free to get on our horses and ride like the troopers did?"

Gray Fox nodded slowly. "Yes. Go now."

"But...but what about Major Garland and Captain Fordham?"

"They stay with us," Gray Fox said.

"Why? What are you going to do to them?"

A scowl passed like a shadow over Gray Fox's face. "No more questions, Lieutenant Creighton Diedrich! You and other lieutenants go *now!* Pick up guns and ride to fort!"

As he spoke, Gray Fox stepped behind the major again, pressing his cocked revolver to the man's head. Little Bull did the same to Fordham with his carbine.

"Do not attempt to catch us off guard," Gray Fox said. "We allow you to have guns as protection against Blackfoot enemies. You cannot take us by surprise. Do not be fools. Go to fort."

The four young officers rose to their feet and looked at the major and the captain with deep concern in their eyes.

"Go on," said Fordham. "Before they change their minds."

Reluctantly, the lieutenants picked up their revolvers, holstered them, and headed for their horses. As they mounted, they looked back once more, then rode away.

When they had passed from view, Gray Fox said to the major and captain, "Get up. We go now."

"Go?" said Garland, as he and Fordham stood up. "Go where?"

"We put wounded Blackfoot on pintos and take to Crooked Foot's village."

"You don't mean we're going there with you?" said Garland.

"Yes, you go with us."

"You can't do that! You know what will happen to us if you turn us over to Crooked Foot!"

Gray Fox waved a hand at Running Antelope and Tall Bird, pointing to the Blackfoot who lay on the ground.

While Running Antelope and Tall Bird were picking up the wounded warriors, the Crow leader said, "Major Blaine Garland will remember his heartless deeds at Buffalo Lodge and that Gray Fox try to stop him. If Gray Fox had not stopped the major today—as Captain John Fordham should have—these Blackfoot warriors would have been tortured to death. Major Blaine Garland must pay for his deeds."

"You're not thinking this through, Gray Fox," said Garland. "Do you realize that you and these other three Crows will be known as renegades for turning against officers of the United States Army?"

"It won't be good, Gray Fox," Fordham said. "You'll have Two Moons on your trail too."

"Right," said Garland. "You know Two Moons wouldn't approve of your taking us to Crooked Foot."

Gray Fox's black eyes flashed. "Two Moons would not approve of what you did to those wounded Blackfoot warriors at Buffalo Lodge, either, Major Blaine Garland! The Crow are enemies of Blackfoot, but Crows not torture wounded men... not even enemies!"

"But if you turn us over to Crooked Foot," said Fordham,

"you'll be at odds with your chief. It's best not to get on the wrong side of Two Moons! Remember, he recommended you and these other men to Colonel Bateman as army scouts. In Two Moons's eyes, you will have betrayed the trust he had in you."

Gray Fox ran his dark gaze to Little Bull, who held his carbine pointed at Fordham. Little Bull's features were like stone. The Crow leader looked toward the other two Indians, who had just hoisted one of the wounded warriors onto a pinto. Both glanced at Gray Fox with an impassive look in their eyes.

Gray Fox turned his gaze to the two army officers and said, "Running Antelope, Tall Bird, Little Bull, and Gray Fox rather be renegades than to scout for U.S. Army that have men who have no heart, as Colonel Blaine Garland, and men who have no courage, as Captain John Fordham."

It was midmorning at Fort Bridger when the combined patrol unit led by Major Darrell Crawley and Captain Ron Phillips trotted through the gate.

Hannah Cooper and little Patty Ruth were alone in the general store and heard the pounding hooves and blowing horses.

Patty Ruth, who was sitting at the small table near the potbellied stove where male customers sometimes played checkers, said, "Some of the so'jers mus' be back already, Mama."

"Sure sounds like it, honey," said Hannah as she closed the cash drawer.

Mandy Carver had worked that morning at the store, since it was her normally scheduled day, but she had been summoned to the school. Her son, Tyrone, age seven, had taken a spill at recess and needed some stitches in his arm.

A short time after the patrol unit entered the fort, Patty Ruth was helping her mother stock some shelves when the little bell above the door jingled. Two army wives, Alice Barker and Maxine Phillips, entered. Maxine, wife of Captain Ron Phillips, hurried to Hannah and said, "Did you hear what happened at the Morley ranch?"

"No, I didn't," said Hannah, straightening up and pressing both hands against the small of her back. "Did it have anything to do with the patrol that just rode in?"

"Yes. That was my husband's unit combined with Major Crawley's. I happened to be near the stables when they came in. Before he went to meet with Colonel Bateman, Ron quickly told me the story. Leah and the children were almost attacked by a Blackfoot war party!"

Hannah gasped. "Oh, how terrible! Are they all right? Is David with them?"

"They're fine," said Maxine, "and David is with them." She gave Hannah the details as she had heard them from her husband, telling her how amazed the soldiers had been at seeing God's hand at work.

"I'm so thankful none of the Morleys were hurt," said Hannah.

"Me too," said Maxine and Alice in unison. Then both ladies made their purchases and left the store.

Town marshal Lance Mangum entered the store and picked up shaving soap and a new razor. When Mangum's turn came, he laid his articles on the counter and smiled at Hannah. She returned the smile, arching her back, and pressed her fingers where the ache hurt the most.

Mangum's eyes showed concern as he looked around and said, "I thought there was supposed to be a lady here to help you at all times, Hannah. At least that's what Glenda Williams told me."

"There usually is, Marshal," Hannah said as she began totaling his bill. "Mandy Carver was here, but Tyrone got hurt at school and she's with him at Doc O'Brien's office."

"Was Tyrone hurt bad?"

"I don't think so. He needed some stitches taken, but I don't think it was real serious."

"Hope not. Would you like for me to see if I can find someone to come and help?"

"That won't be necessary, thank you. I expect Mandy back soon."

After Mangum left, there were a few more customers, then traffic slowed as the noon hour approached.

Patty Ruth noticed her mother's hands pressing her back again and said, "Mama, shouldn' you go see Grandpa O'Brien? Maybe he could make your back feel better."

"There's nothing he can do, honey. This is just part of bringing babies into the world. I had lots of backaches when I was carrying you."

"Really?"

"Mm-hmm."

"But I was worth it, wasn't I?"

Hannah leaned over Patty Ruth and kissed the tip of her nose. "I'll say! You're *still* worth it too! I love you."

"And I love you, Mama."

The bell jingled and Mandy Carver entered the store. "I's back, Miz Hannah. Tyrone's cut took four stitches. It's in his lef' knee."

"But he'll be all right?"

"Yes'm. He's already back at school. He'll jis' have to curtail runnin' fo' a few days till Doc takes the stitches out."

"Mama's back's been hurtin', Miss Mandy," said Patty Ruth. "Did your back hurt when you were carryin' your babies?"

"Oh, did it ever! But that's part of what a mama has to endure to have babies." She turned to Hannah and said, "You go over there and plop yo' little self on that chair, y'hear?"

Hannah had just eased onto one of the chairs behind the counter when the bell jingled again and Corporal Benny Huffman entered, carrying a small satchel marked "U.S. Mail." Twice a week, army wagons made a trip to Cheyenne City, where the mail came from all over the country by rail.

"Hello, ladies!" Huffman said cheerfully. "That includes you, Patty Ruth."

"'Course," said the five-year-old. "How are you, Corporal Benny?"

"A little tuckered from the trip, but I'll get over it. Have your mail here, Hannah."

Mandy reached out and said, "I'll take it, Benny. Miz Hannah is sittin' down fo' a while."

Hannah thanked Huffman and began sorting through the mail as soon as he was gone.

"Oh!" she gasped. "Patty Ruth! It's a letter from your Uncle Adam!"

While Hannah tore open the envelope, Patty Ruth drew close to hear what Uncle Adam had to say.

"Who's Uncle Adam?" Mandy asked.

Hannah now had the letter in her hand and was unfolding it. "He's Solomon's brother. Two years younger than Solomon. His wife, Theresa, has had some health problems. They have a six-year-old boy, Seth. Adam works for a newspaper in Cincinnati."

Hannah's eyes ran across the line and down the page swiftly. The letter was only written on one side of the page.

When she was finished, Patty Ruth said, "What's Uncle Adam say, Mama? Is Aunt Theresa all right?"

"Aunt Theresa is doing better, honey."

"I'm glad."

"Me, too. And Uncle Adam and your cousin Seth are doing fine. They...they are very sad to hear that your papa died. And Uncle Adam wants to know if we need him to send us some money."

"He's a nice man, like Papa."

Hannah sighed as she folded the letter and placed it back in the envelope. "One down and one to go. Now, if we would only hear from Grandma and Grandpa Singleton."

"We will, Mama," Patty Ruth said. "We'll get a letter from 'em soon."

"You haven't heard from yo' parents yet, Miz Hannah?" asked Mandy.

"No. Has me concerned too. I've written more than once, but so far there's been no reply."

"Did yo' brother-in-law say anythin' 'bout 'em in his letter?"

"No."

"Well, then, they must be all right. You jis' keep yo' pretty li'l chin up. I'm sure you'll hear from 'em soon."

Colonel Bateman was talking in his office with the four officers whose units had chased the Blackfoot war party from the Morley ranch.

"I'm convinced, gentlemen," said the colonel, "that if we could bring Crooked Foot down, this whole uprising would go away. He's the core of the trouble."

"I agree, sir," said Major Crawley. "He's the source of it, all right. But as we've discussed before, the way he moves around, he's almost impossible to find."

"That's for sure," Captain Phillips said. "It's going to take another Indian to find him. And though our Crow scouts could no doubt track him down, they aren't in the assassination business."

"I've been thinking about this, Colonel," said Lieutenant Dobie Carlin. "How about us posting one or two of our Crow scouts near Crooked Foot's village every day until he shows up? We know Indians have a way of blending with the land in a way no white man can. We could have one of our combined patrol units doing what appears to be a routine patrol not too far away. This wouldn't arouse suspicion in the minds of the Blackfoot because they're used to seeing the patrols moving about in that area. So, when Crooked Foot comes riding in, the scout or scouts can advise the patrol leader real quick. Our beefed-up unit would launch an attack on the village, making Crooked Foot the main target."

There was a brief silence as the other officers thought about Carlin's proposal.

"Colonel, I like the idea," said Crawley.

"Me too," said Lieutenant Hanks. "This way we can utilize the Crow scouts to help bring about Crooked Foot's demise, but none of the Crows will be asked to do any killing."

"Sounds good to me, Colonel," said Phillips.

Colonel Bateman nodded. "Sounds good to me too. Lieutenant Carlin, that's good thinking. The sharpest of the lot amongst our scouts is Gray Fox."

"For sure, sir," said Crawley.

"It'll be best," Bateman said, "if we send Gray Fox alone. Less chance of being seen and caught spying."

The others nodded.

"By putting this idea to work immediately, we'll gain a good advantage too," said the colonel. "We know that the only time Crooked Foot has all his warriors in the village is in the dead of winter. By striking now, we won't have a large number of warriors to contend with. Once we know Crooked Foot's in the village, we can hit it hard, kill him, and get out fast. I don't want any more women and children to get hurt than is necessary to get their leader."

"How soon will you put the plan into action, Colonel?" asked Major Crawley.

"Tomorrow. When the patrols come in this evening, I'll talk to Gray Fox about it. I'll have him spying on the village before the sun rises in the morning."

There was a knock at the door.

"Yes?" called Bateman.

The door opened and the colonel's adjutant said, "Sorry to interrupt, Colonel Bateman, but Corporal Early is here and needs to see you immediately."

Bateman rose to his feet. "Show him in."

Ted Early, who was on duty at the fort's gate, stepped in and saluted. "Colonel, sir, you'd better come to the gate. I think something bad has happened."

CHAPTER SIXTEEN

W hen Colonel Bateman and the other officers arrived at the gate, Corporal Early led them up the tower stairs to the platform. A second sentry, Corporal Watson, was studying the eastern plains through binoculars.

Watson handed the binoculars to Bateman. "Here, Colonel. Take a look. They're almost close enough to distinguish faces."

As Bateman focused the glasses on the incoming riders he said, "Something's wrong, all right. For one thing, they're returning over two hours early. For another, they're more than trotting those horses...and they're in no semblance of order."

"It looked to me, sir," said Watson, "that it's all troopers. No officers and no Crow scouts among them."

Bateman held the glasses steady, his mouth grim. "You're right, Corporal—no Major Garland, no Captain Fordham, no lieutenants, and no Indian scouts. I'd say they met up with a large war party, but I count thirty-two troopers. The same number who went out with Major Garland and Captain Fordham this morning. It would be some strange battle if only the officers and scouts were killed. It's got to be something else."

"I guess we're about to find out," said Lieutenant Carlin.

Five or six more minutes brought the galloping troopers to the gate, where they skidded to a halt. Colonel Bateman and the other officers were on the ground to meet them.

Sergeant Frayne was the first man out of his saddle, followed by Sergeant Wilkins; the other men stayed on their mounts.

Frayne stepped up to Bateman, saluted, and said, "Sir, may Sergeant Wilkins and I talk to you in your office? I'd like these other officers, here, to come with us."

Bateman looked puzzled but nodded his assent.

"And, sir," said Wilkins, "could the rest of the men go on and put the horses in the corral?"

"That will be fine, Sergeant, but I would rather they didn't tell anyone the story you're about to tell me. I want to hear it first."

Wilkins turned to the mounted troopers. "You men hear that?"

All responded with nods and verbal assent.

Colonel Bateman addressed the men. "I'd like for you men to just stay at the stables until I say differently. If the wives of your missing officers get word that the patrol is back without their husbands, we could have some real problems on our hands. Just go quietly to the stables and stay there until further notice."

Inside the colonel's office, Sergeants Wilkins and Frayne sat front and center before the colonel's desk, with Crawley, Phillips, Carlin, and Hanks flanking them.

Sergeant Frayne started with the horrible scene they found at the settlement early that morning. He then described the attack Crooked Foot launched against the unit and how the war chief wheeled his warriors about when he saw the howitzers. Frayne paused and looked at Wilkins, then back to the colonel. "We...ah...hit some of Crooked Foot's warriors with the cannon fire, sir. Some were killed outright. Others were wounded." Frayne glanced at Wilkins again.

"We've got to tell him, Sergeant," Wilkins said.

"Tell me what?" Bateman said.

"Well, sir," said Frayne, "it's not easy to be a tattletale on a fellow soldier. Especially a commanding officer."

"Go on."

Bateman was shocked to the core to hear about Major Garland's treatment of the wounded Blackfoot after the Buffalo Lodge massacre…and the command Garland had given his men today to torture wounded Blackfoot with burning sticks.

Sergeant Frayne then said that Captain Fordham had refused to go along with it and had commanded his own men not to obey Garland.

Bateman shook his head in astonishment. "This hits me like the kick of a mule. I knew Major Garland held a deep hatred for Indians, but this…"

"Sir," said Frayne, "if you have any doubt that what we're telling you is true, you're free to talk to the other men."

Bateman threw up a palm. "It's not that I don't believe you, it's just that I never dreamed Major Garland would be like that. Go on."

Sergeant Frayne told how Gray Fox had pled with Garland not to mistreat the wounded Blackfoot warriors today. When Garland ignored him, Gray Fox, in desperation, had put a gun to Garland's head. The other scouts joined Gray Fox in disarming the rest of the unit by threatening to kill Garland. Then Gray Fox let the troopers return to the fort.

Bateman's features were drawn and gray as he rubbed a hand across his forehead. "I'm glad to know Captain Fordham refused to go along," he said. "My worry now is what is going to happen to the officers who are in Gray Fox's hands."

"I fear they're already dead, sir," said Sergeant Wilkins. "I think the reason Gray Fox sent us away was so we couldn't swarm him when he started executing the officers."

Bateman nodded, looking ill. "The…the wives of those officers have a right to know what's happened—even though we can't yet tell them the fate of their husbands."

"I agree, sir," said Crawley. "We mustn't keep this from them. Sooner or later, word will get out that the unit is back."

Bateman called his adjutant in and sent him to bring the officers' wives to his office.

While they waited for the women to arrive, Colonel Bateman asked the sergeants questions about Gray Fox and the other scouts. The only good thing they could say about Gray Fox was that he let the troopers have their guns in case they ran into a Blackfoot war party on the way back to the fort.

"I appreciate that," said Bateman, "but for the rest of it, and for whatever he's done with the officers, how's he going to face Two Moons?"

"I don't think Gray Fox and the others have any intention of facing Two Moons, sir," said Wilkins. "They know what would happen. Two Moons would have their hides. We think he'll join up with Crooked Foot. They were boyhood pals. I guess you know that."

"Yes, but I figured that friendship went by the wayside when the two tribes went to war with each other many years ago."

"Maybe so, but after what Gray Fox and the other scouts did today, they won't be in the good graces of Two Moons. Crooked Foot will love them for it."

The men discussed the situation for several minutes, then Lieutenant Carlin said, "Well, Colonel, this news scraps our plan for using Gray Fox to spy on the Blackfoot village."

"You're right about that, Lieutenant. We'll have to come up with some other way to get Crooked Foot. But it's got to be—"

Bateman was interrupted by a knock at the door and the entrance of the five women. The men rose to their feet. There was a look of dread on each woman's face and then surprise as they recognized the two sergeants. None of them had been told the troopers who served under their husbands and Lieutenant Anthony, who was single, had returned to the fort.

Since there were not enough chairs for all, the men remained on their feet and allowed the ladies to be seated.

Colonel Bateman was visibly nervous as he cleared his throat and said, "Let me get right to the point, ladies. Your husbands have been taken captive by the four Crow scouts who rode with the patrol today."

"Captive!" Flora Garland said. "What do you mean? Those scouts are U.S. Army employees!"

"I knew it!" said Betsy Fordham. "I knew it! I've said all along those Crows couldn't be trusted! Where's my husband, Colonel? Where is he?"

"Now, ladies, you must remain calm," said Bateman. "We have no reason to believe your husbands have been harmed, but I'm going to tell you the truth about their capture. You need to know what happened today, and I have Sergeants Frayne and Wilkins here to answer your questions."

Betsy and Melissa Sullivan gripped each other's hands as the colonel began the story. Bateman held back nothing, not even for Flora Garland's sake. When he finished, there was silence.

Finally, Flora said, "I...I must apologize to all of you for my husband's actions. Blaine has had a strong hatred toward Indians for a long time. I will say that he has seen some cruel and inhuman things done by Indians to white people. But this doesn't excuse what he caused today. I'm sorry."

Betsy, her lips quivering, said, "Flora, you have nothing to be sorry for. This is none of your doing."

Then Betsy turned penetrating eyes on the colonel. Her voice rose in pitch as she said, "Colonel, I've told John for some time that you were foolish to use those Crows as scouts. Why would you trust them? They're Indians, and you should have known better! They have probably tortured our husbands to death by now, and it's your fault! You shouldn't have trusted them! And you shouldn't trust that Two Moons either! Can't you see you're courting disaster? Can't you see—"

Betsy broke into sobs, covering her face with her hands.

Melissa wailed and burst into tears, crying, "Greg's dead! He's dead! I know it! Those treacherous Crows killed him! Oh, Greg! Oh-h-h-h, Greg!"

Flora and Darlene Stewart went to Betsy and tried to calm her, and Janet Diedrich wrapped her arms around Melissa, saying, "We mustn't give up. Listen to me! We mustn't give up! We don't know that our husbands have been killed. We've got to believe they're still alive and all right. Please! Get hold of yourself."

Tears were spilling down Melissa's cheeks as she looked at Janet and nodded. Betsy continued to sob. The men looked on helplessly.

Colonel Bateman finally left his chair and went to the inconsolable woman. "Betsy," he said, "we're going to do all we can to get John and the other men back."

"Colonel," said Flora, "Betsy's very close with Hannah Cooper. Perhaps if we could get Hannah in here…"

"Right away," said Bateman. "I'll send my adjutant to bring her."

"No need," said Darlene. "I'll get her."

Hannah Cooper and Mandy Carver were busy at the counter in the general store when Darlene Stewart came in. Darlene excused herself politely and slipped past the customers who were waiting in two lines, going straight to the counter. Hannah glanced at her as she handed change to a customer.

"Hello, Darlene," Hannah said. "Can I help you?"

"Hannah, I've just come from Colonel Bateman's office. We need you there if you can possibly get away."

"You need me? I don't understand."

"Colonel Bateman asked me to come and see if you would help him with a particularly delicate matter. I can't tell you any more than that, but it's very important, and it's urgent."

Hannah looked at Mandy. "I hate to leave you with all these customers, but—"

"It's all right, Miz Hannah," said Mandy. "These folks will understand. I'll get to them as soon as possible."

Julie Powell was one of the customers in the store, and she stepped close and said, "Hannah, I'll take your spot. You go on."

"But Casey and Carrie…"

"They can play over here with me, Mama," spoke up Patty Ruth, who sat at the checkers table close to the potbellied stove.

"I can see them from behind the counter, Hannah," said Julie. "Now go on."

Hannah thanked her, told Patty Ruth she would be back soon, and hurried out the door with Darlene. As they walked across the compound toward the colonel's office, Darlene filled Hannah in on everything that had happened.

"I'll do what I can," Hannah said, as they stepped up on the porch. She could hear Betsy's cries even before Darlene opened the door.

The colonel's adjutant was waiting for them and opened the door of the inner office. Flora was sitting beside Betsy, who was leaning forward with her head down and eyes closed. Hannah swiftly moved toward the grieving woman.

"Betsy, look who's here," said Flora, making room for Hannah.

Betsy's head came up. When she saw her friend, she sucked in a shuddering breath and said, "Oh, Hannah, our husbands are dead! Those savages killed them! My John is gone forever!"

Hannah took Betsy in her arms and said, "Yes, Darlene

told me what happened, but you don't know that John's dead. Let's not accept that as long as there's no proof of it."

The frightened woman looked into Hannah's eyes through a wall of tears and said, "I want to believe he's alive, Hannah, but those Indians are such beasts! Why would they capture him and the other officers except to kill them?"

"I can't give you any answers, honey. But there could very well be some other reason. You must do as your friends here are doing. Hold on to the hope that your husband will come back to you alive and well."

A calm began to slowly descend over Betsy. There was something in Hannah's touch…something in her voice. Betsy stopped crying and used the hanky she had pulled from her dress pocket earlier to dab at her tears.

"That's it, honey," said Hannah, patting Betsy's hand. "Don't give up believing that John is all right."

"I'm trying. I really am trying."

"Colonel," said Hannah, "what are you going to do about finding the captured officers?"

"There's nothing I can do till morning. For one thing, I need to send one of the combined units, and they won't be in till sundown. It would be dark before they could get to the spot where the troopers left the officers with Gray Fox."

"So you're sending a unit out at dawn?" asked Flora.

"That's my plan, but before I finalize it, I want to talk to Two Moons. I need his advice, and he needs to know that four of his trusted men have become renegades."

The colonel saw a look of disbelief cross Betsy's face, and he said softly, "Betsy, I know how you feel about Indians. But Two Moons is our friend. I'm going to need him to help bring John and the other officers home safely."

Hannah squeezed Betsy's hand and whispered, "Please, don't say anything. He's right. We need Two Moons's help."

Betsy bit her lip and looked at the floor.

"Sergeants Frayne and Wilkins," the colonel said, "I need you to ride up to the Crow village and ask Two Moons to come as soon as possible."

The sergeants squared their shoulders and saluted.

"How much shall we tell him, sir?" asked Sergeant Wilkins.

"Don't give out any information other than the fact that I need to talk to him until you're on your way back. Then tell him all of it so he'll have time to think the situation over before he gets here."

The sergeants disappeared through the door. Then Colonel Bateman said to the officers, "Gentlemen, you're free to go. I'll walk outside with you."

As the men started for the door, Bateman said, "Ladies, I'll be right back. If there's anything you want to talk about, we'll do it then."

When Colonel Bateman and the other officers were outside, Bateman said, "Major Crawley, would you go to Dr. Blayney and tell him what's happened? I think it best to alert him that if any or all of our officers have been killed, we'll need him to help with the widows. Especially Mrs. Fordham."

"I'm on my way, sir," said Crawley. "And I assume you want him to keep it under his hat until it's public knowledge?"

"I guess there's no reason to keep it a secret any longer, now that the wives know."

"All right, sir."

Bateman told Lieutenant Carlin to go to the troopers at the stable and tell them they could return to their barracks. When questioned by others, they were to go easy on throwing too much blame on Major Garland.

As soon as the door closed behind Colonel Bateman and the other officers, Betsy said, "Hannah, didn't I tell you those Crows couldn't be trusted? I was right, wasn't I? Look what they've done! I don't trust Two Moons, either."

The other wives sat quietly, listening.

"Betsy," Hannah said, "just because you were right about Gray Fox and those other three scouts doesn't mean the rest of the scouts are traitors. And it certainly doesn't mean that Two Moons is…or that all Crows are bad. You've known some pretty bad white people, haven't you?"

"Well…yes."

"Does that make all white people bad?"

A sullen look captured Betsy's face. "No."

"Then can't you make room for the same rule of thumb toward Indians?"

"No, I can't," Betsy said.

"Why not?"

"Because there are good white people. But there aren't any good Indians! They're all savages, and they have a hatred toward white people that they cover up till they get a chance to turn on them…like Gray Fox and those others did. I don't trust any of them, Hannah. Not one! And if somehow John is still alive, I'll get him out of"—the door opened—"this horrible Indian country."

Betsy paused as the colonel set inquisitive eyes on her, having heard her last few words.

She wasn't embarrassed in the least and repeated for his ears, "If somehow John is still alive, I'll get him out of this horrible Indian country right now, no matter what it takes!"

The colonel closed the door quietly and moved to where Betsy sat. "Betsy, I understand your anguish. I've been in the military through two wars, and now this Indian fighting. I've seen many a wife in the position of not knowing whether her husband lived through a certain battle or was still alive in a prison camp. I can't blame you for being angry at what you're facing. And I can't blame you for feeling that I'm responsible because I brought the Crow scouts in. My heart is heavy for you and for these other wives. I want you to know that I'll leave no stone unturned to bring back your husbands alive and well."

The door suddenly flew open. "Colonel," said the adjutant, "forgive me for the intrusion, but we've got more riders coming in from due east!"

The women were on Bateman's heels as he plunged through the door into the outer office where Corporal Early stood waiting.

"You think these riders are part of Major Garland and Captain Fordham's units, Corporal?" asked Bateman.

"Yes, sir. They're a long way out, but the group is too small to be another patrol unit, and there isn't another one in that direction anyway, sir."

"Oh, Hannah!" said Betsy. "It must be John! He and the others have somehow escaped from Gray Fox!"

The anxious wives, along with Hannah, hurried to the gate behind Colonel Bateman and Corporal Early. Corporal Watson was in the tower, studying the plains to the east through binoculars.

Colonel Bateman, who paused at the bottom of the steps while Early bounded up to the platform, called out, "Are they close enough for you to tell how many there are, Corporal Watson?"

"Yes, sir. Four of them, sir."

Colonel Bateman led the women outside the open gate so they could see for themselves. The riders were too far off to identify.

"Corporal Watson…" called Bateman.

Watson removed the binoculars from his eyes and looked down. "Yes, sir?"

"Let us know when you can identify any of them."

"I will, sir," said the young corporal, looking through the glasses again.

Betsy took Hannah's hand as she strained to focus on the incoming riders. "One of them just has to be John, Hannah. He has to be alive!"

"One thing is for sure," said Flora Garland, "if one of them is Lieutenant Udall, two of us are still missing our husbands."

The women's hearts were beating rapidly as they linked hands and waited for the galloping men to draw nearer.

CHAPTER SEVENTEEN

T he breathless silence was broken when Corporal Watson called from the tower, "I can make out Lieutenant Sullivan!"

Melissa let out a whine of relief as tears filled her eyes. Everyone let go of the hands they were holding, except for Hannah, who kept a grip on Betsy. The other four women waited in icy numbness.

"Lieutenant Udall," called Watson.

"Creighton Diedrich!"

Janet broke into sobs, which she tried to muffle. Hannah felt Betsy's grip turn to steel as she peered toward the oncoming riders without blinking.

"The last one is…Lieutenant Stewart!"

"Flora…Betsy…" said Darlene, wiping tears from her cheeks, "don't give up yet. Maybe we'll hear good news."

Flora Garland compressed her lips and drew in a sharp breath to keep the tears from her eyes. Betsy Fordham clamped a hand over her mouth and closed her eyes, releasing a tiny whimper.

"Hang on," Hannah said, as she put an arm around her friend. "Maybe it's not as bad as it seems."

Betsy's entire body was quivering.

Flora moved up on Betsy's other side, her own nerves

strung like a tightwire. "Let's face this thing together," she said, taking hold of Betsy's hand.

The four riders drew up, with Sullivan, Diedrich, and Stewart quickly sliding from their saddles as their wives ran to them.

Colonel Bateman waited a moment before moving in to ask about Major Garland and Captain Fordham.

Betsy could stand it no longer. "Where's John? Where's my husband?"

"What about our husbands?" Flora said. "Tell us!"

The lieutenants looked to Colonel Bateman.

"The troopers arrived about an hour ago," said the colonel. "They told us the whole story up to when Gray Fox sent them to the fort. Lieutenant Diedrich, you've been a soldier the longest. You do the talking. What about Major Garland and Captain Fordham?"

Diedrich kept an arm around Janet and turned to face Flora and Betsy. "Mrs. Garland…Mrs. Fordham…your husbands were still alive and unharmed when we were released by Gray Fox and the other Crow scouts."

Flora choked a bit, then said, "Lieutenant Diedrich, why is Gray Fox holding our husbands? Why did he let you four go?"

"Ma'am, he really didn't tell us anything. We figured he was going to kill all six of us and was sending the enlisted men away so they wouldn't interfere. But after an hour, he told the four of us to get on our horses and ride for the fort. When we asked what he was going to do, he wouldn't give us an answer. We were told to get on our horses and ride immediately. Captain Fordham told us to go before the Crows changed their minds…so we did."

"In your opinion, Lieutenant," said Bateman, "what do you think Gray Fox is going to do with them?"

"We've talked about it, sir. We think Gray Fox is going to

take Major Garland and Captain Fordham to Crooked Foot."

Flora's face lost color. "Colonel! If our husbands are put in Crooked Foot's hands, it will mean torture and death for both of them!"

"Flora…Betsy…" said Bateman. "Listen to me. You know I've sent Sergeants Frayne and Wilkins to bring Two Moons here. He will know the best way to go about rescuing your husbands. If the assumption is correct—that Gray Fox will take them to Crooked Foot's village—it's at least a half-day's ride from where they are right now to the village. This will give us time to intercept them."

Bateman paused, then added, "I assure you, I will do whatever it takes to save them from the fate Gray Fox has planned for them…whatever it is."

"Thank you, Colonel," said Flora. "I have no doubt of that."

"Yes. Thank you, Colonel," Betsy said weakly. "You will keep us informed?"

"Yes, ma'am. Once I've talked to Two Moons and made plans, I'll let both of you know what we're doing."

Greg and Melissa Sullivan accompanied Flora to her house, and a weary Hannah Cooper headed for the store with an arm around Betsy. Hannah tried to comfort her friend as they moved across the compound.

"Here's one thing to keep in mind, Betsy. Even if Gray Fox is able to get John and the major into the hands of Crooked Foot, it doesn't mean torture and death. Crooked Foot fears the army. He wouldn't do anything to enrage Colonel Bateman and cause him to launch a full-scale attack against his village."

Betsy thought for a moment, then said, "Hannah, I know you're trying to encourage me, but what you're saying doesn't exactly make sense."

"What do you mean?"

"It hasn't bothered Crooked Foot to enrage Colonel

Bateman by massacring white people all over southwest Wyoming. Why should it bother him to stir the colonel's wrath by killing John and the major?"

"Because they're military."

"Military lives aren't any more important than civilian lives."

"Of course not, but Crooked Foot knows that to kill two of Colonel Bateman's officers would make it very personal…it would cause the colonel to react differently and more severely."

Betsy sighed as they neared the store. "I hope you're right, Hannah."

By nightfall, everyone in the fort and town knew that Major Garland and Captain Fordham were in the hands of Crow Indians who might turn them over to Crooked Foot.

Pastor Kelly led a special prayer meeting in the town hall. The building was packed as both military personnel and civilians showed their concern for the two men. Before the service began, Kelly chose seven men of the church, including Dobie Carlin, to lead the congregation in prayer. When it was time to start, Kelly turned the pulpit over to Dr. O'Brien to lead off. Many tears were shed as, one by one, the men prayed for the safety and deliverance of the two officers.

When it was Carlin's turn, he talked in simple, childlike faith to the Lord about the two men. Just before he finished, he said, "And Lord, one more thing to ask You about again. Would You bring my wife and son back to me and restore our marriage and our home? In Jesus' name I pray. Amen."

As the people were putting on their coats to leave, Flora and Betsy went to Pastor Kelly and thanked him for calling the special prayer meeting. Many of the church members gathered round the two women and said they would continue to pray for the safe return of their husbands. Flora and Betsy were deeply touched by the prayers and expressions of concern.

Mary Beth Cooper and Abby Turner came up to say hello to Dobie Carlin.

"We came to tell you we have prayer every night after supper at the Williams home," Mary Beth said, "and we've been praying for your wife and son."

Dobie's eyes filmed with tears. "Thank you, girls. It means more to me than I could ever tell you."

Just then, Hannah Cooper appeared, and on her heels were Chris, B. J., and Patty Ruth. "Dobie," Hannah said warmly, "I want you to know that the children and I are praying harder than ever for Donna and Travis. We're not going to give up."

"I appreciate that, ma'am," Dobie said.

Patty Ruth's eyes danced as she looked up at the lieutenant. "I been prayin' to Jesus before I go to sleep at night, Mr. Lieutenant Dobie Carlin. I don't want Mrs. Carlin to dishorse you."

Dobie smiled down at the little girl.

"Honey, it's divorce," Hannah said. "You don't want Lieutenant Carlin's wife to divorce him."

Patty Ruth sighed. "Yeah, that." She took a deep breath. "An' I don' want his boy to do that to him neither."

Hannah smiled at Dobie, who was barely able to keep from laughing, and said, "We've got to be going. See you soon. Let's go, children. I need to talk to Mrs. Fordham before she leaves."

As Hannah and the other children walked away, Chris gave Dobie a quick hug and said, "I'm excited about what the Lord's going to do, Dobie." With that, he hurried away to join the others.

Dobie shook his head back and forth slowly. "Thank You, Lord, for bringing these wonderful people into my life."

Betsy and Flora were thanking the Williamses for their

words of encouragement just as Hannah drew up with her brood and Abby Turner. Ryan, Will, and little Belinda were now standing beside their mother.

While Patty Ruth and Belinda struck up their own quiet conversation, Hannah said, "Betsy, I can't leave you and the children alone tonight. I've already spoken to Glenda about it. If you'll let me come and spend the night at your house, Glenda will see that my four are put to bed at the hotel."

"Oh, Hannah, it's awfully sweet of you, but you don't have to do that."

"Oh, yes I do. I won't sleep a wink for thinking of you and the children being alone with this heartache hanging over you."

"Let her do it, Betsy," said Flora. "I've already got two army wives going to spend the night at my house."

Betsy blinked at her sudden tears and said, "All right, Hannah. But carrying that baby, you need lots of rest."

"Like I said, I wouldn't sleep if I was in my own bed because I'd be thinking about you and the children. This way I'll know what's going on at the Fordham house, and I can get some rest."

Hannah kissed her children goodnight, gave Glenda a hug and Gary a smile, and watched them file out the door.

As Hannah and Betsy walked along Main Street toward the fort, Betsy said, "Hannah, I'm having a hard time understanding how God would allow this horrible thing to happen to John…to be in the hands of those savages."

"We'll talk about it after the children are in bed, Betsy. Maybe I can help."

Chief Two Moons and four of his warriors entered Colonel Bateman's office with Sergeants Frayne and Wilkins at eight-thirty that night. Colonel Bateman shook hands with the chief and with each warrior, then gestured toward the chairs he had placed in front of the desk. "Please be seated, my friends."

Two Moons shook his head. "Sitting is for pleasant pow-wow. This news not pleasant."

Bateman shrugged. "All right. We'll stand."

The chief's black eyes flashed fire as he said, "Two Moons very angry at what has happened. He makes apology to Colonel Ross Bateman for conduct of Gray Fox, Running Antelope, Tall Bird, and Little Bull. This chief gave Colonel Ross Bateman good word on these men so they be hired as trusted scouts for United States Army. Now they do bad thing."

"I'm not blaming you, Chief," said Bateman. "I've had men under my command who've made me ashamed to wear the same uniform and serve under the same flag."

Two Moons nodded. "Then Colonel Ross Bateman understands."

"Yes."

"Sergeant Del Frayne and Sergeant Barry Wilkins say they think Gray Fox and other Crow scouts will join Crooked Foot."

"That's what we all figure," said Bateman.

Two Moons nodded. "Two Moons think so too. Gray Fox and other Crow scouts know they be in deep trouble if come back and face Chief Two Moons and tribe. This Crow chief not hold with torture of wounded enemy. Agree with Gray Fox that Major Blaine Garland bad wrong to do that to wounded Blackfoot warriors. Know Colonel Ross Bateman agree."

"I do agree, Chief. Major Garland was dead wrong to give such an order. If we're able to get him back alive, he will face serious discipline for doing so and for his treatment of the wounded Blackfoot warriors at Buffalo Lodge."

The chief nodded. "Two Moons glad Gray Fox stand against Colonel Blaine Garland. But Two Moons very much angry at Gray Fox and other scouts for make Major Blaine Garland and Captain John Fordham prisoners. Be even more angry if take them to Crooked Foot."

"We've got to get them away from Gray Fox before he can do that, Chief," said Bateman.

"Two Moons wish Crooked Foot not attack white towns and settlements. Wish he and Blackfoot warriors be at peace with white eyes."

"Me, too," said Bateman. "But it doesn't look like Crooked Foot has any plans of making peace. The only thing I've been able to come up with is to concentrate on finding a way to kill him. Then I think the hostilities against the whites will cease."

Two Moons agreed.

The colonel told Two Moons the plan he and some of his officers had developed earlier in the day. Now they had lost Gray Fox for the job of sneaking up on the Blackfoot village to determine when Crooked Foot was there. None of the other Crow scouts were as good at such a thing as Gray Fox.

Two Moons nodded. "Plan might have worked with Gray Fox. Maybe not. Crooked Foot keep plenty warriors at village all times. Many bluecoats would have died in attack. Best let Two Moons make attempt to bring Major Blaine Garland and Captain John Fordham back."

Bateman's eyebrows arched. "You mean, without our troops?"

"Umm."

"Chief, I appreciate your willingness to help us like this, but what will you do?"

A cryptic smile tugged at the corners of the chief's mouth. "Though Two Moons and Crooked Foot enemies, we also brothers. Both Indian. Have respect for each other."

"Okay. I'm with you up to this point."

"Two Moons ride into Blackfoot village with small band of warriors…give sign of peace. If Major Blaine Garland and Captain John Fordham still alive, it is possible Two Moons bring them back."

"I don't understand how, Chief," said Bateman. "If I know Crooked Foot like I think I know him, he'll delight in having those two officers in his hands. How can you say it's possible he would turn them over to you so you could bring them home?"

"I'd like to know that, myself, Chief Two Moons," said Del Frayne.

Once again, a smile tugged at the corners of the chief's mouth. "There are many Indian ways of which white man know nothing. Not good that white eyes know everything about Indian. Colonel Ross Bateman trust Two Moons to speak truth. He say it is possible to bring officers back to fort alive."

Bateman smiled for the first time since early that morning. "Oh, I believe you, Chief. You've just got me a bit mystified."

"Mystified?" said Two Moons. "Do not know word. What is mystified?"

"Ah…puzzled. Bewildered."

"Confused?"

"Yes. Confused."

"Is good. As Two Moons say, not good that white eyes know everything about Indian."

"I can live with that," said Bateman, "but I have a suggestion. How about if you pull out at dawn and aim in a direction to intercept Gray Fox and the others as they head for the Blackfoot village?"

The chief shook his head. "Too late."

"Too late?"

"Mmm. Colonel Ross Bateman can believe that Gray Fox, Running Antelope, Tall Bird, and Little Bull already moving toward village with prisoners."

"They're traveling at night?"

"Mmm. Get there fast. Want to be protected from Two Moons and Crow."

"Then maybe you should get up a good bunch of warriors and go after them right now."

The chief shook his head. "Gray Fox know where village is. Can travel in dark. Two Moons not know where Gray Fox is. Travel in dark not work. Best to go to village tomorrow."

"But if they get my men to the village by early morning, Crooked Foot could have them dead and buried before you get there."

"Possible, but not think so. Blackfoot village one hour ride from Crow village. Nothing happen to Major Blaine Garland and Captain John Fordham if Crooked Foot not there. Other Blackfoot warriors not harm them or kill them without chief's orders. This time of year, Crooked Foot not there much. Must hope he not arrive until after Two Moons and small band of warriors."

"So if Crooked Foot is there, or arrives there before you do, my men will be killed?"

"Possible. But Crooked Foot may wish to keep them alive for a while. Main thing is for Two Moons to get to village by daylight. We leave hour before dawn to arrive at Blackfoot village when dawn give light. Not wise to arrive in dark. Blackfoot think they are being attacked."

"And we don't want that, do we?" said Bateman. "Chief, this means a lot to me. And it will mean a lot to everybody in this fort—especially to Mrs. Garland and Mrs. Fordham if you bring back their husbands. I don't know how to thank you."

"No need. We friends. Two Moons return as soon as possible. Hope return with Major Blaine Garland and Captain John Fordham."

"I'll pass your words on to Mrs. Garland and Mrs. Fordham, Chief. It will give them something to hang on to. Thank you."

Two Moons looked at the colonel warily. "Does wicked deed of Gray Fox, Running Antelope, Tall Bird, and Little Bull make Colonel Ross Bateman wonder about other Crow scouts? Maybe they become renegades too?"

Bateman shook his head. "No. I won't distrust your men who have served us well because of what Gray Fox and his friends have done. I will still take the scouts you tell me are good men. I trust you completely."

The chief let a smile curve his lips. He shook hands with the colonel and the sergeants Indian-style, then left with his warriors.

"Well, gentlemen," Bateman said to his sergeants, "I'm going to go home and bring my wife up to date, then take her with me to visit Mrs. Garland and Mrs. Fordham."

CHAPTER EIGHTEEN

R yan and Will Fordham were shedding quiet tears in their room as they put on their night clothes. Both were afraid their father was dead.

Hannah Cooper was in Belinda's bedroom, brushing the little girl's long black hair, and Betsy was in the kitchen, building a fire in the stove. When the children were in bed, she and Hannah would have some hot tea while they talked.

Betsy set the teapot on to heat up and went down the hall toward Belinda's room. As she drew near the boys' room, she heard sniffling. She stopped and looked in. The boys were sitting on the edge of their beds, looking as if their hearts were broken.

Betsy's heart seemed to melt within her at sight of them. She sat down beside Will, putting an arm around him. She looked at Ryan and patted the spot next to her. "Come, sit by Mama."

Their mother's attention caused the boys to cry harder. She sat silently with an arm around each one, holding them close.

"Papa's never coming home, is he Mama?" said Will.

"He's dead, isn't he, Mama?" said Ryan, wiping tears from his cheeks.

Betsy steeled herself against her own fears and said, "Now, boys, we mustn't despair. As long as we have no proof your father has been killed, we must believe he's still alive."

In Belinda's bedroom, Hannah laid the hairbrush on the small dresser and said, "There, sweetheart. All done. Your hair looks beautiful."

"Thank you, Miss Hannah," said the child, looking at herself in the mirror.

Belinda's gaze went to Hannah, who stood behind her, and she said, "Papa stands there sometimes after Mama brushes my hair. He always looks at me in the mirror and says I'm his beautiful princess."

A lump rose up in Hannah's throat.

Belinda turned and looked up with misty eyes. "Miss Hannah, isn't Jesus going to bring my papa home?"

Hannah led Belinda to her bed and sat down on the edge before lifting the little girl onto her lap. "Sweetheart, Jesus loves you, and He loves your brothers and your mama and papa. He will do what is best for all of you."

"Then He will bring Papa home, 'cause that's what's best."

Hannah felt helpless to find the right words to give a five-year-old. Before she could speak, Betsy appeared at the door with the boys at her side.

"The boys want to tell their sister goodnight," said Betsy.

Ryan and Will hugged and kissed Belinda, then gave Hannah a goodnight hug and headed for their room.

"Well, Belinda," said her mother, "your hair sure does look pretty."

"Mm-hmm. Miss Hannah brushed it real good."

"You give Miss Hannah a hug and get into bed."

Betsy then hugged her daughter goodnight and told her she loved her, then blew out the lantern.

Moments later, in the kitchen, Hannah put aside her own fatigue and sat down at the table to try to help her friend. She watched Betsy pour two cups of steaming hot spicy tea.

Hannah inhaled the aroma and said, "My mother always

told me there were calming effects and restoring properties in a hot cup of tea."

Betsy set the teapot back on the stove and sat down corner-wise from Hannah. "Well, let's hope it works that way tonight. I need both calming and restoring and a good night's rest. And so do you."

"Sleep is very important," said Hannah, "but there's something more important than sleep. Something I already have that you need, Betsy."

"I know. I need to be born again. I need to open my heart and let Jesus come in."

"Being saved doesn't solve all your problems, Betsy; we still live in a trouble-filled world. But when Jesus lives in your heart, He helps you face your problems and your tormenting fears. Without Him you face them alone. You have only your own finite strength to lean on. And when it comes your time to leave this world, if you go without Jesus, there's only an eternal hell to face."

Betsy stared at the steam rising from her teacup but didn't respond.

"Remember what I told you before, Betsy, about God being love, and that there is no fear in love, but perfect love casts out fear? Right now, you are tormented by fear over John's situation."

Betsy raised her eyes to Hannah's and said, "I can't concentrate on the salvation thing right now, Hannah. What I need is to understand why God allowed my husband to be taken captive by those heartless savages. You said we'd talk about it. Please help me to understand."

Hannah prayed in her heart for wisdom to say the right thing. "The best way for me to answer your question is to say that John's being taken captive is all in God's plan."

Betsy's eyebrows arched. "God's plan? God's plan for what?"

"For your lives. He loves you and—"

"If that's the case, why put us through this? If God is all-powerful, like I've been told so many times, He could've prevented Gray Fox from doing what he did. I've always been told that God is kind and merciful. If that were true, He wouldn't have let John fall into the hands of those devils! If God were merciful, John would be home with his family tonight!" Betsy choked up and began to whimper. "But God is not kind and merciful, Hannah. John may even be dead. What's kind and merciful about that?"

"Betsy, I can't speak for God and His plan for people's lives, but you can't go to Calvary and see Jesus hanging on that cross—having been sent by the Father to suffer and die for our sins—and tell me God isn't kind and merciful."

Betsy was staring at her teacup.

"Can you?" pressed Hannah.

Suddenly there was a knock at the front door. Betsy went to answer it.

A moment later, she returned to the kitchen with Colonel Bateman and his wife, Sylvia. They greeted Hannah, then Betsy said, "Colonel Bateman says he has some encouraging news for me, Hannah. I told him I would listen to it over a cup of tea."

Betsy poured tea into two more cups, then refreshed hers and Hannah's and sat down. "All right, Colonel," she said, "I can use some good news."

Colonel Bateman told her of his conversation with Chief Two Moons. The chief had taken the responsibility squarely on his shoulders to make the rescue attempt.

Betsy was skeptical. "Colonel, the Blackfoot and the Crow are bitter enemies. How can he possibly get John away from Crooked Foot?"

"I asked him the same question. He said Indians have ways that white men don't know anything about. He's confident he can go into that village and bring John home."

"If he's still alive."

"Well, yes, of course."

Betsy brushed a nervous hand over her mouth. "And you really have confidence that Two Moons can do this?"

"Yes, I do."

"And you're sure he isn't going to pull something like Gray Fox did?"

"Betsy, I can't blame you for being uneasy, but I assure you, Two Moons is trustworthy. If anybody can get John and Major Garland out, it's him."

Hannah patted Betsy's hand. "See, there's still hope. You mustn't give up."

At midnight, Corporal Tim Farr and Private Bob Cullen relieved two other men of duty at the tower above the fort's gate. They had dressed warmly for the long, cold night on the platform.

It was near three o'clock in the morning when the two watchmen stood at the platform railing and looked up at the great canopy of twinkling stars against the black sky. There was no moon. They turned up their coat collars and pulled their hats low against the chilly wind.

Although the two men had already discussed everything they knew about the kidnapping of Garland and Fordham, they came back to the subject once more.

"I was really disappointed in Major Garland when I learned about his cruelty to those wounded Indians," Cullen said, cradling his carbine in one arm.

"Yeah, me too," said Farr. "I'm glad to know, though, that Captain Fordham stood against him. I really like the captain."

"So do I. He's the kind of man I could follow. 'Course, as much as the major disappointed me, I still don't wish him any harm at the hands of the hostiles."

"Oh, me neither. I just think I'd have a hard time being in an outfit he was leading."

"Yeah. If he's still alive and makes it back here, I'd think he'd have to transfer somewhere else. I don't think any of the men in this fort would have confidence in him anymore."

"That's probably what'll happen. It's his wife I feel sorry for. This thing coming to light has got to be an embarrassment for her."

"Speaking of feeling sorry for someone...I really feel sorry for Mrs. Fordham. Here she is with three kids to raise, and he may not be coming back."

"Well, if that happens, she's got a great friend in Hannah Cooper. That little gal has had it to bear. She knows what it's like to become a widow all of a sudden and have youngins to bring up and provide for."

Both men fell quiet, letting their gaze sweep over the starlit hills as they listened to the normal night sounds.

"I miss the crickets," Cullen said, adjusting the rifle in the crook of his arm. "Too bad summer's so short around here."

Farr sighed and watched his breath plume out before him in the dim starlight.

Suddenly the night sounds were punctuated with the distant rumble of galloping hooves. Both men readied their carbines.

"Coming from the northwest," said Farr, peering in that direction.

"That's where it's coming from, all right. Sounds like just one horse."

They waited for the rider to draw closer, then Cullen said, "You don't suppose the major or the captain made an escape and is coming home."

"I sure hope that's the case."

The hoofbeats grew louder. Both men raised their rifles to

fire, if necessary, and peered into the darkness.

"There he is!" Farr whispered.

They could barely make out the white markings on the pinto and the dark form of the rider guiding the pony in a wide swing to head due south. The rider came parallel with the west side of the fort underneath the tower. He didn't slow as he drew near the gate, but thundered past it, dropping something that made a whump when it hit the ground. In seconds, he was swallowed by the night.

The sound of hoofbeats faded as Corporal Tim Farr fired a lantern. Both men hurried down the steps and opened the gate. Private Cullen picked up a cloth bundle held together with a thin hemp rope.

As he held the bundle close to the lantern, his eyes widened. "You know what this is, don't you?"

"I think you're right," Farr said. "But before we take it to the colonel, we'd best make sure."

When they were back on the tower platform, they untied the thin rope and unrolled the bundle. It was made up of two sets of blood-soaked uniforms, boots, and crumpled army hats.

Sylvia Bateman heard it first. She rolled over in the bed, opened her eyes to look at the surrounding darkness, then heard it again. She raised up on an elbow and shook her husband awake.

"Ross! Someone's knocking at the front door."

The colonel groaned, rolled over, and mumbled, "What'd you say?"

Before Sylvia could repeat her words there was another loud knock on the door.

Bateman threw the covers back. He sat up, reached toward a nearby chair for his robe, and stood unsteadily to his feet. "This better be important," he grumbled, as he donned the robe and started toward the bedroom door.

The knock came again.

"I'm coming! I'm coming!" The colonel paused at a small table and fumbled till he found a match and lit the lantern before going downstairs.

Whoever it was already had a lantern, for there was a heavy glare against the curtains.

Bateman could hear his wife padding down the stairs behind him as he opened the door and saw Corporal Tim Farr.

"Colonel," said Farr, saluting, "I'm sorry to disturb you at this hour, but Private Cullen and I figured you'd want to know about this immediately. He's still on duty at the gate."

Sylvia drew up beside her husband as the colonel looked down and saw the bundle, which Farr had re-tied. The crimson stains drew his gaze like a magnet. "Where'd you get this?" he asked.

"Rider on a pinto horse galloped by the gate, dropped it, and kept on riding, sir."

"Ross, what is it?" asked Sylvia.

"One or both?" Bateman asked Farr.

"Both of them, sir. Two uniforms with the insignias of major and captain…two pair of boots, and two flattened-out hats. They're Major Garland's and Captain Fordham's all right."

"Those are Major Garland's and Captain Fordham's uniforms?" Sylvia said.

"Yes, ma'am."

"They've got blood on them!"

"Yes, ma'am."

"Oh, Ross! Does that mean—"

"I think so, dear, but I want an Indian's opinion on it. Corporal, I want you to roust Sergeants Frayne and Wilkins out of their bunks and send them over here immediately."

When the colonel closed the door, Sylvia gripped his

upper arm. "Ross, what else could it mean?"

"Maybe it's just Gray Fox's way of making us think they're dead. You know…fear tactic. I'll know better when the sergeants get Two Moons here."

In less than an hour, Two Moons and four of his braves stood in the Batemans' parlor. The colonel and Sylvia had dressed, and Sylvia stood at the foot of the staircase as the sergeants looked on with Corporal Farr.

Bateman had not yet untied the bundle. When he handed it to Two Moons, he explained how a rider on a pinto had galloped by and dropped it at the gate around three o'clock.

The chief shook his head when he saw it.

"Does it mean they're dead?" Bateman asked.

Two Moons turned the bundle in his hands. "Uniforms, boots, hats inside? Both men?"

"Yes."

"You are sure they belong to Captain John Fordham and Major Blaine Garland?"

"They do, Chief," Farr said.

Two Moons nodded solemnly. "Major Blaine Garland…Captain John Fordham dead. This Blackfoot way of telling whites they have killed men who belong to uniforms, hats, and boots."

Sylvia's hand went to her mouth. "Oh! Poor Betsy. Poor Flora."

"So this is not Gray Fox's doing?" said the colonel.

"No. This Blackfoot way. Not Crow. Colonel Ross Bateman can be sure Gray Fox take them to Crooked Foot. Crooked Foot kill them."

Bateman looked at Two Moons. "I didn't want to tell Mrs. Garland and Mrs. Fordham their husbands were dead unless I was sure this was what the bundle meant."

Two Moons nodded and hissed through his teeth, "Crooked Foot will pay for this!"

When Two Moons and his braves were gone, Corporal Farr looked at the bundle near his feet and said, "Colonel, sir, what should I do with this?"

"Leave it with me," said Bateman. "Mrs. Garland and Mrs. Fordham have a right to claim what belonged to their husbands. But I hope they will tell me to burn it."

"Dear," said Sylvia, "you're not going to awaken Flora and Betsy at this hour, are you?"

"No. Morning will be here soon enough. We'll let them sleep the night through."

It was almost six-thirty the next morning when Colonel Bateman and his wife stepped off the porch of the Garland house, leaving a sobbing Flora with the two army wives who had stayed with her the previous night.

As the Batemans moved down the boardwalk that edged the compound, the colonel said, "It's times like these I wish I was a ditchdigger."

Sylvia slipped her hand into the crook of her husband's arm and looked up into his careworn face. "I understand. It's...it's going to be even harder to tell Betsy."

The colonel sighed, ejecting a puffy cloud of vapor on the cold morning air. "Right now I wish I was one of those army mules over there in the corral. They never have to do anything like this."

Betsy and Hannah were up at dawn. Though the children were still sleeping soundly, the women had spent little time in sleep. Betsy hadn't even wanted to change into her night clothes, but Hannah finally persuaded her to take off her shoes and lie down on top of her coverlet with a heavy quilt thrown over her.

Hannah tried to sleep on the couch, but her heart was so heavy for Betsy and the children that she had spent most of the night in prayer.

At daybreak, Betsy rolled off her bed, the aroma of hot coffee tempting her. As she moved down the hall, she heard a cheery fire crackling in the parlor fireplace. Hannah was drinking coffee at the table in the cozy blue-and-white kitchen when Betsy came in.

"Good morning, Betsy," Hannah said wearily. "Sleep at all?"

"A little." Betsy covered a yawn and moved to the stove where the coffeepot was steaming. "You?"

"Some."

"I'm sorry, Hannah. You should've been in your own bed last night."

"No. I should've been right here with you."

Hannah indicated a cup on the table for Betsy, and as she poured it full, Betsy managed a small smile and said, "Nobody ever had a friend like you."

Hannah smiled in spite of her fatigue. "I'm glad you feel that way."

Just as Betsy placed the coffeepot back on the stove, there was a knock at the front door. Betsy's heart skipped a beat and she caught her breath. "Hannah, it's too early for someone to be making a routine visit."

Hannah rose to her feet. "Maybe it's John!"

"No. He would come in…we never lock the doors. I'll see who it is."

"I'm going with you," said Hannah, hurrying behind Betsy to the front of the house.

There was another knock as the two women reached the door. Betsy looked fearfully at Hannah. "There's some kind of news waiting on the other side of this door, Hannah. I just don't know which kind."

"You have to find out sooner or later," Hannah said.

Betsy took a deep breath and turned the doorknob.

Pastor Andrew Kelly and his wife, Rebecca, left the Fordham home at ten minutes shy of eight o'clock. Glenda Williams and Julie Powell were just coming up the walk. After they had greeted each other, Glenda said, "Must have been difficult for you to go in there."

Pastor nodded. "So you already know?"

"The whole town knows by now, Pastor," said Julie. "Have you been able to see Mrs. Garland yet?"

"Yes. We went there first." He shook his head. "Neither of these women knows the Lord. Neither did their husbands. It was very hard to make them feel better and remain truthful. And Betsy's so angry at God, she didn't hear a thing we said, I'm sure."

"Were you hoping to see Betsy?" Rebecca asked.

Glenda shook her head no. "We'd probably be extra baggage right now. We came to let Hannah know we'll be running the store for her today. We know she'll want to stay with Betsy. Gary's bringing Patty Ruth to the store. We'll take care of her too."

"Mighty nice of you," said Kelly. "Betsy needs Hannah, that's for sure."

"Is she close to a breakdown, Pastor?" Glenda asked.

Kelly shook his head. "I don't think so, unless she gets a lot worse. Right now she's grieving over John, naturally, and she's filled with hate toward Indians—all Indians. She keeps saying over and over that she doesn't trust Two Moons or any other Indian."

"Maybe she'll get over it in time," said Julie.

"That's what Hannah told her, but Betsy swears she'll never get over it. She'll hate every Indian in this country for the rest of her life."

"That will change when she gets saved," said Glenda.

"That's what we pray for," said Rebecca. "Not only for Betsy's sake, but for those boys, who are such young Christians. They need guidance in the home, and there's no one to give it. And then there's little Belinda."

"We'll sure be praying for them at our house," said Julie.

"Us too," said Glenda.

Kelly nodded. "I offered to hold a memorial service for both men if Flora and Betsy wanted me to. They both said they did. It'll be at eight o'clock tomorrow evening at the town hall. I set it a little later than usual to allow as many military people as possible to attend."

"We'll be praying about that, Pastor," said Julie. "It's not going to be easy for you since both men went into eternity without the Lord."

"I have no hope at all for Major Garland," said Kelly. "He never attended a regular preaching service. But with John…well, I know he heard the gospel in our services many, many times, though he never responded. I can only hope that, possibly, he had time before they took his life to call on the Lord to save him."

CHAPTER NINETEEN

A cloudy sky hung low over Denver, Colorado, dropping lightly falling snow, as a buggy swung off Stout Street and pulled into the alley behind the Great Western Hotel. Donna Carlin leaned close to the man who held the reins, kissed his cheek, and said, "See you tonight, Daddy."

Hugh Wooldridge smiled. "Pick you up at five. Don't work too hard."

Donna's breath misted out in a small cloud as she said, "Oh, sure. There's a cattlemen's convention in town, the hotel is full, and my father tells me not to work too hard."

Wooldridge laughed, then said, "I know how you hotel maids are. When you clean, you also take time to stretch out on the beds and take a nap between rooms."

"Get out of here!" Donna said in mock anger.

"'Bye, honey," said Hugh as he put the buggy in motion.

Donna shook her head and smiled to herself. She entered the back door of the hotel and stepped into a room where other maids were removing their coats.

Soon Donna was on the fourth floor—her usual assignment—pushing her little cart from the supply room. By nine o'clock she had finished three rooms and was knocking on the door of 407, calling, "Maid service!"

The door opened to reveal a handsome young man in

army uniform, wearing insignias on his shoulders that identified him as a lieutenant.

"Good morning, sir," said Donna. "Would you like your room serviced now? I see by my chart that you'll be staying over tonight. Are you Lieutenant Bradley Smith?"

"Yes."

"If you'd like, sir, I can come back this afternoon."

"Oh, right now would be fine, ma'am," said the lieutenant. "Please, come ahead."

Donna adjusted the cart close to the door, picked up fresh sheets and pillowcases, and stepped into the room. A pretty lady seated at the desk looked up and smiled.

"This is my wife, Susan," said Smith.

"Pleased to meet you, ma'am," said Donna.

"And I'm glad to meet you, Miss..."

"Carlin. Donna Carlin."

The lieutenant went to the window, which faced west, and parted the curtains. "Can't even see the mountains today with the clouds so low."

Donna began pulling the sheets off the bed. "They'll be beautiful when the storm's gone, sir. They'll have a fresh white coat on their peaks."

"We'll have a good view of them in Fort Collins," said the lieutenant's wife.

"Oh, you're going to Fort Collins?" asked Donna.

"I'm being transferred there from Fort Marcy, New Mexico," Smith said. "We came by rail from Santa Fe, and we'll be taking a train to Fort Collins in the morning."

Susan chuckled. "He'll go from fighting Apaches, Navajos, and Hopis to fighting Cheyenne, Arapahos, and Kiowas. And then the army will transfer him to some other fort where he can fight some other kinds of Indians. Oh, well...such is army life. At least, being married to a soldier, I get to see a lot of the country."

Donna felt a wave of anguish wash over her that she couldn't quite hide.

"Oh, my," the lieutenant's wife said. "Did I say something that upset you? I'm sorry."

Smith turned from the window in time to catch the sad look on Donna's face and noticed her blinking back a tear.

"You don't have to be sorry, ma'am," Donna said, "it's just that—"

Susan left her chair and came closer. "Is there something I can do, Miss Carlin?"

"Not really, ma'am." Donna felt more tears welling up and willed them not to spill onto her cheeks.

A compassionate look came over Susan's face. "Would it help to talk about it?"

Donna cleared her throat and said, "I…I have to get your room done."

"Well, while you work, we'll talk if you want to. Here, let me help you."

Donna objected, but Susan took the opposite side of the bed and began pulling the bottom sheet in place. "Tell us about it," she said.

Donna swallowed hard, tucked the sheet into place on one corner, and said, "What you just said about army life got to me, Mrs. Smith, because I was married to an army lieutenant. Well, I still am, but there's a divorce pending."

"Oh, I'm sorry to hear that."

"My husband's name is Dobie Carlin. We have a fourteen-year-old son, Travis. I…I lost two babies during pregnancy, after Travis was born. I can't have any more children. Anyway, we were at Fort Auger, Wyoming, up until several weeks ago. There was continuous Indian trouble. I never liked army life to begin with, but when we were at forts back east, at least there were no whooping savages to fight."

The Smiths exchanged knowing glances.

"I finally came to the place where I couldn't stand it anymore. I told Dobie I wanted him to get out of the army altogether and go back East where we came from. He said he couldn't just quit. He had signed up for another five years and had an obligation to the government. I argued with him about it. I reminded him of army men we'd known who had gotten out before their terms expired.

"He said it was a matter of honor. Well, it made me angry that he cared more about the government and his honor than he did me. I told him that if he didn't get out of the army right now, I'd leave him, go back to my parents, and divorce him. I told him if he loved me, he would resign and leave Fort Auger, even if it meant shame in the eyes of the government."

The lieutenant and his wife, who were listening with sober expressions, nodded for Donna to continue.

"Well…he still insisted that his sense of honor wouldn't allow him to do it. I hope, Mrs. Smith, that you can understand this. One day after I asked Dobie to leave the army and take me away from Fort Auger, a wagon supply train stopped at the fort on its way to Denver. Dobie was out on a two-day patrol. I told the man in charge of the wagon train that my son and I needed to get to Denver. He was kind enough to let us ride in one of the wagons. I left a note for Dobie, telling him where Travis and I were going, and that I was going to file for divorce."

Donna was crying freely now as Susan said, "Do you still love Dobie?"

Donna squeezed her eyes shut and nodded. "But I cannot and I *will* not go back to army life."

"Mrs. Carlin," said the lieutenant, "did you file for the divorce?"

"Yes, but it hasn't yet been granted. From what my attorney says, the judge is very slow to grant divorces."

The bed was now made up and Donna went to the cart to get a broom. Before she could begin sweeping, Susan moved close to her and said, "Donna, if a woman loves her husband as she should, she will stay by him, no matter what his chosen profession, if it's honorable.

"Brad could tell you that when we were first married and he was stationed at Fort Stockton, Texas, I had a horrible time. He was fighting the Comanches, and I was having my own battle. I put pressure on him to get out of the army. I told him that if he loved me, he would do it. He was giving it serious thought, but I could see what it was doing to him. He's a West Point graduate. The army is his life, and he loves it. I saw how selfish I was, to use his love for me as a leverage to get him out of the army. I—"

Susan choked up, and the lieutenant picked up the story. "She came to me and said she wanted whatever I wanted in life. And we've been superbly happy ever since."

"Yes, we have," said Susan, dabbing at her eyes with a hanky she had produced from her sleeve. "Donna, I won't tell you it doesn't get tough for me at times, but I'll stay by Brad because he loves being an army officer, and the army is his chosen profession."

Donna nodded and began her sweeping job. When she didn't say another word and went on to dust the furniture and clean the mirrors, the Smiths politely said no more.

When she had finished cleaning and was ready to leave, Donna stopped at the door and said, "Lieutenant and Mrs. Smith, I want to thank you for listening to me…and for talking to me about your own experiences."

Susan rushed up to her and put a hand on Donna's arm. "You said you still love your husband. If my advice means anything to you, take your son and go back to him."

Donna backed out the door and closed it softly.

That evening, when Donna and her father arrived at the Wooldridge home, Iris Wooldridge greeted them in the front hallway. "Hello, you two," she said. "Hard day today, Donna?"

"You might say that, Mom. But I met some nice people."

"Cattlemen?"

"Yes, and others."

"Well, get washed up. Supper's almost ready. Travis has been helping me." With that, Iris disappeared into the kitchen.

Travis came and helped his mother remove her coat. "So…are you teaching Grandma how to cook?" Donna asked.

"Oh, sure. *I'm* teaching Grandma how to cook!"

"And how about the homework? All caught up?"

"Yes, ma'am. Took care of it right after I got home from school."

"Good boy. Keep it up. Someday you'll be president of the United States."

Travis wanted to say that the man in the White House was there because he had been a great soldier, but he knew better than to voice it. Ulysses S. Grant—next to Lieutenant Dobie Carlin—was his biggest hero. But his mother would be upset if he said so.

Hugh followed his daughter and grandson as they moved down the hall toward the kitchen.

"Travis…"

The boy glanced over his shoulder. "Yes, Grandpa?"

"You didn't tell your mother what came in the mail today."

"Didn't you tell her?"

"Nope. I was leaving that for you."

"So what came in the mail?" asked Donna as they turned into the kitchen.

Travis hesitated, then said, "A letter from Pa."

Donna went to the washstand, where she dipped water from a bucket, and began washing her hands. "You open it, Travis?"

"No. It was addressed to both of us, so I figured we'd open it together."

"After supper," she said in a flat voice.

Hugh set loving eyes on his daughter and said, "Donna, when are you going to give in?"

"To what?" she asked, lifting her chin.

"To the fact that you still love Dobie and that you and this boy belong with him."

"It's not as simple as that, Daddy."

"Sure it is. You're the one who's making it complicated. Fact is, you married that fine young man *for better or for worse*. Isn't that what you said in your marriage vow?"

Donna could feel everyone's eyes on her as she said, "Yes, that's what I said in the marriage vow, Daddy. But the *worse* was more than I bargained for. I didn't know how hard army life would be."

"So you really didn't keep your vow, did you?"

Donna looked her father in the eyes and said, "If Dobie cared anything about me and Travis, he'd get out of the army and come after both of us."

Iris looked intently at her daughter. "So Dobie's chosen career—that which is his life's profession—has to be sacrificed because you don't like the army. Donna, if a woman loves her husband, she'll stick by him, no matter what he does for a living."

"Travis," Donna said, "after we've had dinner, and the dishes are done and the kitchen is all cleaned up, we'll go upstairs and read the letter together in your room."

"All right, Mom."

It was after nine o'clock when Donna descended the stairs and entered the parlor where her parents sat by the fireplace, reading by lantern light. The flickering flames made dancing shadows on the walls and ceiling.

"Get your boy put to bed, honey?" asked Hugh, lowering his copy of the *Rocky Mountain News* to gaze at Donna over his half-moon glasses.

"Mm-hmm."

Donna chose a third overstuffed chair that faced the fireplace and sat down with a sigh.

"Is that a sound of being tired or upset?" asked Iris.

"A little of both."

"Well, we know what caused you to be tired," said Hugh. "Was it Dobie's letter that upset you?"

"You might say that."

"Do you mind telling us what he said?"

"It's the same old thing that's been in the last three letters. Since he's become one of those born-again Christians, he wants Travis and me to get born again too. He keeps asking me to seek out a church that preaches the Bible so we can learn more about salvation and all that."

The room was quiet for a long moment, except for the sound of the crackling fire.

Hugh broke the silence. "Well, Donna, I know we've never been church-going people, but it might not be so bad to cross the line. We're not atheists."

"No…but Dobie talks like a religious fanatic. Almost every other word is *Jesus* or *God* or *saved* or *born-again*. Travis and I don't need this. If there's a heaven, we'll go there just like you and Mother will, Daddy. We've always been decent people. If there's a hell, we certainly haven't been bad enough to deserve to go there. This family has gotten along fine without church."

Later, when Donna wearily turned down her bed, her eye caught sight of the envelope on the dresser. What was Dobie's letter doing in her room? She had left it on Travis's night stand.

Donna blew out the lantern next to her bed and crawled between the cool sheets. She tried to force the day's events from her mind—the conversation with the Smiths, what her parents had said at the supper table and by the fireside, and Dobie's letter, even the part where he had said how much he loved her.

After she tossed and turned for better than an hour, Donna threw back the covers and padded to the closest window. She pulled back the curtain and saw that it had quit snowing. There was a mantle of snow on the roofs of neighboring houses and on the ground below. The sky was clear, and the stars twinkled above like lights in a fairy palace.

Donna wondered how far heaven was above the stars…if there was a heaven.

It was chilly in the room. She rubbed her arms and headed back for the comfort of her feather bed. As she passed the dresser, the white envelope, barely visible in the gloom, caught her attention.

She ignored it and slipped back into bed, fluffed her pillow to get it just right, and closed her eyes.

Sleep would not come.

"Oh, all right, Donna. If you insist…"

Her practiced hands found a match in the dark and fired the wick of the lantern. She raised the wick to get good light, went to the dresser and picked up the envelope, then padded back to bed and sat with her back against the pillow. Dobie's words of love soon had her crying. She admitted to herself that she missed him. Even though she had filed for divorce, Donna knew in her heart of hearts that she was still in love with Dobie.

She muffled her sobs with the edge of the blanket and said aloud in a trembling voice, "Oh, Dobie, I do love you! If only you would leave the army, I'm sure we could have a wonderful life together."

She wept into the blanket for a long moment, then said in a half whisper, "I feel so guilty about taking Travis from you, but it's still all for the best. Maybe it will be your love for him that will bring you to us."

She stopped crying, dried her tears, and read the letter again. Three times he had put in the words of Jesus, "Except a man be born again, he cannot see the kingdom of God."

Donna folded the letter, slipped it back into the envelope, and laid it on the bedstand. "Travis Carlin," she said with a grin, "you're a little sneak."

She blew out the lantern and slid back under the covers. Jesus' words continued to echo through her mind. "The kingdom of God," she whispered. "That's heaven. Of course, Donna, you know there's a heaven. But hell…well, I guess if there's a heaven, there's a hell."

She was starting to feel drowsy when those words came thundering through her mind again and cut all the way to the center of her being: *"Except a man be born again, he cannot see the kingdom of God."*

For what seemed like a long time, those words reverberated through Donna's mind and heart. Finally, she was able to drop off to sleep.

Donna slept lightly, as mothers are prone to do, and was awakened in the darkness by groans coming from her son's room. She threw back the covers and once again lit the lantern. By its light she found her robe and hurried out the door.

When she entered Travis's room, he was doubled up in a fetal position, gripping his midsection. "Oh, Mom, I hurt ba-a-ad!" he moaned.

Donna's parents heard Travis's cry, and moments later met Donna in the hall as she carried a pail of water and two towels. She moved into the ring of light cast by the lantern in her father's hand.

"What is it, Donna?" asked Iris.

"Travis is sick. Really sick. He's vomiting and has terrible pain in his stomach."

"Do you suppose it was the chocolate cake? He ate two pieces."

"I don't know. This may be more serious than that."

Travis's grandparents followed Donna into the room and saw their grandson frantically moving his legs, trying to get comfortable and ease the pain. His face was ashen, and his eyes had a glazed look.

Donna gave the boy home remedies through the remainder of the night, but nothing helped. By sunrise, he was worse, and a high fever had set in.

"Daddy," said Donna, "would you hitch the horse to the buggy? I think it's appendicitis. We've got to get him to the hospital."

The Wooldridges and their daughter arrived at Denver's Mile High Hospital with a very sick boy just as the late shift personnel were leaving.

When the young woman at the reception desk saw Travis and heard Donna say *appendicitis*, she quickly called for a cart. The boy was immediately wheeled to the surgical wing and met by a lady in white who introduced herself to Donna and her parents as Mary Donelson. Donna gave Travis's name, then her own, and explained that the man and woman with her were her parents.

Mrs. Donelson directed the cart attendant to move the boy into an examining room, then called to a young doctor who was coming down the hall. After Donna told him Travis's symptoms, he hurried toward the examination room, saying, "Mrs. Donelson, Breanna Baylor is in room 112 with a student nurse and patient. Would you get her for me?"

Mary got the attention of a nurse who was near room 112 and asked her to send Miss Baylor quickly. To the family, she said, "Dr. Jack Myers is very good. He'll do an examination and let you know the diagnosis. If it is appendicitis—and I think it is—he'll perform surgery immediately."

At that moment they saw a blonde nurse hurrying down the hall. When she reached them, Mary said, "Breanna, Dr. Myers has a possible appendectomy to do on this lady's son. He asked for you."

"All right."

"Folks," said Mary, "This is Breanna Baylor. She's absolutely the best. With Dr. Myers and Miss Baylor, Travis is in good hands."

"That's comforting to know," said Donna. "I'm glad to meet you Miss Baylor. I'm Donna Carlin, Travis's mother. These are my parents, Hugh and Iris Wooldridge."

Breanna flashed a smile at them, then said, "Mrs. Carlin, we'll do the very best we can for your son."

Donna thanked her and they started toward the examining room together. They stopped abruptly as Dr. Myers came out, face grim, and said, "It's definitely appendicitis, Miss Baylor. The appendix just burst. Dr. Carroll is with him—he's going to do the surgery. He's in operating room number one and needs you *now*."

As Nurse Baylor disappeared down the hall, Dr. Myers

joined Mary Donelson, who was trying to reassure Donna. Donna's lips quivered as she interrupted Mary's words and said, "I know what that means! I had a good friend whose appendix burst, and she died!"

"Listen to me, ma'am," said Myers, "the doctor who is doing the surgery is also the chief administrator here, Dr. Matthew Carroll. He's the *very* best surgeon this side of the Mississippi, believe me. He said to tell you he would have come and met you first, but time is of the essence. You understand."

"Yes," said Donna, biting her lip.

"You folks can sit in the waiting room right across the hall. Mrs. Donelson will look in on the surgery and keep you posted. I'm going in there now to watch Dr. Carroll at work."

Donna suddenly remembered that she needed to let her boss at the hotel know that she wouldn't be in today.

"I'll go tell him, honey," her father said. Thirty minutes later, Hugh was back with the message that Donna's boss understood and would be pulling for the boy.

Donna began to think how wrong she had been to keep her son from spiritual teaching and guidance. Travis had a right to hear about God and make his own decision about his relationship with Him. Things were going to change. When Travis recuperated from the surgery, she would find a church like Dobie had described.

But what if he didn't make it? What if—

Mary Donelson came through the door.

Donna jumped to her feet and asked the question with her eyes.

Mary smiled and said, "Everything's going well. Dr. Carroll said to tell you he was able to contain the poison from the ruptured appendix. It didn't get into the bloodstream. Travis is going to be fine."

"Oh, thank God!" said Iris.

"Yes! Thank God!" echoed Hugh.

Donna's relief was so great that speech was impossible. All she could do was weep and nod her head.

An hour later, Dr. Carroll entered the waiting room to give Donna and her parents the details of the surgery.

"Travis won't be clear-minded for another three hours. We gave him ether, and it takes time to wear off. Nurse Baylor will stay with him until her shift is over at two this afternoon. But you will have spoken with him before then."

Donna nodded and said, "How long before he can come home, Doctor Carroll?"

"Travis will have to stay in the hospital about ten days, maybe longer, depending on how quickly his strength comes back. But don't worry, he's going to be just fine."

It was almost noon before the family was allowed to enter the boy's room. They found Nurse Baylor sitting in a chair beside the bed, keeping a close eye on him. Travis was awake but groggy.

"Miss Baylor," Donna said, "is there any way I could sleep at the hospital, at least for tonight?"

Breanna smiled and said, "Our head nurse, Mary Donelson, would have to approve it, but I'm sure it would be all right."

The head nurse indeed approved it. Donna's parents went home, saying they would be back the next day, and that night, Donna slept in her son's room on a cot.

Donna awakened at first light to find Travis sleeping peacefully. She tiptoed from the room and went down the hall to the hospital's dining room for breakfast. The shift changed while she was eating, and Donna was pleased when Mary Donelson came to her table to greet her and ask about Travis.

After breakfast, Donna made her way back to Travis's

room. When she opened the door, she found Breanna Baylor sitting beside the bed with an open Bible in her hand, talking to Travis. His head was propped up with an extra pillow, and he looked bright-eyed.

"Well, what's going on here?" asked Donna, smiling warmly.

"Good morning, Mom. Miss Baylor and I got to talking about how close I came to dying yesterday. She asked me if I had died, would I have gone to heaven. I said I didn't know. She was just showing me in the Bible how Jesus died on the cross to save sinners from hell, and how I could be saved. It's exactly the same as Dad has been writing in his letters. You know…'Except a man be born again, he cannot see the kingdom of God.'"

Tears welled up in Donna's eyes. "Oh, Miss Baylor," she said past the lump in her throat, "would you show us both how to be saved?"

CHAPTER TWENTY

S aturday evening, in Fort Bridger, a tired Hannah Cooper closed up the store and thanked Christel Crawley for helping her all day. Then she headed for the hotel.

After a tasty meal with the Williamses, Hannah took her children to the hotel and ordered up hot water for their baths. The boys bathed in their room as usual, and while Mary Beth bathed in the girls' room, Hannah took Patty Ruth with her.

Hannah washed the little girl's hair and marveled anew at the riot of red curls when Patty Ruth's hair was wet. She toweled her off, hugging her a few times, then put a flannel nightgown on her. After brushing out her daughter's long hair, she took her back to the girls' room.

While Mary Beth finished getting ready for bed, Hannah went to see about the boys and pray with them. After she'd kissed them goodnight, she returned to the girls' room and found Mary Beth and Patty Ruth on their knees, praying for Dobie Carlin's wife and son. Hannah knelt beside them and joined in their prayers, then tucked them in their beds and kissed them goodnight.

Just before blowing out the lantern, she said, "I'm so glad you girls care about people the way you do and that you faithfully pray for Dobie Carlin's family. The boys prayed for them extra hard tonight too. Good night, my lovely girls."

"Goodnight, Mama," came the voices in unison.

When Glenda Williams answered the knock on her door, she looked surprised. "Hannah, I thought you'd be in bed by now."

"I will in a little while, but I want to spend some time with Betsy. Will you just look in on my brood in a half hour or so?"

"I'll be glad to, but you need to get some rest, dearie."

Hannah gave her a sheepish look. "I will. Soon."

"You'd better, or Aunt Glenda is going to be on your back about it."

Hannah threw up her hands in surrender and said, "I will. I will."

"Promise?"

"Yes, I won't be too long. I'll tap on your door so you'll know when I'm back."

Hannah unbuttoned her coat as she made her way down Main Street toward the fort. A warm wind had come in from the south. *Maybe this means winter won't come so soon,* Hannah thought.

Betsy's eyes were red and swollen when she opened the door to Hannah's knock. She tried to smile as she said, "Come in."

Hannah waited until Betsy closed the door, then said, "I had to come over and see how you and the children are doing. You've been crying."

Betsy embraced her, then took her by the hand and led her toward the kitchen. "The children are sleeping. We've had our crying times together, but they're doing better than their mother is. I've got some coffee heating up. Want some?"

"Sure."

When they reached the kitchen, Betsy gave Hannah a tender look and said, "What would I ever do without you?"

"Oh, you'd manage. But as long as I'm here, I'm going to look after you."

Betsy shook her head in wonderment. "And here you are, practically a new widow yourself. A pregnant one to boot, and you're here to look after me."

"Because I care about you, Betsy. I know what it's like to lose a husband."

Betsy went to the stove to check the coffeepot. It wasn't boiling yet. There was iron in her voice when she spoke over her shoulder. "I wouldn't be a widow, Hannah, if God had taken care of John. Here he was, just doing his duty as a soldier to protect the white people in this territory, and God let those devil savages kill him."

Betsy's eyes were black, bitter pools, and her lips were set in a thin line. "It's the army's fault that I'm a widow too. If they hadn't been using those Crow scouts, John would still be alive. And it's those filthy Indians' fault, Hannah! Crooked Foot murdered him!"

Hannah was casting about for what the Lord would have her say when Betsy hissed, "So you see, it's the fault of all of them! God, the army, and the Indians!"

Hannah drew in a deep breath and said, "Being bitter against God will only dry up your soul, Betsy. All I can tell you is that He had a reason for what happened to John. Just like He had a reason for letting that rattlesnake take my Solomon."

"Then you ought to be mad at God too."

"I can't be, because I trust Him thoroughly. The Lord doesn't have to explain everything He does in my life. I'm sure if I wasn't saved, I'd have been angry at God when Solomon was taken. But— Oh, Betsy, there's no way to explain it. All I can say is that if you would open your heart to Jesus and trust Him to save you and guide your life, you'd have His help to overcome your grief, your bitterness, and the fear you still carry."

Betsy tried to keep her anger from spilling toward her friend as she said, "How do you know I still have fear? I can't fear for John any longer. He's dead."

"But I know what kind of fear wormed its way into my heart when I realized I was facing the task of going on in life without Sol, and raising my children and making a living for them. Not to mention that I was also going to bring another child into the world without a husband at my side."

Betsy stared at her for a long moment, then turned back to the stove and said, "The coffee's hot."

As they sat at the table and drank coffee, Betsy said, "Hannah, I'm sorry for spouting off. I shouldn't take my frustrations out on you."

"I didn't think you were. I just want you to know my Jesus. When you do, everything will look different to you...in a better way."

Betsy stared into her cup but didn't respond.

"Will you come to church with me tomorrow?" Hannah said. "Your boys need it, and so does Belinda."

A weak smile curved Betsy's lips. Nodding, she said, "All right. We'll come to church tomorrow."

Sunday was a banner day for Pastor Andrew Kelly and his congregation as they held their first service in the brand-new building. Many people from the town and fort who did not ordinarily attend were on hand.

Betsy Fordham and her children sat with the Coopers, the O'Briens, and the Williamses. Just before the sermon, the pastor called on Gary Williams to offer a dedicatory prayer for the new building.

Hannah watched Betsy from the corner of her eye during the sermon. The new widow sat woodenly, listening but not concentrating on what the pastor was saying. Hannah was sure she was dwelling on her loss of John but not her own lost soul.

On Sunday afternoon, Broken Wing came to Fort Bridger, escorted by a band of braves, to take a ride with Chris Cooper. The warm south winds were still blowing, and the boys enjoyed their time together, wearing only light wraps.

Word was out that Crooked Foot's war parties were still on the prowl. Under the watchful eyes of the Crow braves, and for safety's sake, Chris and Broken Wing rode only the perimeter of the town and fort.

As the sun was lowering, Two Moons and Sweet Blossom emerged from their tepee at the sound of horses thundering into the village. They waved as their son rode his pinto up to them.

"Did you enjoy your ride with Chris Cooper?" asked Two Moons.

"Very much, my father. I am sad, though."

Sweet Blossom frowned. "Why are you sad?"

"I am sad for Mrs. Betsy Fordham."

"Yes," said Two Moons. "It is sad that Crooked Foot killed Captain John Fordham."

The boy slid off his horse. "I am sad because Mrs. Betsy Fordham lost her husband, yes, but I am also sad because she is full of hate for Indians. Not just Blackfoot, Crow—all Indians. She does not trust even the great Chief Two Moons."

"How do you know this?"

"Chris Cooper told me. Mrs. Hannah Cooper is very sad because Mrs. Betsy Fordham feels this way about Indians. Especially the great Chief Two Moons."

The chief nodded, his features grave. "Gray Fox, Running Antelope, Tall Bird, Little Bull…Crooked Foot…they did a bad thing. They will pay. My heart hurts for Mrs. Betsy Fordham."

The next morning at the Crow village, Chief Two Moons was bridling his horse at the rope corral when Broken Wing stepped up behind him. "Where are you going, father?"

"Fort Bridger."

"Are some braves going with you?"

"Only to the gate of the fort. I am going to see Mrs. Betsy Fordham alone. She must learn that the Crows are not her enemies; she can trust Two Moons."

"What if Mrs. Betsy Fordham will not talk to the great Chief Two Moons?"

The chief looped the reins over his horse's head and swung aboard. "I will not force her to talk. If she is not willing to talk, at least I will know I tried."

"May I go too?"

"Not today."

The boy watched his father ride toward the south edge of the village where a band of braves awaited him. They followed Two Moons as he threaded his horse among the tepees. Soon the small band was out of sight.

Two Moons had scouts watching Crooked Foot's village. They had already reported that the renegade Crows were now riding with Crooked Foot and were away from the village. Broken Wing considered his father's plan for vengeance and thought that Crooked Foot and the renegade Crows might as well start digging their graves.

At Fort Bridger, the sun was midway in the morning sky when Betsy Fordham came into Cooper's General Store, her face a dismal mask. Glenda Williams, who stood behind the counter, looked up and smiled, then turned to the customer who had just walked up to the counter with several items in her hands. When Glenda had finished with the customer, she turned and greeted Betsy.

"Hello, Glenda." Betsy's voice sounded flat yet full of some tamped down emotion. "Is Hannah here?"

"Yes. She's in the storeroom."

Betsy thanked her and headed down the narrow space between shelves. Just as she got to the back door, Hannah emerged, carrying a small box. Patty Ruth was at her side, carrying a smaller one.

"Hello, Miss Betsy," Patty Ruth said. "Where's Belinda?"

"She's staying with Darlene Stewart for a little while, honey. I need to talk to your mama." Then to Hannah, "Could we take a little walk?"

"Sure."

After planting Patty Ruth at the table by the potbellied stove and telling Glenda she would be back shortly, Hannah walked out into the warm sunshine with Betsy.

"What do you make of this chinook we're having?" Hannah asked. "Isn't it something, not having to wear a coat, or even a shawl?"

Betsy nodded. "I like it. The cold winter days will come soon enough."

Soon they were passing the fort's gate and turning toward Main Street.

Hannah glanced at her friend. "What was it you wanted to talk about?"

"I'm having some problems with Ryan and Will."

"What kind of problems?"

"Well, I've been keeping a close eye on them since…John was killed. With all these Indians around, I just don't want them in any danger. I'm going to walk them to and from school every day, and they're going to stay inside the house when they're home. I don't care if our house is inside the fort; if Crooked Foot wanted to kidnap them, he'd find a way to grab them in their own yard. This morning I walked them to school and told them I'd be there this afternoon to walk them home."

"And I take it the boys are rebelling against it?"

"They say it embarrasses them in front of their friends. And…and they say I'm suffocating them because I won't hardly let them out of my sight. What do you think, Hannah?"

"Well, I can understand it. Part of it is the male ego. The other boys at school will no doubt look down on them for having to be escorted by their mother. And obviously they don't share your fear of the Indians."

"They should, Hannah. The Indians killed their father!"

"Yes, but it was Crooked Foot. And I really don't think there's any way he or his warriors are going to get into the fort and take your sons. Betsy, you can't coop them up inside the house when they're not at school."

Betsy's lower lip quivered. "I…I thought you might understand, Hannah. That maybe you'd talk to the boys and help them see that I don't mean to smother them; I'm only interested in keeping them safe."

"Betsy, you know I want to help you any way I can, but I'm in agreement with the boys. I think you're being overly cautious, and your constant hovering could very well cause them to turn away from you. You sure don't need that."

Betsy pondered Hannah's words. "Well, I asked for your opinion, and I got it."

"I'm sorry I can't agree with you, Betsy, but I really think you're making a mistake."

"Even if I only keep a tight rein on them for a little while? Till I get over my loss of John?"

"If it will ease your fears to hover over them for a little while, go ahead, but tell Will and Ryan why you need to do it, and let them know it's only temporary. If I were you, I'd make the 'little while' a very little while."

"All right. I just need to make sure they're safe. I couldn't stand to lose even one of them."

"For that matter," said Hannah, "if Crooked Foot wanted to take the boys from you when you're walking them to school, you couldn't stop him."

"Maybe not, but he'd have to get past six .45 caliber bullets. I carry one of John's revolvers."

"Oh. Well, I doubt you'll ever have to use it."

"I hope you're right, but if any of those red-skinned beasts try it, they'll get a surprise."

Their walk had taken them almost to the center of town.

"I'm facing some other problems too, Hannah. When a new captain is assigned to the fort to take John's place, the children and I will have to move out of the house."

"But that won't be for a while, will it?"

"Depends on how soon the army can get him here. Could be a month. Could be three months."

"What are you planning to do, Betsy?"

"Stay right here."

"Oh, good!"

"We'll have to get us a house to live in. And I'll have to find a job. There'll be some pension money from the army, but it won't be enough to live on."

Hannah thought on it for a moment. "I could hire you as a clerk at the store…but I probably couldn't pay you enough for you to support three children and yourself. Especially since you have to buy or build a house."

"It's sweet of you to even consider it," said Betsy, "but I've already been offered a couple of jobs."

"Oh, really? Wonderful! Tell me."

"Well, after church yesterday…did you see Justin and Julie Powell talking to me?"

"Mm-hmm."

"They offered to hire me as a clerk in their store. I don't know much about hardware, and I don't know a lot about guns, but they said they'd teach me what I need to know, and the pay is pretty good."

"What's the other offer?"

"Heidi Lindgren has seen the dresses I've made for myself and Belinda. She likes my work, so she also approached me at church yesterday."

"I saw you talking to Heidi and Sundi. Is Heidi wanting you to do seamstress work for her?"

"Yes. She wants me to work right there at the shop. I'd be working mostly on commission, but the way her business is growing, I'd probably do all right."

"Well, it's great that you've had the offers. Any idea which one you'll take?"

"Not yet. Oh, and I had another kind of offer too. The Morleys asked how long we'd be able to stay in the house. When I told them, they offered to let us move in with them till we could come up with a place of our own."

"That's kind of them. Have you had any other job offers or offers of a place to live?"

"No, not really."

"Then I see something very significant."

"What's that?"

"All these people who have made offers are Christians. They're showing you love and concern because they have the mind of Christ. They think like Jesus does. And He loves you even more than anyone else ever could."

Suddenly Betsy stopped and stared at something across the street. Hannah followed her gaze and saw Chief Two Moons on his horse. He was looking right at Betsy.

"I think Two Moons wants to talk to you," said Hannah.

Betsy glared at the chief and said loud enough for him to hear, "I don't want to talk to any Indian!"

Embarrassed by her friend's rudeness, Hannah turned away for a moment. When she turned back, Betsy was still glaring in the same direction, but Two Moons had ridden away.

When Betsy arrived at Darlene Stewart's house, she found several of the military children who were Belinda's age playing in the yard. Belinda begged to stay longer, and Darlene interceded for her, persuading Betsy to let the little girl stay until after Betsy had walked the boys home from school.

Betsy arrived at the school a few minutes late after meeting up with friends who detained her to give their condolences for the loss of John.

When she saw Ryan and Will on the playground, talking to a couple of boys, she rushed up to them with skirt flying, and said, "What are you doing out here? I distinctly told you that if I was ever late getting here after school, you were to wait inside!"

Ryan and Will ducked their heads in embarrassment, and Betsy hurried them away.

When they were a few yards from the school grounds, Ryan said, "Mom, we play out here at recess. We didn't think anything about it."

Betsy hadn't yet calmed down, and her voice came out in a more scolding tone than she intended. "It's different when Miss Lindgren is out here, and all the other children, but I want you inside the schoolhouse when school's out till I'm here to walk you home."

"Aw, Mom," said Will, "those Indians aren't gonna come after us. It makes us look like little babies, you having to walk us to school and back."

Betsy marched her sons home in silence. When they reached the house, she told them to go inside, she had to go to the store for a few things, then to the Stewart house to get Belinda. She would be back within an hour or so.

A few minutes after Betsy had gone, Ryan said to Will, "I hate being closed up here in the house. Let's just take a walk over to the forest. There aren't gonna be any Blackfoot coming this close to the fort."

"Let's go," said Will. "We can be back before Mom gets here."

"I really had fun, Mama," said Belinda, as she and her mother left the Stewart house, hand-in-hand.

Betsy gave her daughter a slight smile and said, "That's good, honey."

Soon they were home. As soon as Betsy closed the front door, Belinda went running to the boys' room, calling, "Ryan! Will! I had lots of fun today!"

Betsy was in the kitchen, preparing to start a fire in the cookstove, when she heard Belinda's footsteps hurrying down the hall.

Belinda entered the kitchen and said, "Where's Ryan and Will, Mama?"

"They're not in their room?"

"Huh-uh. They're not in any room. I can't find 'em."

Betsy dashed through the house, calling her sons' names, but there was no reply. She hurried toward the front door, telling Belinda to stay inside. There was no sign of the boys in the yard.

She returned to the house and called for her little girl. "Come with me, Belinda. We've got to find your brothers."

Betsy went first to the general store and approached the counter where Hannah and Glenda were waiting on customers. Belinda spotted Patty Ruth at the small table and hurried to her.

"Hannah," said Betsy breathlessly, "have Ryan and Will been in here?"

"No, they haven't. What's wrong?"

"The boys are gone. I can't find them anywhere."

"You said they were at the house when you were in here a little while ago."

"Well, they're not there now. When Belinda and I got home, they were gone."

"They couldn't have gone far," said Glenda. "They must be somewhere in the fort."

Betsy let out a sigh. "Oh, I hope so, Glenda. Could I leave Belinda here while I make a search?"

"Certainly," said Hannah. "I'll come with you."

"That's not necessary. If I don't find them right away, I'll have the soldiers help me."

Outside, Betsy decided to go to the gate tower and see if the sentries had seen her sons. When she had brought her boys home earlier, she had spoken to Corporals Eddie Watson and Cliff Beemer. She looked up now and saw Watson looking down at her.

"Eddie," she said, "have you seen Ryan and Will since we came in a while ago?"

"Yes'm. They came by here oh...probably an hour ago. The gate was open. We just waved them on through."

"Did they seem upset?"

"No, ma'am. Is there something wrong?"

"Yes. They were told to stay inside the house while I was away for a while. When I got back, they were gone. Did you see which direction they went?"

"Didn't really pay that much attention, Mrs. Fordham."

"Cliff," said Eddie, "did you see which way the boys went?"

"Nope. Probably went into town, though, I'd think."

The sun was low in the western horizon when Betsy

ended up at Marshal Lance Mangum's office. Mangum quickly gathered a group of men to search the town. They would have to work fast; it would be dark in a couple of hours.

CHAPTER TWENTY-ONE

Ryan and Will Fordham were enjoying themselves in the dense forest of spruce, birch, and cottonwood that stretched toward the Uintah Mountains. They wandered over the sun-dappled woods, unmindful of the lengthening shadows, as the late afternoon sun heightened the colors of the leaves that still clung to birch and cottonwood.

Squirrels chattered at the intruders who disturbed their domain by snapping twigs underfoot and scuffing through leaves.

High in the limbs of a spruce, a pair of hawks screeched then spread their wings before lifting themselves skyward. As the boys watched the hawks ride the airwaves, the birds swung around to the west, and Ryan took note of the position of the sun.

"Guess we'd better get back," he said to his younger brother. "Mom'll skin us alive if we're not in the house when she gets there."

"Have we stayed too long?" asked Will.

"I don't think so, but we'd better run just to make sure."

Will suddenly took off, calling "Race ya!" over his shoulder.

On the southern side of the forest stood a huge rock formation, thrust up through the earth's crust by some ancient upheaval. It was surrounded mostly by slender birch trees. The boys had played around it often when exploring the forest with their father in days gone by. Once, in a game of hide-and-seek, Ryan and Will had squeezed themselves into narrow vertical apertures in the rugged rock walls.

Now, Ryan ran after Will and caught up with him about twenty yards away from the rock formation, then passed him and ran around the base of it, disappearing.

When Will came around, he found Ryan looking at two black bear cubs, who were playfully rolling with each other on the ground.

"Wow!" said Will. "I've never seen little bears like these before."

A raven fluttered its wings in a treetop nearby, squawked, and took flight. The boys watched it for a few seconds, then froze at the sound of a roar from the deep shadows of the forest nearby. They pivoted about and saw a large female black bear charging them with her head down.

"Rya-a-a-an!" wailed Will.

"Get in the rock!" shouted Ryan at the same time he grabbed the smaller boy and shoved him toward the nearest aperture.

Ryan followed Will into the narrow cleft and pressed him as far inside the shelter as he could. The mother bear drew up to the cleft, a horror of snarling teeth and protective rage. Her claws were distended as she reached into the aperture. The boys flattened themselves even further, the deadly claws only inches from Ryan's face.

Will's high-pitched wails seemed to infuriate the bear, and she stayed in front of the cleft, growling fiercely. Finally, she backed away, snorting, then whirled about and went to her cubs.

"Stop it, Will! She can't get to us! Stop crying!"

The younger boy sucked in a ragged breath and looked

around Ryan's shoulder. "Are you sure?"

"Yes. She reached in as far as she could, but she still couldn't claw me."

"Will she go away?"

"I don't know."

"What are we going to do?" asked Will in a quavering voice.

"Let it get dark and try to make it out of the forest."

"Maybe she'll come after us."

"She might."

"Then we better not try it."

"We can't stay here all night, Will."

"Be better than getting eaten by that bear."

"We'll just have to move slow and quiet so she doesn't hear us."

"Can she smell us?"

"I don't know. We have to try to get home. Mom's had enough to upset her with Pa getting killed. We—"

Suddenly there was a deafening roar and the deadly paw thrust deep into the cleft again, swinging wildly.

Will screamed, and Ryan let out a loud yell, shouting at the bear to go away.

A lantern burned brightly on the front porch of the Fordham house, throwing a mixture of light and shadow on the faces of the men who stood in a half-circle. Darkness had fallen about thirty minutes earlier.

Betsy Fordham stood on the porch, squeezing her hands together until the knuckles turned white. Hannah Cooper stood next to her, keeping a hand on Belinda's shoulder as the little girl watched her mother's face.

Colonel Bateman and Marshal Mangum, who led the group of men, had just asked Betsy about the likeliest place the boys would have gone.

Tears filled her eyes as she said, "I don't know where to tell you to look. They could've gone anywhere. But I know something terrible has happened to them. Ryan and Will wouldn't torture me like this. They wouldn't stay out there this late if they could help it."

"We'll spread out and cover as much ground as possible, Betsy," said the colonel. "If we don't find them tonight, we'll be back on the search come daylight."

Betsy nodded and bit down hard to still her quivering lips.

Marshal Mangum stepped up and said in a soothing tone, "Don't you despair, ma'am. We'll find them."

Hannah took hold of little Belinda's hand and said to Betsy, "Let's go inside. These men will do everything they can to find Ryan and Will."

Each man in the search party carried a lantern, and the compound filled with a yellow glow as the men lit them.

With Bateman and Mangum in the lead, the group headed for the fort's gate, their lanterns gleaming brightly against the darkness.

Inside the Fordham house, Betsy's shoulders gave an involuntary shudder. "Oh, Hannah," she sobbed, "where could they have gone? Would they have run away from home because they felt I was…I was smothering them?"

"I don't think so. They may have gone for a walk to ease the feeling of being closed in, but it's not like those two boys to run away from home."

"Maybe some wild animals have eaten them!" Betsy wailed. "Or…maybe Indians have captured them like I've feared all along! Maybe they're dead, just like their father!"

Hannah took hold of Betsy's arm. "Let's go in the kitchen,

and I'll fix you and Belinda something to eat."

"I'm not hungry," Betsy said.

"Me neither," said the child. "I want my brothers."

"How about some tea, Betsy?" Hannah said softly. "Can I fix you some tea?"

"Why, Hannah? Why did God let this happen to my sons? Why is God doing this to me? He let the Indians kill John …and now this! The savage devils will probably bring my boys' bloody clothes and dump them at the gate, just like they did John's! What horrible thing have I done to be punished like this?"

Hannah took hold of Betsy's shoulders and looked her square in the eye. "I can't answer all of your questions. But I can tell you this: God is good and He is merciful. He wants you to be saved, Betsy. And it's quite possible He's allowed all of this to happen to get your attention—to get you to turn to Jesus and open your heart to Him."

"Why would He do that? Why would I want to turn to Him if—"

Betsy's words were cut off by the sound of excited voices outside, punctuated with happy laughter.

"They've found them, Betsy!" said Hannah as she headed for the door.

Betsy and Belinda followed close behind.

When Hannah opened the door, the entire area in front of the house was filled with the men of the search party and some of the women of the fort. In their midst were seven Indians on horses. Two of the Indians had Ryan and Will in their arms. Betsy didn't know the name of the brave who sat behind Will, but Ryan was sitting with Two Moons.

She burst into tears and leaped off the porch, opening her arms to the boys who were sliding groundward. Everyone applauded as the ecstatic mother gathered her sons to her and held them tightly as they wept together.

More people had gathered by the time Betsy finally loosened her grip on the boys and settled them in the crook of her arms. "Why did you boys leave the house?" she asked. "I told you to stay inside."

Ryan calmly explained that her hovering made them feel like prisoners. They knew they shouldn't have disobeyed, but they were just going to take a walk into the forest and be back before she got home.

Every ear in the crowd was attentive as Ryan told his mother about running onto the bear cubs, and how the mother bear had charged after them. He explained about the rock formation, which he and Will had discovered when they'd come to the woods with their father, and how they had jumped into one of the slender openings to escape the angry mother bear.

"The bear had us trapped, Mama," said Ryan. "But Chief Two Moons and these braves were riding nearby and heard the bear roaring. The sun had gone down, but it was still light enough for them to see us. They chased the bear and her cubs away, put us on their horses, and brought us home."

"Oh, thank God!" Betsy said, as she wept for joy. "Thank You, God! You are merciful and You are good! Thank You!"

Two Moons and the brave who had carried Will on his horse dismounted. Betsy looked at the smiling chief and the brave beside him. Her throat felt constricted, and her mind was in a whirl, but she was able to look at the chief with gratitude as she said, "I...I want to thank you, Chief. It was very kind of you and your braves to drive away the bear and rescue my boys."

Two Moons smiled. "Two Moons glad we hear bear growling. It is his and his braves pleasure to bring Ryan Fordham and Will Fordham to their mother."

As the chief turned to mount his horse, Colonel Bateman and Marshal Mangum expressed their appreciation, and people in the crowd called out their thanks. The Indians gave a friendly wave and trotted out of the fort.

Betsy's gaze fell on the colonel and Marshal Mangum. "Colonel Bateman, I want to thank you and the marshal…and all of the men who joined in the search party. Thanks to all of you and Chief Two Moons, I have my boys back."

The crowd began to disperse, and Betsy and Hannah herded the children into the house. Once inside, Hannah hugged the boys, telling them how glad she was they were home safe. She then hugged Belinda and said, "I guess I'd better go see if my kids are driving the Williamses crazy."

"I doubt that," said Betsy. She grabbed hold of Hannah's hands and said, "I love you, my friend. Thank you for being here for me. You'll never know how very much I appreciate you."

"And I love you too, Betsy. Now, I'd better get home."

Ryan rushed ahead and put his hand on the doorknob. Before opening it, he said, "Thank you, Miss Hannah, for being such a good friend to Mama and us kids."

"I'm glad I can be," said Hannah, as she ran her fingers through his hair. "And keep in mind that Chief Two Moons and his people are your friends too."

"Yes, ma'am," he said as he opened the door.

Hannah stepped onto the porch, gave a little wave, and started toward the steps.

"Hannah…"

Hannah turned back and saw Betsy at the door.

Betsy swallowed hard and said, "I…ah…maybe I've been wrong about the Crows."

Hannah took a step toward her friend. "Yes, maybe you have. But there's no maybe that you've been wrong about the Lord, Betsy."

It took Hannah's words a moment to sink in. When they did, Betsy grimaced and her eyes flooded with tears. "You're right. I've been so wrong about Him, Hannah. Would you—"

Betsy choked up.

"Would I what?" asked Hannah.

"Would you help me? I want to be saved."

Hannah rushed to take Betsy's hand and led her back into the house.

The next Sunday Betsy Fordham walked the aisle at invitation time. Pastor Kelly, who already knew what she was coming for, smiled and shook her hand. The news of Betsy's salvation had spread all over town, and there was much rejoicing in the congregation when they saw her standing beside the pastor in front of the platform.

Kelly smiled at the congregation and said, "Folks, Betsy has asked if she could give a word of testimony."

Betsy told of how Hannah Cooper had witnessed to her lovingly, kindly, and consistently for the past two months. She thanked God for such a friend as Hannah, which drew many "Amens" from the crowd.

"Then, a few nights ago, Hannah introduced me to the greatest Friend of all—the Friend of sinners, the precious Lord Jesus Christ. I never had real peace and joy until I came to know Him. Hannah could tell you that I became bitter against God for allowing John to be taken from me. But that bitterness left my heart when Jesus came in."

The place rang with "Amens."

Betsy wept softly as she turned to Pastor Kelly and said, "I want to obey my Lord and follow His command to be baptized."

The service ended with great rejoicing, for many people had been praying for Betsy's salvation. As the crowd filed slowly by to rejoice with Betsy, Belinda stood nearby with her best friend, Patty Ruth.

"When I get a little bit older I'm gonna get saved," Belinda said.

"Me too," said the little redhead. "An' after I get saved, I'm gonna get bapatized too."

Belinda thought on it. "Patty Ruth…"

"Huh?"

"If we died now, would we go to…to—"

"To the hot place?"

"Yeah, the hot place."

"Nope."

"But don't we have to be saved to go to heaven?"

"Well, my mama says that until we're old enough to understand 'bout all that, Jesus keeps us safe."

"Why does He do that?"

"'Cause we're jis' little girls, an' He loves us."

"Oh. I'm sure glad."

"Me too."

David and Leah Morley had finally worked their way up the line to Betsy. After they told her how happy they were that she had come to the Lord, David said, "We meant it when we said you and the children could come live with us until you have a permanent home. So whenever you have to leave your present house, ours is open."

"That's right," said Leah. "We'll be glad to have you."

Betsy thanked them and said she would take them up on it.

Heidi and Sundi Lindgren were next. After they embraced, Heidi said, "My offer still stands on the seamstress job, Betsy. Just want you to know that. No hurry on giving me an answer. Whenever you're ready to make the decision, let me know 'yea' or 'nay,' all right?"

"I sure will…and thank you."

Behind the Lindgren sisters were Justin and Julie Powell. After they embraced their new sister in Christ, Justin said, "The job we offered you is still open too, Betsy. But we'll certainly understand if you decide to go to work for Heidi."

"Thank you," said Betsy. "Your kind offer means so much.

I'll be making my decision soon."

The Williamses and Abby Turner, and the Coopers, were next. As Abby hugged Betsy, she said, "I'm still new at this myself, Mrs. Fordham, but I can tell you for sure, having Jesus in my heart is the best thing that ever happened to me!"

"Isn't that the truth," Betsy said. "God is so good!"

When Betsy heard herself say those words, she marveled that praising God came so effortlessly now. She had undergone a complete change in such a short time. Truly, Jesus made all the difference in a person's life, she thought.

That evening after church, the Fordhams and the Coopers were at the Williamses' house for a snack. As they sat around the table, talking about salvation and spending eternity with the Lord, Mary Beth noticed a sad look come over Betsy's face."

"Mrs. Fordham," she said, "are you all right?"

All eyes went to Betsy, who put a trembling hand to her mouth. "It's hard for me to talk about it." She cleared her throat, then said, "It's about John. Unless he called on Jesus to save him before...before he died, he won't be there in heaven. And I have no way of knowing whether he did or not. I have this fear that I'll never see him again."

Hannah reached over and patted Betsy's hand. "That's true, we can't know for sure. But remember what I showed you in 1 John chapter 4?"

"About there being no place for fear in the love of God? And that if I let fear torment me, I'm not letting God have control?"

"See how much you've learned since the Holy Spirit opened your eyes?" said Hannah.

Betsy shook her head slowly. "It's amazing how the things of God are so much easier to understand now."

"And you're just getting started!"

On Tuesday, an elderly couple in a wagon drove into Fort Bridger with two well-dressed men riding horseback beside them. The wagon was loaded with cargo covered with a large tarpaulin. They hauled up in front of the new Wells Fargo building and the old man said, "Wal, lookie there, my li'l rose blossom! That's our new home!"

"The second floor, at least," the woman said. "That there bottom floor is where we're gonna carry on the stagecoachin' business an' the U.S. mail!"

"I imagine the army will be glad to turn the mail delivery over to us," said Fargo executive Winn Haltom.

"They always are," said the other Wells Fargo man, Stanley Mills. "Well, let's get inside and let these people take a look at their new place of business!"

Word spread quickly that the Wells Fargo executives were back with the new agents. Soon a crowd of curious onlookers gathered.

Cade Samuels, the town barber and chairman of the town council, arrived about the same time as bank president Lloyd Dawson. Winn Haltom introduced them to Curly and Judy Charley Wesson. They were a bit amused at the old couple but found them charming.

Several men and women offered to help the Wessons carry their goods to the upstairs apartment, which had been completely furnished by the Wells Fargo people.

By the time the wagon was unloaded, many more people had gathered, including all the school children. Word had filtered to the school that the couple had arrived, and Sundi Lindgren agreed to take the children to the Wells Fargo office just before it was time for school to let out.

When official introductions were over, the people welcomed

Curly and Judy warmly. Hannah's children joined her and took their turn to introduce themselves to the old couple. Curly and Judy were glad to meet the proprietor of the general store and told Hannah they had also run the general store on Luther Pass.

Curly looked a Hannah's youngest daughter. He winked at her and said, "Now what did your mommy say your name was?"

The little redhead's eyes bulged. "P-Patty Ruth, sir."

"Patty Ruth! Y'hear that sugar? Her name's Patty Ruth!"

"I hear it," Judy said, admiring the child's auburn hair.

"Patty Ruth, how old are you?" Curly said, bending over to look her in the eye.

Patty Ruth swallowed hard. "Five."

"Five! You're five years old?"

"Uh-huh."

"Do you know what I do when I meet a li'l girl what is five years old an' her name is Patty Ruth?"

The child blinked and shook her head.

"I hug her!" Curly said. "That's what I do!" He put his arms around her and won her heart. Patty Ruth hugged him back.

CHAPTER TWENTY-TWO

The next few days were difficult for Betsy Fordham as she tried to adjust to widowhood, but with Hannah Cooper's counsel and daily Bible studies with Pastor and Rebecca Kelly, she grew stronger.

On a Tuesday, a week after Ryan and Will's incident with the bear, Betsy entered Cooper's General Store with Patty Ruth after keeping her all day. Hannah and Nellie Patterson were just closing up.

As Nellie excused herself, Hannah looked around the store once more and saw that everything was in order, then turned to her little girl and said, "I guess you and I better be going too, Patty Ruth. Did you and Belinda have lots of fun today?"

"Wal, we shore did, Mama," said the little redhead, hitching up Tony the Bear in the crook of her arm. "Belinda an' me practiced talkin' like Mr. Curly an' Miss Judy."

"Oh, you did, eh?"

"Shore did, sugar lump!"

Hannah and Betsy laughed.

"Now, Patty Ruth," said Hannah, "I don't want you doing that in front of Mr. Curly or Miss Judy. You might hurt their feelings."

"I wouldn' hurt their feelin's, Mama. I really like both of 'em. An' I enjoyed sittin' between them and Grandpa and

Grandma O'Brien in church las' night."

"That's good, honey. Did you thank Miss Betsy for taking care of you today?"

"No, but I will right now. Thank you for takin' care of me, Miss Betsy. I had a nice time. But—" Patty Ruth broke off speaking and pushed out her lower lip.

Betsy waited a moment, then said, "But *what,* honey? What's the matter?"

"When you get a job, I won't get to come on Tuesdays and Thursdays and play with Belinda no more."

Betsy smiled at the little girl and said, "It's Belinda's turn to stay with someone while I work…and although I don't yet know who that will be, whoever it is might take care of you on Tuesdays and Thursdays like I've been doing."

That gave the little girl something to think about, and the pouty lip disappeared.

Hannah had started toward the door with her key in hand when Betsy said, "Before you go, could I ask you something?"

Hannah turned back. "Of course."

"You've been a widow for well over two months now. How long did it take you to get to the point where you didn't miss your husband all day every day and cry yourself to sleep at night…then dream about him?"

"Betsy, I'm not too far past it yet. Getting over the grief comes very slowly, even for a Christian. I still dream of Sol about three nights out of four, and at times I feel like I'm just going to fall apart for want of him. But the Lord has been so good to give me that extra amount of strength, just when I need it."

Betsy gave a tentative smile and said, "I've experienced a little of that."

Hannah nodded in agreement. "As you learn to walk with the Lord, you'll find inner strength because the Holy Spirit lives inside you. He'll help you day by day in a way that no mortal can."

"Now that I'm saved, I believe that's possible," said Betsy. "I never did before."

"It gets better as the days go by and you continue to grow in your spiritual life."

Betsy nodded, satisfied. "Thank you. I'd better get home to Belinda and the boys."

"Could I ask one thing of you?" said Hannah.

"Sure."

"My heart is heavy for Chris's friend, Lieutenant Carlin. He wants to go to Denver and see his wife and son, especially before the divorce is final. Would you pray for Dobie and ask God to intervene? Pray that he will be able to get to Denver on time and that she'll be willing to reconcile. And pray that he'll be able to lead his wife and son to Jesus."

"Oh, I sure will," said Betsy. "I sure will!"

At midmorning, Colonel Bateman was reading a telegram from Washington that gave him details on the new men who would replace those killed in the past few weeks. He laid it on his desk when he heard a knock and his adjutant opened the door a few inches.

"Sir, Chief Two Moons just rode into the fort with about three dozen warriors. He would like to see you."

Bateman quickly rose to his feet. "Send him in."

Seconds later, Colonel Bateman shook hands Indian-style with the Crow leader and said, "Would you like to sit down this time, Chief?"

"Yes. Sit this time. I bring good word."

As Two Moons sat on one of the chairs in front of the desk, the colonel returned to his own.

"What is this good word, Chief?"

"Blackfoot uprising is over."

"What? Tell me more!"

"Chief Crooked Foot is dead." The stoic Crow chief's features never altered. "Two Moons and warriors kill him. Set trap. He ride into it."

"When did this happen?"

"Three days."

"Three days ago! I could have used this good news then!"

"Two Moons wait to bring word. Want to see what Crooked Foot's warriors do. Yesterday, they pack up village and go north to Montana to join village there. Bother you no more."

"But how did you do it?"

When the Crow chief remained silent, Colonel Bateman didn't press him. Instead, he said, "Well, my friend, I congratulate you. The people in this part of Wyoming will be glad to hear the Blackfoot threat is over."

"May happen again someday," the chief said solemnly, "but over for now."

"We'll have to face that if it ever comes," said Bateman, "but when I make this announcement, I'm going to have some very relieved soldiers and soldiers' wives!"

Although most of his men were on patrol, Colonel Bateman made the announcement to those in the fort immediately after the Crows had ridden out. Word spread quickly throughout the town.

Colonel Bateman was at his desk late in the afternoon when he heard the patrol units arriving, one by one. He knew the moment each unit learned the good news at the gate, for the cheers could be heard throughout the fort.

Bateman was about to call it a day when his adjutant knocked on the door and told him Lieutenant Dobie Carlin was in the outer office and needed to see him.

When Carlin sat down after saluting his commanding officer, Colonel Bateman said, "Don't tell me, Lieutenant. Let me
guess."

Carlin raised his eyebrows. "All right, sir."

"You want time off from your duties here in order to go to
Denver and try to get things reconciled between you and your
wife."

"Why, yes, sir! That's it exactly, sir!"

"And you will be going as far as Cheyenne City with one
of our supply wagon trains?"

"Not if I can get a seat on a stagecoach, sir. I'll check that
out first. If I need to travel with one of the wagon trains, I'll let
you know."

Bateman was already filling out an official form for Carlin
to carry with him. "How long will this take, Lieutenant?"

"Well, sir, it would help if I had a couple of weeks."

"How about three?"

"Oh, that would be great, Colonel!"

"All right. Three weeks it is. The time will start the day
you leave here."

At the Wells Fargo office, Curly and Judy Charley Wesson were
busy at the counter, working side by side. Earlier in the day,
two spare six-up teams of stagecoach horses had been delivered
by Wells Fargo personnel and placed in the corral behind the
stage office. While Curly spent some enjoyable time getting to
know his horses, the Wells Fargo people had told him they'd
booked some passengers out of Fort Bridger.

"Wal, that's really good, honey bunch," said Judy. "We got
three passengers already for the very first stage!"

The door opened, and Curly looked up and grinned. "Well, lookee who's here! It's Lieutenant Carlin. Howdy, Lieutenant!"

"Howdy, yourself," Dobie said with a smile. "And howdy to you, Mrs. Wesson."

Judy showed him her snaggletoothed grin. "Glad to see ya, son. What kin we do for ya?"

"You heard about the Blackfoot situation, I assume?"

"Shore did! We was plenty glad to hear of it too! Wasn't we, honey love?"

"Yes, ma'am!" said Curly. "So I guess that means your wantin' to get to Denver real pronto. Right, Lieutenant?"

"Right. When does the first stage go? And can you put me on it?"

"The first stage goes tomorra about ten o'clock in the mornin'. And yes, I can put you on it."

"Good!"

Curly smiled. "The stage will be a-comin' in here from Cheyenne City 'bout nine-thirty and will pull out jist as soon as the passengers comin' in have their luggage off the stage an' a fresh team is hitched to it. Won't take no more than a half-hour and you'll be on your way. We got three other passengers fer Cheyenne City so far. You'll make number four!"

On Saturday morning, most everyone in the town and fort were gathered in front of the Wells Fargo Stagelines office to welcome the first stagecoach to Fort Bridger. Curly Wesson had painted a large white banner with big red letters to announce the event and had strung it over the street. All the businesses were closed for the occasion.

At 9:15, Curly and Judy stood on the boardwalk in front

of the stage office, chatting merrily with the people around them. Three elderly women, who were booked on the stage, sat on a bench near the door.

Lieutenant Dobie Carlin waited near the Wessons with several friends who had come to see him off—Pastor and Rebecca Kelly, Betsy Fordham and her children, and Hannah Cooper, with three of her children. Mary Beth was at the Crow village, teaching with Sundi Lindgren.

The preacher laid a hand on Dobie's shoulder and said, "You know our prayers go with you, Dobie. We've put this whole situation in God's capable hands, and we're trusting Him to work it out."

"Yes, sir. I know He will do it."

"The whole church has been praying and will continue to pray for you and your family."

"That means more to me than I could ever put into words, Pastor."

Betsy smiled at the young soldier and said, "Dobie, if the Lord can get to a sinful wretch like me, I know He can save your wife."

"Thank you for the encouragement, ma'am."

"Dobie…" said Hannah.

"Yes'm?"

"When you get to Denver and the Lord answers our prayers, will you let us know what's happening?"

"I sure will, ma'am. I'm sure I can send a message through the army's telegraph service. I'll send it directly to Colonel Bateman, and he can advise you."

"I just know it's going to turn out real good, Dobie," said Chris.

Dobie made a fist and playfully clipped Chris's chin. "It all started to turn right when you got me under the gospel, my friend."

Chris grinned from ear to ear.

"Hey, everybody!" shouted someone on the edge of the crowd. "Here comes the stage!"

A cloud of dust appeared where the road ran over a hill about a mile to the east. Then the six-up team and stage crested the hill. A roar went up from the crowd as people began to wave and cheer. When the coach reached the east edge of town, the cheering grew louder. The horses puffed and snorted as driver and shotgunner waved their hats to the crowd.

Curly stepped off the boardwalk, asking the people to clear a path so the stage could pull up in front of the office. When it came to a halt in a cloud of dust, Curly and Judy stepped up and introduced themselves to the crew as the Fargo agents, then Curly opened the door, looked inside and said, "Howdy, ma'am. Howdy, son. Welcome to Fort Bridger!"

Dobie's gaze rested casually on the open stagecoach door when suddenly the face he saw put a shock through him like a bolt of lightning.

Donna!

Curly helped the woman descend from the coach. Right behind her was a young boy.

Dobie pushed his way through the crowd. When Donna saw him coming toward her with tears streaming down his cheeks, she broke into tears herself, and opened her arms.

"Pa!" Travis cried, pressing himself to his father's side.

While the Carlin family stood holding on to each other, Pastor Kelly said, "Look at that, Rebecca! The Lord's way ahead of us!"

"I knew it!" said Chris. "I knew the Lord was going to do something special for Dobie! I didn't think it would happen like this, but—wow!—isn't it great, Mama?"

Hannah, like Betsy, was wiping tears. "It sure is, honey," she said. "It sure is."

Patty Ruth held her stuffed bear in front of her face and

said, "See there, Tony? Aren't you glad we asked Jesus to help Mr. Lieutenant Dobie get his wife and son back?"

As Dobie held his wife and son close, Donna said, "Darling, I can't wait to tell you how this trip came about. I have to tell you right now."

"I'm listening!" said Dobie.

"A couple of weeks ago, Travis had an appendicitis attack. Daddy and I rushed him to the hospital in Denver, and they did an emergency appendectomy on him. The appendix had burst, but the doctor was able to keep the poison from getting into his bloodstream."

Dobie squeezed his son's shoulder, but his eyes never left his wife's face.

"As you can see, he came through it fine. What—" Donna's voice caught, and she paused for a moment, then said, "What we want you to know is that while we were at the hospital, a sweet Christian nurse named Breanna Baylor led both of us to the Lord. Your wife and son are saved, Dobie!"

Dobie wept with joy and hugged them closer. The family stayed that way for a long moment, then Travis pulled back to look up into his father's eyes and said, "We'll be in heaven together, Pa!"

"Yes, son. Praise the Lord!"

"Dobie..." said Donna. "The divorce was never finalized. I was such a fool to ever begin the proceedings, anyway. But I'm willing to live the army life if you'll have me."

"If I'll *have* you!" Dobie threw his hat in the air. "Whoopee-e-e! I sure will!" He then kissed her right in front of everybody.

"Pardon me fer buttin' in, here," said Curly Wesson, "but I'd like to say somethin' to your missus and your boy, Lieutenant."

"Be my guest!"

"Well, I heard you tell your husbin', ma'am, that you and

your boy was led to Jesus by Nurse Breanna Baylor."

"Why, yes," said Donna. "Do you know her?"

"I shore do, ma'am. It was Miss Breanna who led me to the Lord on a wagon train just over a year ago!"

Donna impulsively reached out and grasped Curly's hand, acknowledging the bond between them.

"Praise the Lord for Nurse Breanna Baylor!" said Hannah, and everyone who had gathered round the Carlins laughed and murmured their assent.

Betsy laughed along with them, then said, "Well and good…but I say praise the Lord for Hannah Cooper!"

Dobie scanned the joyful faces around him and then looked down at Donna and Travis, and said, "I want you to meet my brothers and sisters in the Lord. They're your brothers and sisters now too."

When Dobie came to Chris, he told his family that it was Chris who had brought him to the Lord.

Chris had watched Travis closely throughout the reunion and thought they would probably become good friends. He wasn't disappointed. He and Travis hit it off immediately. Hannah smiled with pleasure as she watched Chris and Travis enjoying each other's company.

The stagecoach driver handed Curly a big sack of mail, then helped the shotgunner unload Donna's trunk and luggage. Dobie decided to put Donna and Travis up in the hotel until he could make arrangements to move from the single-men's quarters to a house inside the fort.

It was almost noon. Hannah was stocking shelves with the help of Chris, B. J., and Patty Ruth, while Mandy Carver waited on customers.

Hannah was at the back of the store when she heard the

little bell above the door jingle, and she soon made out the voice of Curly Wesson as he greeted Mandy and other customers.

"Is Miss Hannah around?" she heard Curly ask.

"Yes, sir. She's right back there at the end o' that row of shelves."

Seconds later, the little man came around the end of the row, and said, "Well, there's that li'l mama an' her chilluns!"

"Hi, Mr. Curly!" Patty Ruth said as she ran to him.

Curly smiled down at the little girl.

"Mr. Curly…?" Patty Ruth said, her blue eyes flashing.

"Yes, ma'am?"

"How old are you?"

Hannah started to scold her daughter, but Curly held up his hand to stop her.

"Well, li'l punkin, how old do ya think I am?"

Patty Ruth frowned in concentration. "'Bout thirty-six."

Curly winked at Hannah, and said, "Well, what do ya know! You guessed it 'zactly!"

Patty Ruth giggled. "Do you know what I do when I meet a nice man whose name is Mr. Curly and he's thirty-six years old? Do you know what I do?"

Curly bent down and said, "No. What do ya do when ya meet a nice man whose name is Mr. Curly and he's thirty-six years old?"

"I hug him!"

Hannah and Patty Ruth's brothers looked on, smiling, as the little girl reached her arms around Curly as far as she could.

Curly held on to Patty Ruth's hand as he drew up to Hannah and the boys and extended an envelope to Hannah. "Mail fer ya, Miss Hannah."

"Why, thank you." Hannah let her glance fall to the return address on the letter. "Oh! It's a letter from Grandma and Grandpa Singleton, kids!"

When Curly was gone, Hannah ripped open the envelope and pulled out the letter. At first she smiled. Then the smile drained away. She looked up from the letter and said, "Grandma says they never got the first two letters I mentioned I had sent. They were sorry to hear about your father's death, and they're praying for us. She says Grandpa has gotten over being mad at us for moving away, and she has too."

"That's good," said B. J. "But what were you looking so serious about as you read the bottom of the letter?"

"It's your grandpa. He's been pretty sick with influenza. Grandma asks that we pray for him."

"Grandpa will get well," said Patty Ruth. "'Cause if God can bring Mrs. Carlin an' Travis to Mr. Lieutenant Dobie, He can make Grandpa well!"

"They want us to move back to Independence," said Hannah.

"Do you think we should do that, Mama?" asked Chris.

"No, honey. We're right where God wants us. We're staying put."

"I wish Grandma and Grandpa would move out here," said B. J.

"Maybe someday they will," said Hannah, as she folded the letter and placed it back in the envelope.

At 10:15 that night, Pastor Kelly and Rebecca bid Flora Garland goodnight and left her house. The compound was dark, and the Kellys picked their way toward the gate.

"Andy," Rebecca said, as she held on to her husband's arm, "why don't they light up the inside of the fort like they do the streets of the town? You'd think they'd have lanterns burning at the gate."

"It's because of the Indians, who might just decide to

attack at night. Some of them do that, I've been told. Anyone standing near a glowing lantern would be a perfect target—especially the men in the tower."

Corporal Tim Farr and Private Bob Cullen stood in the tower in silence. There was only a quarter moon, and the thin clouds overhead filtered out most of its light. All was quiet in the town and fort.

When the sentries heard voices from inside the compound, followed by the sound of a closing door, Cullen said, "That'll be the Kellys coming from Mrs. Garland's house."

The soldiers peered through the darkness in that direction as they picked up the sound of the Kellys' conversation. The voices grew louder as the couple walked toward the gate.

Suddenly, a shuffling sound came from outside the gate. The sentries whirled about, bringing their carbines to bear on the deep shadows beneath the tower. They waited tensely as a vague form emerged from the darkness.

"Halt right there!" commanded Farr.

"Identify yourself!" said Cullen.

The pastor and Rebecca were about thirty yards from the gate when they saw the flare of a match in the tower, and the wick of a lantern come to life. Both sentries hurried down the stairs to open the gate.

"Wonder what's going on?" Kelly said. "They wouldn't light a lantern unless there was a very good reason."

The Kellys quickened their pace. As they drew nearer, they saw the sentries usher a man in buckskins through the open gate. When they saw the man's features, Rebecca Kelly gasped.

CHAPTER TWENTY-THREE

T he tired man smiled slightly as everyone spoke at once.
"It's Captain Fordham!"

"What a sight for sore eyes *you* are, Captain!"

"I can hardly believe my eyes!" said Rebecca.

"Sir," said Tim Farr, "we figured Crooked Foot had killed you. They brought two sets of blood-soaked uniforms and dumped them right here at the gate."

"Maybe I could just sit down for a moment...on the tower stairs over there?" Fordham said. "I've walked a long way in the last three days." The guards helped Fordham to the stairs, where he gingerly sat down. "I'm alive because I tried to keep the major from torturing the wounded Blackfoot warriors. Gray Fox pleaded my case with Crooked Foot. And yes, Major Garland is dead. It was his blood on both uniforms."

"Well," said Bob Cullen, "we can chalk up at least one good thing for Gray Fox."

"Crooked Foot agreed to let me live," Fordham went on, "but said he would hold me captive for the rest of my life. He wanted to punish the army by making them think I had been killed too."

"How did you escape?" asked Kelly.

Fordham looked at the two soldiers, "Do you know yet that Two Moons and his warriors killed Crooked Foot?"

"Yes, sir," said Tim Farr.

"Well, when word came to the village that Two Moons and his warriors had set a trap for Crooked Foot and killed him—along with about a dozen warriors—the Blackfoot people panicked. They were afraid that with Crooked Foot dead, the army might launch an attack on the village. There was a mad scramble to pack up their tepees and head for Montana to join another village of their tribe. During that mad scramble, I managed to escape."

"Captain, would you like us to alert Colonel Bateman of your return, sir?" asked Farr.

"That can wait till morning, Tim. I want to see Betsy and my children right now."

"Of course, Captain. We've got an extra lantern in the tower, sir. I'll run up and get it for you."

"Be obliged," said Fordham. "I could make it to the house in the dark, all right, but it might be best that when I knock on the door, Betsy can see who's standing there."

"It's going to be quite a shock for her, John," said Kelly, "especially with you standing there in those buckskins. However, it will be a *pleasant* shock."

Fordham grinned. "Before I go, Pastor, I want to tell you something."

"Yes?"

"Until Gray Fox pleaded my case, it looked like I was going to die. That's when I realized I wasn't ready, and I faced head-on for the first time that my religious philosophy was wrong. I could live by it all right, but I couldn't die by it. I repented on the spot and asked the Lord Jesus to save me."

"Oh, wonderful!" exclaimed Kelly, grabbing his hand and pulling the man into an embrace.

John's smile grew wider as he said, "Pastor, it happened in the dark of night, and I was bound hand and foot, but I've never felt such peace and freedom."

"Oh, I'm so happy to hear it!" cried Rebecca. Tears began

to flow freely down her cheeks, and she gently touched her husband's arm. "Andy, don't you think you should let him know about Betsy?"

John looked at Rebecca, then the pastor. "Where's Betsy? What's wrong?"

"Everything's right, John," said the preacher. "I've got some good news for you too. Just a few days ago, Hannah Cooper led Betsy to the Lord."

"Oh, praise God!" John said.

Just then Bob Cullen came down the tower steps with a lighted lantern in his hand.

John glanced at him, gave a sigh, and said, "Well, folks, it's time for me to go see my family. Thank you, Pastor, for preaching the Word straight to me."

Andy Kelly smiled and shook his hand, then gave him a gentle shove toward the married officers' quarters.

"I know we have to let them have their private moment," said Rebecca, wiping tears, "but I'd sure like to see Betsy's face when she opens that door!"

When he thought no one was looking, Corporal Farr quickly wiped a hand across the wetness on his cheeks and murmured agreement as they all watched Captain John Fordham walk toward his house in a circle of light.

OTHER COMPELLING STORIES BY
AL LACY

Books in the Battles of Destiny series:

☞ *A Promise Unbroken*

Two couples battle jealousy and racial hatred amidst a war that would cripple America. From a prosperous Virginia plantation to a grim jail cell outside Lynchburg, follow the dramatic story of a love that could not be destroyed.

☞ *A Heart Divided*

Ryan McGraw—leader of the Confederate Sharpshooters—is nursed back to health by beautiful army nurse Dixie Quade. Their romance would survive the perils of war, but can it withstand the reappearance of a past love?

☞ *Beloved Enemy*

Young Jenny Jordan covers for her father's Confederate spy missions. But as she grows closer to Union soldier Buck Brownell, Jenny finds herself torn between devotion to the South and her feelings for the man she is forbidden to love.

☞ *Shadowed Memories*

Critically wounded on the field of battle and haunted by amnesia, one man struggles to regain his strength and the memories that have slipped away from him.

☞ *Joy from Ashes*

Major Layne Dalton made it through the horrors of the battle of Fredericksburg, but can he rise above his hatred toward the Heglund brothers who brutalized his wife and killed his unborn son?

☞ *Season of Valor*

Captain Shane Donovan was heroic in battle. Can he summon the courage to face the dark tragedy unfolding back home in Maine?

Books in the Battles of Destiny series (cont.):

☞ *Wings of the Wind*

God brings a young doctor and a nursing student together in this story of the Battle of Antietam.

☞ *Turn of Glory* (February 1998)

Four confederate soldiers lauded for bravery mistakenly shoot General Stonewall Jackson. Driven from the army in shame, they become outlaws…and their friend must bring them to justice.

Books in the Journeys of the Stranger series:

☞ *Legacy*

Can John Stranger bring Clay Austin back to the right side of the law…and restore the code of honor shared by the woman he loves?

☞ *Silent Abduction*

The mysterious man in black fights to defend a small town targeted by cattle rustlers and to rescue a young woman and child held captive by a local Indian tribe.

☞ *Blizzard*

When three murderers slated for hanging escape from the Colorado Territorial Prison, young U.S. Marshal Ridge Holloway and the mysterious John Stranger join together to track down the infamous convicts.

☞ *Tears of the Sun*

When John Stranger arrives in Apache Junction, Arizona, he finds himself caught up in a bitter war between sworn enemies: the Tonto Apaches and the Arizona Zunis.

☞ *Circle of Fire*

John Stranger must clear his name of the crimes committed by another mysterious—and murderous—"stranger" who has adopted his identity.

☞ *Quiet Thunder*

A Sioux warrior and a white army captain have been blood brothers since childhood. But when the two meet on the battlefield, which will win out—love or duty?

☞ *Snow Ghost*

John Stranger must unravel the mystery of a murderer who appears to have come back from the grave to avenge his execution.

Books in the Angel of Mercy series:

☞ *A Promise for Breanna*

The man who broke Breanna's heart is back. But this time, he's after her life.

☞ *Faithful Heart*

Breanna and her sister Dottie find themselves in a desperate struggle to save a man they love, but can no longer trust.

☞ *Captive Set Free*

No one leaves Morgan's labor camp alive. Not even Breanna Baylor.

☞ *A Dream Fulfilled*

A tender story about one woman's healing from heartbreak and the fulfillment of her dreams.

☞ *Suffer the Little Children*

Breanna Baylor develops a special bond with the children headed west on an orphan train.

☞ *Whither Thou Goest*

As they begin their lives together, John Stranger and Breanna Baylor place themselves in danger to help a friend.

Books in the Hannah of Fort Bridger series (co-authored with JoAnna Lacy):

☞ *Under the Distant Sky*

Follow the Cooper family as they travel West from Missouri in pursuit of their dream of a new life on the Wyoming frontier.

☞ *Consider the Lilies*

Will Hannah Cooper and her children learn to trust God to provide when tragedy threatens to destroy their dream?

☞ *No Place for Fear*

A widow rejects the gospel until the disappearance of her sons and their rescue by Indians opens her heart to God's love.

Available at your local Christian bookstore

Printed in the United States
by Baker & Taylor Publisher Services